nF421065

STALKING -NOT- REQUIRED

CORINA BAIR

*I wrote this in 2025.
Lighting shit on fire (metaphorically—you'll see)
was how I coped.
I hope it's as healing for you to read it
as it was for me to write it.*

AUTHOR NOTE

Hello lovely romance readers,

I have two important things to share with you before you read Stalking ~~Not~~ Required.

First, this story takes place in a queer-normative world. There are multiple characters who are part of the LGBTQ+ community, but they do not experience discrimination, prejudice, fear of coming out, or any of the atrocities we experience in the real world by being part of this community. I understand that the characters' experiences are not representative of the world we live in, and I have done this intentionally. I hope you find relief in not only the lack of conflict and hate, but the unconditional love and acceptance this book brings.

Second, although this is a feel-good contemporary romance with significant paranormal elements, please review these content notes:
- Generational trauma
- Vague references to (past) childhood neglect

- All the mental health stuff (panic attack, depression, anxiety, trauma responses, OCD-type symptoms, etc)
- Arson. Lots of fire setting.
- Stalking (but not written in a dark/malicious way)
- Arrest / incarceration

Thank you, and happy reading!
Corina

1

———

DEMONS REALLY NEED THERAPY

Ro

"No more fires. No more stealing. No killing."

I mumble the words under my breath, repeating them like a mantra as the afternoon sun beats down on me. I kick a pebble down the sidewalk, scuffing my sneaker and sending the stone skittering off the curb into a pile of leaves. My inner demon perks up. Those leaves would go up in flames *so easily.*

Ugh. I rake my fingers through my hair, irritation bubbling. I was literally reciting my mantra seconds ago, yet my brain went to setting another fire at the first opportunity. My therapist says I need to change my thought patterns, and that'll help me control the urges. She also says it takes time, patience, and practice, all of which are a struggle for me.

My hands clench at the nape of my neck as I tip my head back, letting out a heavy sigh before checking for traffic and crossing the road. I need to get my thoughts back in order before my bartending shift at Tempo, one of many queer clubs in the gayborhood.

Last time I let the demon out too close to work, I flirted with everyone who so much as looked at me with interest, and hooked up with two different guys before my shift was over. Then I ended up stealing a grand total of $103 dollars, a sleek black watch, someone's phone (which I later put in the lost and found bin behind the bar), and a tube of lipstick.

I don't even wear lipstick.

And *that's* why I'm in therapy. Because even though I'm a demon, I want to be good. I yearn to be a good person, someone who contributes to society rather than being a menace who breaks laws every day. I know it's not in my nature as a demon, but people can change, right? My therapist seems to think so, anyway. If she has hope for me, then I will too.

A flash of silver in the sunlight catches my attention and my steps falter. I do a double take, but only see a glimpse of a woman in black before she disappears around the corner of the next building. Her hair was shimmery silver, shining like starlight even though it's mid-afternoon. I've never seen anything like it, and the demon inside me is more intrigued than I've felt in ages.

Already on edge, he's desperate to follow her. The urge bubbles and rises, filling my chest until it's hard to breathe, and I instinctively take a step in her direction.

But no, I have to get to work. My shift starts in... I check my phone. Five minutes ago.

Shit.

I jog the remaining half block to Tempo and fling the door open, reminding myself that this is the exact type of impulse my therapist wants me resisting anyway. I try to feel good about ignoring it, like I'm doing the right thing, but all I feel is a staticky type of anxious. Denying my demonic urges never feels good. It brings fire to my fingertips, a flash of wavering heat flickering in and out, and I grimace, clenching my fists to douse it.

I steel myself for another rough shift as I clock in. Tempo

doesn't open for twenty minutes yet, so I go through the motions on autopilot, falling into the familiar routine of setting up my space behind the bar while my brain obsesses over that millisecond glimpse of *her*. The girl with the starlight hair, black combat boots, and skintight black pants.

I need to see her again.

"Hey, man," Finn says. My friend thumps his fist on the bar as he saunters in, heading to the stage.

"Hey," I mumble a reply, giving an absent nod in greeting.

I wish I had caught more. I've never seen her before, but then again, I only recently started working here when Finn told me there was an opening bartending at the club where he DJ's. I resolve to keep my eyes peeled and be at that corner five minutes earlier tomorrow, just in case she and I are on a similar schedule.

Tempo opens and people trickle in for a couple hours. Then it turns to a steady pour, and before I know it, the club is filled. Music thumps beneath my feet as I shake cocktails and pour shots. The fire at my fingertips is eager, making my hot pink nails glow each time it flares to life.

I flex and clench my hands every few minutes to try to erase the prickling itch beneath my skin, the impulse to set fire to the next thing I see, to swipe or steal the next thing I touch. Even the itch to strangle this guy who won't stop talking to me is getting hard to ignore.

I've never killed anyone, thankfully, but that's not to say it's off the table. Plenty of demons have. It's part of why we're called demons, after all, because we're known criminals with urges that used to get us institutionalized and locked away. Now, most of us live in hiding or work for various levels of law enforcement; still largely responsible for many of the horrors that happen in the world, but some of us aren't so bad.

My parents are the type of demons whose inclinations mostly revolve around drugs and sex, much to my discomfort as a teenager. I think that's why I don't view sex as something serious; it's just another fun activity that's been normal since I was old enough to understand it.

My mom and dad have always been open about who they are and embracing their lifestyle, accepting their demon urges. And while I love that for them, it doesn't exactly work with the demonic impulses I was born with. Mine are much more destructive and harmful to others, rather than only myself, and my parents never knew what to do with me.

I don't know what to do with me either.

"You're distracted today."

I nearly leap out of my skin and fire shoots from my fingers down to the floor. Thankfully, it sputters out before catching.

"Finn! Holy shit, man. Don't sneak up on me like that," I gasp, my heart hammering in my chest.

Finn looks around, eyebrows raised. "Sorry about that?"

I laugh it off with a wave and Finn tilts his head at how clearly fake it sounds.

"What's up with you? I've been watching that guy flirt with you all night and you'd normally have banged him in the bathroom by now, but you look ready to murder him instead."

His tone is joking, which tells me he has no idea how close that is to the truth. One look from the curly-haired, muscled daddy of a man and I'd have been on my knees before the words were out of his mouth—if the demon inside me didn't have a new obsession. Instead, every suggestive word and heated glance he sends my way have my hackles rising in irritation.

"Yeah, I don't know. Just feeling off today I guess."

"Riiiiight," he says, still skeptical.

I refill the glass of water he helped himself to when I wasn't paying attention and slide it back to him.

"Thanks." He's still eyeing me like he can figure out what's wrong if he looks hard enough.

"Sure. So what's up with you?" I ask, forcing the words through my teeth even though I'm a terrible friend today and couldn't care less what he has to say.

"I've got this new beat in my head, thinking I might give it a spin later." Finn's head is bobbing and his fingers are tapping on the bar like he's playing it right now. It finally pulls a grin to my face, dissipating some of the angst that's been simmering under my skin the last couple hours.

"Yeah? That's awesome, it's been a while since you came up with something new. You should give it a go!"

Another patron waves me over and Finn grins with a nod, understanding I can't stay and chat even though he's on his break. I pour shots and refill drinks, and finally come to the conclusion that maybe sexy-bear-daddy is exactly what I need tonight.

I need to get out of my own head, and he seems like he's ready for the challenge. I check him out again, glancing over the too-tight tee he's wearing and knowing the scruff along his jaw would feel delightfully rough against my own skin. I try to imagine it, where he'd put his hands, what he might say, how I'd feel in response.

A few minutes later, I groan in defeat. Despite my best efforts at returning his flirting, I can't get into it. I end up shaking my head at him with a shrug of apology, and he winks at me before turning around to survey the dance floor. I don't blame him. I'm a lost cause at this point. My thoughts are stuck on long, wispy silver hair and wondering what color eyes go with it.

My single memory and multiple daydreams cause me to hallucinate, and I start catching flashes of shimmering hair through the throngs of dancers. I roll my eyes at myself, half hoping I don't see her again because this woman is clearly a problem for the demon.

I yank the tap in front of me, frothy beer pouring into the glass I'm holding, then I slide it across the bar and do a double take. There's a woman leaning on the bar next to the person I just served.

A woman with silver hair reflecting the colored lights in the club.

The woman I'm newly obsessed with is right in front of me, ordering three shots of tequila with a voice like velvet.

My eyes trace as much of her as I can see, which isn't much. Dark eyes—too dark to tell the color in this lighting—a dainty nose and slightly pointed chin. Her shoulders are thrown back, daring anyone to mess with her, and it immediately makes me want to give her trouble.

I grin, and it feels manic on my face. I'm definitely showing too many teeth, but I can't possibly rein it in. She's stunning and fierce and terrifying.

I drop the shot glasses in front of her and wait until she meets my eyes before raising the bottle to pour. I sink into her dark gaze and hold eye contact with her, having poured enough shots in my day to know exactly when and how much to move the bottle to fill up all three glasses. I wink when I lower it, my grin never leaving my face, and my fingers itch to light the shots on fire. My inner demon wants to give her a show, but I set the bottle down and grip the edge of the bar instead.

She narrows her eyes, not breaking our eye contact, and downs one shot after the other, slamming each empty glass on the bar in front of her. When she throws back the third, my eyes travel down her slim neck, watching her throat bob as she swallows. She has a tattoo, sparrows taking flight behind her ear and part way down her neck.

My gut clenches, and it feels like there's fire behind my

eyes. It's a new feeling, one I have no idea what to do with, and I wonder if there might be flames reflected in my eyes. That's how it feels, anyway, but she doesn't so much as flinch when my gaze travels back up and meets hers again. I raise one eyebrow, waiting for her next move.

Her face doesn't change, her expression remaining stone cold as she turns and strides to the dance floor. I'd be disappointed, but now I can see the rest of her. My eyes snag on the three silver bracelets looped around one dainty wrist, then on the bare skin between her dark crop top and high-waisted pants, and finally on the slight curve of her cute little ass.

She doesn't approach anyone. Instead, she dances alone, losing herself to the beat as her hips roll, and my irritation reignites in my chest. I wish I wasn't working so I could go out there and dance with her. Talk to her. Worship her. *Take her.*

Ooookay, so my inner demon has *strong* thoughts about her. Cool cool cool. My therapist will love this development.

A swanky looking guy grinds up behind my starlight girl and she dances with him for a bit, but then shakes her head when he leans down to speak in her ear. He turns away to feel up someone else, and she dances up behind another girl. Their limbs intertwine and their bodies bump and sway to the beat as colored lights reflect off their sweat-slicked skin.

I get a rush at the bar and she's out of my sight for a few minutes as the bodies on the dance floor shift. Then Finn sets the music to auto play while he takes another break, making his way behind the bar to help himself to a drink.

"Still waiting on that new track!" I say, nodding to him.

He grins in reply and shrugs one shoulder. I take it to mean he hasn't decided yet.

I'm mid-pour on an IPA when the crowd parts and I catch a glimpse of her again—making out with the girl she was dancing with. Time stands still and the image is seared into my brain. Hands on hips and tangled in hair, legs between the others' thighs as they dance and grind on each other, a flash of tongue between parted lips.

The demon howls inside my chest as I freeze. The chilled beer overflows the glass and froths over my hand, startling me. I drop the glass, a loud clang against the floor, though thankfully it doesn't break. The sound shatters the trance that seeing her tongue, her lips, her pleasure put me in, and I whip around to lean my back against the bar. It's the closest I can come to hiding, given the current situation.

Finn stares at me, his drink halfway to his mouth, eyes wide with some combination of amusement and concern as his gaze flits between me and the girl I've been staring at since she arrived.

"Uh-huh," he says, a knowing smirk on his lips.

He takes a gulp of his whiskey, then sets it down and grabs a rag while I suck in a deep breath, then re-pour the beer.

"So she's what's got your panties in a twist tonight, eh?" he says, laughter barely concealed beneath the words.

I don't even bother trying to deny it. "Yeah, yeah. Laugh it up."

He smacks a hand against my back, a wide grin on his face as he tosses the rag aside.

"I don't know if I've ever seen you this messed up over someone before. What's her deal?"

"No deal. I don't even know her," I say, cringing at the wistful note in my voice and hoping he doesn't catch it over the music.

"But you want to," he replies.

"Yeah," I say with a sigh. "I really do."

2

LOR ALSO REALLY NEEDS THERAPY

May 7, 1977: Today is Renée's third birthday.
She's such a sweet, happy child, and I hate to
think of how the curse in our blood is going
to ruin her joy. I haven't seen any signs of
the stars torturing her yet, but it will come.
It's only a matter of time.

LOR

I grip the woman's hips and pull her tighter against me, slotting my leg between hers as she fists a hand in my hair and drags her tongue along mine. Her breasts are soft, her lips taste like tequila, and she's cute as fuck in a sparkly pink dress. It barely covers her ass, and she doesn't seem to mind that it rides up even further as we grind on each other's thighs.

I've been aching for exactly this kind of distraction all week, but apparently her tongue tasting mine isn't enough to push back the darkness in my head, even with three shots to help. I try to stay in the moment, focusing on the music reverberating around us, the feel of her fingers as they tease the bare skin between my black pants and crop top, but as one song rolls into the next, I slowly give up. The darkness bleeds into the edges of my mind, threatening and sapping my strength.

Her hands still as she feels my energy change, and she pulls back, inquiry in her gaze. I try to offer a smile, but it feels more like a grimace. She shrugs and steps back, and I match her movements. We part ways, no words needed, and I'm back to dancing alone while she finds a new partner for the night.

I pretend for a few songs.

Pretend to have fun, that I'm dancing my heart out, that I'm enjoying myself and lost in the music. This club has brought good luck in the past, and I was hopeful someone would catch my eye tonight. That maybe someone could spark something inside me. Anything to distract from the desolate loneliness yawning through my soul, but nothing fills the void.

Sometimes I can escape for a few hours with a night of lust, but even that is losing its effectiveness lately. Nothing works, and the burden of being profoundly alone creeps ever closer, increasingly darker, weighing heavier.

There's a moment of deliberation when I consider trying again, and another when I wonder if more alcohol is the answer. I know it in my bones though—neither will help.

So I call it a night.

I don't even turn the lights on when I get home, knowing the sight of my empty, undecorated apartment will only depress me further. I strip out of my clothes, drop them in the hamper, then swish some mouthwash before falling into bed and hoping for oblivion.

THE NEXT MORNING is more of the same, a dull ache deep inside. I wake up late to a bleak apartment, poor job prospects, and the unwelcome sound of loud meowing outside my third floor bedroom window. I roll over and push it open, letting in the stray tabby cat that seems to have decided it lives here. The cat leaps inside, then sits primly on the floor and glares at me with startlingly evil looking green eyes.

"What?" I say, defensive that it's mad at me for doing what it wanted. Why are cats so hard to please?

Its tail twitches.

I groan and get out of bed, noticing there's also a relentless hum in my blood today. It brings a wave of relief, followed quickly by resentment. I don't know if I'd rather feel this, the persistent urge to follow—to *seek*—or nothing.

I think numb is worse, so I welcome the unrelenting urge for now.

The coffee maker splutters and I inhale the aroma of a cheap medium roast as I pull open my laptop. The buzzing hum running through my veins tells me another star has fallen, and about time too. I'm low on funds, and my employer/evil boss man who I suspect might be part of the mafia won't wait on me forever. He hasn't given me any sort of name other than 'boss' but he seems to hate it when I call him 'partner' instead, so naturally that's what I do.

We both know we aren't partners.

After all, it's hard to be partners with someone who is blackmailing you.

Especially when they're also your only source of income. It's my fault he figured out that I'm a star-chaser, a rare descendent of the stars. I don't know of any others besides my mom, and most people think we're a myth—that's how uncommon we are. We're ruled by the curse in our blood to retrieve the remains of fallen stars.

I wasn't careful enough when I sold the stardust I found, taking the quick and easy way of making money by selling to my 'partner' repeatedly instead of finding other buyers.

Stardust, it turns out, has magical properties that few people know about.

I mentally kick myself again for being such an idiot in the past. I know not to trust anyone. It's one of the only things my mother was ever consistent on: never trust anyone, ever. Yet here I am, blackmailed by a mob boss because I forgot the most important rule of star-chasing and sold to him a few too many times.

Now I have no other choice.

It takes me the better part of the day, but eventually I scrounge up enough information from NASA on a couple leads and wonder how my ancestors did this. I know how to follow the urge when I get close enough to a fallen star to find the stardust—the remains of my ancestral beings—but I need to at least know what direction to go in first. How did they survive this buzzing without the internet to tell them where they needed to go?

In the end, I guess they didn't. That's the one other thing my mother consistently warned me of: my fate.

Star-chasers go mad. Always.

Every.

Single.

One.

I decide to check out the leads tomorrow since it's already late afternoon, and the urge to move, to find, to *go*, settles a bit now that I have a plan mapped out. I won't be able to resist it for long, but I've learned the hard way that it's better not to go out unprepared. The last thing I need is to get lost again, or caught in a tornado on my bike. I make a mental note to check the weather before I head out tomorrow.

The cat scratches at the table leg across from me and I scowl down at it.

"Stop that."

It turns narrowed green eyes on me, then slowly extends one paw and digs its nails into the wood of my second-hand table. I groan and flop back in my chair. This cat is impossible and I have no idea why I keep letting it inside.

Seemingly satisfied with its destruction of both the table and my will, the cat hops onto the kitchen counter in search of food.

My phone rings from the other room, and I point a finger at the cat as I walk past it.

"Keep your claws to yourself. I'll find you some food in a minute."

I swipe up my phone, then freeze when I see the words 'Partner AKA Evil Blackmailing Boss Man' on the screen. I brace myself for the threats before answering.

"Hello?" I say.

"Alorra." His voice is gruff and angry, which is exactly how he always looks in person too.

"Yes, hi."

"I expect good news. When will you be dropping by?"

"Ah, yeah…" I chew my lip, trying to figure out how to tell him I don't have any stardust yet.

He tsks, clicking his tongue against his teeth.

"Okay, so I don't have any right now," I rush to keep talking. "But I have a lead! A couple leads to follow up on. I'll have more soon."

"You have two weeks to get me double."

"Wait, double?" My voice rises with alarm, an octave too high, but there's no answer.

I pull the phone from my ear to see he's already hung up. I don't know if I can get any more in two weeks, let alone double. Just because I have a lead and the urge to follow it doesn't mean there will be any usable stardust at the impact site. My neck prickles, the sensation of fighting off tears when I have no tears left to give.

The phone drops from my limp fingers onto the bed and I shuffle back to the kitchen. I pull a can of chicken breast from a worn cabinet and pop the top off for the cat, then slouch back in front of my laptop. I don't even have the energy to open it, which is apparently unacceptable to the refueled cat.

It hops from the counter to my table, then sits right in front of me on the other side of my computer, staring me down, tail flicking side to side.

"Fine," I huff, and open the laptop.

The cat flops onto its side and rolls around, looking at me upside down around the side of my screen. I twist my lips to the side to hold in what feels suspiciously like a smile; this cat will not break me.

AFTER A FEW MORE HOURS OF research, an entire pot of crappy coffee, and two slices of leftover pizza, I have four destinations to check out starting tomorrow. It'll be a multi-day trip on my bike, but that's nothing new. If I'm lucky, I'll find some salvageable stardust and the evil boss man will lay off me for a while.

The cat has long since disappeared after demanding to be let back outside, and I don't expect to see it until after I return. My brain is exhausted, but my body is wired from too much caffeine. I didn't get the escape I was looking for last night, and that pathetic, hopeful part of me wants to try again. So I hop in the shower, scrubbing my scalp and rinsing the anxious sweat of today from my body.

I dry my hair and let it hang straight down my back, then wing out my eyeliner, dab an extra layer of mascara, and swipe blood red lipstick across my lips. I loop a jangle of silver bracelets around my wrist, and that's the extent of my jewelry.

Then I pull on my usual outfit: skintight black pants, a black crop top, and black riding boots. I have very few colors in my closet—okay, I have no colors in my closet—and that's exactly how I like it. Quick, easy, no threat of decision paralysis. Plus, fewer people mess with me when I'm dressed like a badass.

I walk the few blocks to Tempo and notice the dance floor isn't as busy as usual. I wonder what day it is? It must be a weekday. There's plenty of space at the bar, so I lean against it and order my usual, three shots of tequila.

The bartender catches my eye, and I remember him from the previous night. A few inches taller than me with messy, brown hair and a smile so bright it makes me cringe. No one has the right to exude so much happiness, especially not in a nearly empty bar.

I haven't seen him here before this week. He must be new, although he clearly knows what he's doing, moving around behind the bar like it's second nature. I take another look, drawn in by the dark eyeliner accenting bright hazel eyes that almost glow in the dim lighting.

I eye him up and down, taking in his colorful look. An eclectic mix of hot pink nails, a tattoo of a moth on the back of one hand, a loose purple shirt with the sleeves cut off and fishnet over the shoulders, and too many piercings to count. My eyes snag on the silver lip ring glinting on the right side of his lower lip.

He's hot, and if the heated look he's giving me is any indication, he's also more than willing.

I consider it, slamming the shots back, and decide to hit the dance floor while I scope things out. I sway my hips to the beat, reach my arms above my head and close my eyes as I try to let the music take me. Hands land on my hips, but I don't acknowledge them, waiting to see what the mystery person will do. I know they're not the bartender's hands; they're much too small to belong to him. Soon enough the hands leave, and I'm swaying on my own again. I feel eyes on me, prickling the hair on the back of my neck, so I tip my head back down and open my eyes to peek over my shoulder.

The bartender is watching me.

I tilt my head to the side as I spin toward him, trailing one hand down my body as I dance. His throat bobs as he pauses shaking a cocktail, arms raised and muscles tense while his gaze blazes heat down my body. I trace my eyes over his biceps, appreciating their definition, but ultimately deciding I don't want to wait.

Another night, perhaps, he'd be what I want, but tonight I don't want it quick and dirty in a back room. I want hours of oblivion, ideally in someone else's bed so I can sneak away when I'm satisfied.

No one else here is doing it for me, though. I wrinkle my nose as I make the decision to walk another couple blocks to the more popular, more expensive club. It's a swanky place that tends to draw more tourists than this one, so I probably have a decent shot of finding what I want there, even if the drinks are pricey. Before I leave, I saunter back to the bar, and the bartender scrambles over to serve me. It's kind of cute, and my lips twitch up before I can stop them.

"More shots?" he says.

"Nah, closing my tab," I reply, dropping a few bills on the bar.

His face falls and I almost feel bad, until I remember that I don't owe him anything and he's hot enough to bag any hookup in this place. I turn away, my gaze roving over the crowd one last time.

"You're all set," he says.

I don't reply, and I don't look back, not wanting to see his sad puppy dog eyes as I leave.

3

LOGIC HAS NO PLACE HERE

Ro

I've been wiping the same stretch of bar for far too long. She's mesmerizing though, the way her body moves with the music, flowing with the beat. Pulsing hexagon light strips on the ceiling scatter rainbows across her silver hair, while the flashing floor tiles cast a mystical glow from beneath. Whispers of color and shadow whirl over her pale skin in time to the beat, like they're dancing with her. The demon in my chest rumbles, envious desire bubbling up in my chest.

There are a few other people dancing, but not many. A gay couple grinding in the corner, and a group of women having a fun, alcohol-free night. Surprisingly, they tip better for their mocktails than most folks who order specialized cocktails do.

My eyes drift back to the sole silhouette dancing alone. Her hands are dainty, reaching high above her head, and I blink, zeroing in on the dark lines of delicate tattoos curving over her fingers. I was too focused on her face to catch them before. I wonder what other details I haven't discovered yet.

Finn slaps me on the back, startling me out of my stupor, and the hand I was leaning on jerks out from under me so my ribs crack against the bar. I rub my side with a wince as I straighten to face him.

"Have you talked to her?" he asks.

I laugh, and it comes out more self-deprecating than I intended.

"No," I say, clearing my throat.

"You should. She's been checking you out."

My gaze is drawn back to her and she turns, opening her eyes again and trailing one hand down her body. It's the sexiest thing I've ever seen, and my dick pulses against my thigh. Next thing I know, she's walking toward me, her hips still swaying to the music. My brain distorts the vision, like in a movie when everything slows down and tunnels.

Nothing exists except her.

And then she's leaning against the bar, reality restored around me.

Finn chuckles as he walks back to the stage with a bottle of water, and I know it's aimed at me. This weird, tongue-tied uncertainty is not my usual vibe. I take a breath and throw my shoulders back, determined to win her over.

Only... she's not even looking at me anymore. Instead, she's dropping cash on the bar to close out her tab.

And then she's leaving without a backward glance.

Dumbfounded, I turn and look at the backlit stage where Finn is spinning his beats. He sees her walking toward the door, then looks back at me, throws his head back, and laughs. I can't hear it over the thumping music, but I roll my eyes, a smile cracking my own face, because it is kind of funny.

I can't remember the last time I was unable to get someone I wanted into my bed.

It's different with her, though.

Something about her makes me stupid, and honestly, I don't want a quick hookup. That thought strikes me dumb again, and I look back at the door that swings closed behind her. I've been thinking about her since I first saw her yesterday, and I'm kicking myself for not asking her name when I had the chance. I didn't expect her to dip out so fast, though. She stayed for hours the other night.

I toss the rag under the bar and search for a customer, but it's slow tonight. No wonder she left. This place is a bore.

My fingers are twitchy; the demon inside wants me to follow her. It's frightening, this new urge, and I try to avoid it, which only serves to make the demon more adamant.

My eyes flick to the door she just left through, and the demon pushes at my chest. He wants me to follow her, kidnap her, fuck her, *claim her*—whatever the hell that means. I shudder at the strength of his desires, pushing back, reminding myself that good people don't do those things, and I want to be a good person.

The thing is, the demon inside me has never been this obsessed before, and I don't know how long I can hold out.

I pocket one of the many metal jiggers lining the shelf below the bar in an attempt to settle my urges, but it doesn't help. Fire licks at my fingers, and I run it along my knuckles, playing with it like humans fiddle with a pen. I can't stop looking at the door, and although it's likely only been seconds, it feels like ages when I finally give in.

I wave to catch Finn's attention, gesturing to ask if he can cover the bar. It's slow enough that he can set an auto-play track if needed. He smirks, then gives me the 'go ahead' chin jerk. I race around the bar, ignoring the wide-eyed looks of the few patrons we have in here as I fling the door open and look up and down the street.

She's a block down, not hard to spot thanks to her bright silver hair. My instincts push me forward, and the feeling of giving in is a painful dichotomy of euphoria and shame. It licks up my spine and settles in my gut, but it's too late for me now.

The demon has too strong a hold.

The cool night air licks at my heated skin. I follow at a distance as she turns a corner, but she doesn't go far. She steps into another club; this one seems to be aimed at tourists rather than locals, and I walk inside a few seconds after her. She only orders one shot at the bar this time, and the demon hums with pleasure that I got to serve her more than this bartender.

It's ridiculous and I silently berate myself.

I keep my distance, settling onto a stool at the far end of the bar and turning my body away from her. The last thing I need is to be caught here, at another club, when she knows I'm supposed to be working at Tempo.

She slams the glass down on the reflective black counter and stands, maneuvering her way into the mass of bodies on the dance floor. The LED lights shine off her hair, dotting spots of color over her face. I sit up a little straighter and shift on my stool, trying to keep her in my line of sight, but it's impossible.

Bodies move and sway, and her silver hair flickers in and out of sight. The demon gets antsy again, urging me to find her, but I force myself to sit back down instead. I order a cheap beer and nurse it, absorbing the delicious flashes of her in the crowd as I bite my lip ring between my teeth.

That is, until the next break in the dance floor shows her dancing with another woman. The woman is standing behind her, one hand pressed to her lower stomach to hold their bodies close as they rock together, the other hand on her jaw. This woman kisses along her neck and my blood heats, both with jealousy and desire. I want to be the one holding her like that, kissing her like that, swaying to the beat with her like that. I'd even be happy to join the two of them, if that's what they wanted. I'm not picky.

Then her hands run up her own body, across her breasts, over her shoulders, and into the hair of the woman dancing behind her. Her arms are raised, baring her pale stomach, and I groan under my breath. I know I can't join them, she already turned me down tonight, but the demon doesn't understand consent.

I realize with horror that I might not be able to hold him back if I stay here. I drop a twenty on the bar and lurch out of my seat.

"No more fires. No more stealing. No killing."

The mantra is supposed to help me resist demonic impulses, and I hope the familiar pattern of reciting it will help in this situation, too. At this point, it's a habit more than anything. I repeat the words under my breath as I duck out of the club, hoping fresh air will snap me out of it. Instead, the distance only riles the demon urges even more.

"Okay," I say to myself. "Harm reduction, that's what my therapist said we're working on. A safe way to let my urges out in small amounts. What can..."

I look around, spotting a metal trashcan in the alley along the side of the building. I stalk over and immediately throw a line of fire at it. It flashes in a blaze of heat when I set fire to the contents, and I don't stop. My arm is outstretched, palm wide open, sending more and more fire into it, allowing myself to release some of the pent up frustration the demon is pumping into me.

My emotions ebb and flow as heat and tension release with the flames. The fire burns hot and bright, flaring into the sky. I let it roar for a few more seconds before smothering it down to a steady smolder.

The last thing I need is someone calling the cops on me.

I shake out my hands, crack my neck, and roll my shoulders. I glare at the glowing coals, take a breath, then clench my fists to douse the remains of the fire. My emotions aren't as close to the surface now, but they're still there, a low roil under my skin.

"Better," I mutter. "Okay, for real this time. No more fires. No more stealing. No killing."

I pace back and forth, up and down the alley a few times as I take deep breaths and repeat the mantra to myself. I yank the stolen jigger from my pocket and squeeze it, the curved metal edges denting my palm. I'm feeling slightly more in control, a little bit more settled, when I freeze, my eyes going wide.

I realize... Nothing in the rules from my therapist says I can't follow her. 'No stalking' isn't on the list. The demon immediately calms, quietly perking up at this idea.

Of course, some deep down part of me knows just because it isn't on the list, doesn't mean it's okay. Obviously, I know stalking is wrong, but the logical side isn't in charge right now.

I decide following her for now—from a safe distance, with no intent to harm—isn't bad. It's simply a coping mechanism, one that allows me to control my urges without putting anyone in danger. Harm reduction, right?

And... yeah, okay. I'll definitely be telling my therapist about it as soon as possible.

With that decided, I lean against the brick wall and wait, flicking a tiny flame back and forth over my knuckles and between my fingers with the demon purring happily in my chest. The chill seeps into my back, but the fire of my demon keeps me plenty warm while I wait.

When she finally steps outside, alone, I frown. I fully expected her to hook up with the other woman, but then again, maybe they already did.

She pauses in the doorway, and the neon lights above and behind frame her in a colorful halo. My eyes track up and down her body, taking in an outfit remarkably similar to the one from the night before. Tight black clothing, boots that could easily kick my ass, curves that would fit perfectly in my palms.

Lust burns low in my belly, but then I tilt my head,

picking up other details now that she's alone and standing still. She's tense, rigid almost, with a defensive, ready for fight-or-flight posture. Not relaxed at all, as she should be if she'd had a successful night out. I study the walls she's built around herself, wondering if they have any cracks.

My frown deepens when her breasts heave with a sigh and her shoulders slump forward. Her eyes are dark wells, unfathomable from this distance, yet they tug at my heart. I want to comfort her, another urge that's new to me.

She steps away from the light and shoves her hands in her pockets as she walks down the sidewalk. I follow, but only because I want to make sure she gets to her next location safely. Obviously.

Although that thought is an excuse, it also rings true, and the demon seems to agree. He's urging me to follow, but the impulse to *take*, to do anything more, is no longer there. Never before has the demon inside me given me such whiplash, but I'll accept any small win I can right now.

I step quietly, doing my best to be stealthy as I follow half a block behind her. She keeps glancing back, like she senses someone following, but it's dark enough that I can slip into a doorway or alcove and remain undetected.

When she turns into the entrance for an apartment building, I look away from her to check where we're at.

Aaaand that's a problem.

She lives only blocks from me, on the same street. This woman with sad eyes and shimmering hair that reflects the moon.

The demon is practically preening at how close I can be to her, how often and easily I can follow her now that I know where she lives. I try to force myself to turn away, to not watch the windows to see which lights flick on, but it's impossible. That demon inside me won't be swayed, but after a few minutes of observation, there are no lights.

Maybe she lives on the other side of the building.

Then curtains drift as a window is pushed open, a lithe shadow with silver hair moves behind sheer fabric, and I know without a doubt.

It's her.

That's where she lives. Eats. Sleeps.

I have *got* to call my therapist.

4

OVEREAGER PUPPY-DOG VIBES

Ro

"What I'm hearing is that you're struggling with a new obsession: your thoughts of this woman, and a new compulsion: your urge to stalk her."

Yikes.

June, my therapist, really isn't pulling any punches today.

"I, uh..." I ruffle the short hair on the back of my head, then drop my hand back to my lap. "Yeah, I guess."

"You guess?" June says, her head tilted and a tiny smile quirking one side of her mouth.

"Fine. That's correct. I have a new obsession and compulsion and..."

June raises her eyebrows, nodding her head for me to continue. She's always patient, never rushing me when I struggle to admit a truth I don't want to face or find words that elude me.

"It's stronger than any of the other urges I've had. The demon..." I grimace. "He really likes her."

June jots a couple notes on the yellow lined notepad in her lap, then looks back up at me.

"We're going to come back to that, but first, is it okay if I share an observation with you?"

"Of course."

That is why I'm here after all, for her help.

"I've noticed in the couple months we've been working together that you refer to the demon as being separate from you, like another entity. Is your inner demon not you?"

"He's..." I trail off, gaping at her. I have no idea how to answer that.

"I don't know," I say. "Is he?"

June chuckles. "I think only you have that answer. I wasn't trying to lead you anywhere, I was genuinely asking."

"Right," I murmur, turning to stare out the window.

She lets me stew for a few moments, but I shake my head and shrug. When I turn back to her with an apologetic smile, she meets it.

"We'll come back to it, after you've had some time to think about it," she says.

"Homework?" I ask.

June grins. "Homework."

Then she looks back at her notebook.

"So, this new, stronger urge. Based on the skills you've learned so far, what have you already tried?" she asks.

And with that, we're off. I relax into the sofa, letting her confidence wash over me as we figure out how I'm going to continue my journey toward being a good person when all I want to do is stalk a mysterious woman whose name I don't even know.

I MANAGE to resist following her—my silver-haired obsession —for a couple of days after meeting with June, and it probably helps that I don't see her anywhere. When she doesn't show up to the club for the fourth night in a row though, I'm feeling increasingly restless. It's all I can do to stop myself from walking by her apartment building on my way to and from work. I've taken to reciting my mantra like it's my only link to sanity, which still has nothing about stalking included, despite my therapist thinking it may be a good idea to revise it.

Denial and avoidance at its finest.

It also doesn't help that it's been over a week now since I've gotten laid, and that's definitely some sort of record. I can't remember the last time I went this long without having sex. It was probably when I was in high school, but even then, my parents (being sex demons) encouraged me to explore my sexuality. Frustratingly, my dick doesn't seem to have interest in anyone besides the elusive, silver-haired woman I'm supposed to be keeping my distance from.

Quite the conundrum.

I'm whipping up a cocktail and contemplating drinking on the job in the hopes that will help me relax, when she slips through the door into the club. My lips pull into a grin and my spine snaps straight, the demon inside me on alert. I quickly pour the cocktail and pass it across the bar, not even bothering with garnish in my haste to serve her. I bound over, not caring one bit if I look like an overeager puppy.

She slides onto a stool and flicks her long hair over her shoulder. Then I notice the dark circles under her eyes, the way her hair seems to have lost its luster, the tense hunch of her shoulders. She looks exhausted.

"Hey," I say, putting on my prettiest bartender voice. "What can I get for ya?"

"Tequila," she says.

"Gonna need to see an ID with that," I reply, deciding a little snooping won't hurt anyone. I nudge my lip ring with my tongue as I wait. The demon preens when her eyes flick to it, then the piercing in my eyebrow, before returning to meet my gaze.

She purses her lips, but pulls the card out of her bra and passes it to me. My stupid dick throbs at the thought of touching something that was pressed against her breast. I feel like a horny teenager again who has no idea how to talk to a pretty girl.

I look down at her ID, confirming the address I followed her to last week, and finally learning her name.

"Alorra Seren," I say, rolling her name along my tongue. It's like a sweet treat in my mouth, making me salivate for more. I pass the card back to her and do some quick math. "Twenty-eight. Checks out. Triple order of tequila, coming right up!"

I grin, but she doesn't return it, instead eyeing me with apathy.

I hate that, so I decide it's a personal challenge.

I set her three shot glasses in front of her, but don't fill them yet. Instead, I turn back to the bar, surveying my options. I get to work, grabbing a clear bottle from the shelves as well as a couple ingredients from below. I measure and pour, shake, then strain my concoction into a glass.

Finally, I turn back with her tequila. I fill the shot glasses lined up in front of her, then set the sparkly purple drink I created right next to them.

Alorra pauses with one hand outstretched toward the row of shots. Her eyes flick up to mine, a dark grey-blue color, and my heart skips a beat. Will she accept my offering? I swear even my inner demon is holding his breath.

Her gaze flits between mine and the gay as hell purple drink I set in front of her. Her hand slowly moves away from the shots and toward the glass as I watch with bated breath. I bite my lip ring, stifling a grin as she picks it up.

Alorra sniffs it first, then she eyes it, skeptical, before turning her narrowed gaze on me.

Her eyes have captured mine, daring me to look away as she takes a sip. Thanks to this unspoken threat, I catch the moment of surprise and pleasure that flits across her face before she manages to conceal it.

I grin in triumph. My chest puffs out on a relieved breath, and tension I didn't realize I was carrying loosens from my shoulders.

Then the beautiful Alorra Seren scowls, sets the drink down, and glares at me.

"What is this?" she demands, her voice husky and low and... weary?

My smile wavers. "It's a moonlight cocktail."

She stares at me, so I swallow and continue. "Gin, creme de violette, lemon juice, simple syrup... and uh, edible glitter."

She blinks, but her stare is resolute. "Why?"

"Because," I falter, sensing again that any hint of sympathy or caring will send her running. "I don't know. I just wanted to try making it and thought you'd give it a go."

Her eyes soften the barest amount, and the scowl lifts when she turns curious eyes back to the fabulous lavender cocktail swirling with sparkles in front of her.

"Is it bad?" I ask, wondering if I misjudged the ingredients.

She shrugs, but then she takes another sip.

The demon howls with glee, rumbling in my chest and I grin again, straightening back up. Her lips twitch when she sees my reaction, and I'd bet money that's the closest she's gotten to smiling in days. That's a win if I ever saw one.

Now I need to learn how to turn that twitch into a full-on smile.

"You gonna finish those shots, or...?"

She pretends to glare at me. It's adorable. We're basically friends now, so I don't take it to heart.

"I haven't decided yet," she says.

I shrug, then snag one and throw it back.

"Hey!" she shrieks, the most animated I've seen her yet, and a number of eyes turn toward us.

I bellow a laugh, waving away the attention when she huffs. Then she grabs the second shot and downs it with a grimace.

"Ah," she says, clicking her tongue. "That's not great after whatever this purple monstrosity is."

"Hey!" It's my turn to protest with a laugh. "I'll have you know that so-called monstrosity is my pride and joy creation."

"Oh, really?" She raises a skeptical eyebrow. "And why is that?"

"Because it *almost* got you to smile."

To my absolute delight, her cheeks turn pink. Of course, it's accompanied by another scowling glare, but that's still another win in my book.

Three points to Ro.

"And now I'm winning," I say, propping my elbow on the bar and my chin in my palm.

I didn't know I could grin so wide when a look of outraged consternation finally overtakes the lethargic apathy that had been clinging to her. She stares at me and I hold her gaze, not letting my smile falter. Her entire body transforms, the defensive tension shifting to an upright, quiet confidence, her blank expression turning to wary interest as her mind tries to make sense of my words.

"Winning *what?*" she finally demands.

"This, of course." I gesture between us and confusion mars her stoic facade.

She shakes her head and knocks back the last shot.

"You're something else," she mutters under her breath.

I hear it, though I'm not sure if I was supposed to.

"You've got that right," I say with a wink.

Her lips twitch again and she turns her back to me, leaning against the bar as she looks out over the dance floor. I take the opportunity to catch up on orders, thankful I'm not working the bar alone tonight. When I glance back over at her, she's raising the so-called purple monstrosity to her blood red lips for another sip.

WHEN ALORRA SWIVELS back to the bar again, I'm ready. She seems to debate her next move, glancing from the dance floor to the exit, so I step in before she decides to leave again.

"Can I take you out on a date?" I ask.

She stares at me, her steely gaze holding me hostage. I straighten my shoulders and do my best to present a 'I'm a good, safe, definitely-not-a-demon-who-wants-to-stalk-you' facade.

After what must be at least a couple years, she finally speaks.

"Why should I let you?" she says.

I was not prepared for that response. A 'yes' would have been fantastic. 'No' I can deal with. But this? I gape at her, feeling like a fish out of water as I open my mouth, but no words come out.

She shrugs one shoulder, throws back the rest of her purple drink, then sets the empty glass on the bar and slides off the barstool. Without a backward glance—again—she leaves.

I can't tear my eyes away from her. Each blink takes her further from me, until she's out the door and it's swinging shut behind her.

"Tough luck, man." Finn claps me on the back as he walks by.

I shake my head, a disorienting jumble of confusion and delight tumbling around my head. I turn my back to the bar and lean against it. Then my hand sneaks into my pocket and I pull out a delicate silver chain.

It's simple, with a few tiny round beads dotted along it, the interconnecting links so minuscule I can barely make them out. I'm lucky I managed to swipe it from her wrist without breaking it, or without her noticing. So much for no more stealing...

Alorra.

I roll her name around my tongue again, whispering it to myself. It's beautiful, but it doesn't quite seem to fit her. I tilt my head, inspecting the bracelet as I contemplate her name, Alorra.

Alorra Seren.

The demon is a satisfied rumble in my chest.

A name and a stolen trinket in the same night. I resist the urge to lift it to my nose to see if I can catch any trace of her on it, and my lips quirk as I curl my fingers around the dainty bracelet. Then I drape it over my wrist and fiddle with the clasp until it snaps into place, holding my arm out to admire my newest treasure.

The rest of the shift passes with dull tedium as I work on autopilot filling drinks, wiping the bar, swiping cards, until finally I'm free. The world kicks back into focus and I make a beeline for the door.

June would be disappointed, but I don't even try to curb the urge as I stride with single-minded determination down the sidewalk to Alorra's apartment. I lean against a wide tree across the road, my eyes fixed on her dark window.

My leg starts to bounce when I don't see any movement, and fire lights at my fingertips. I douse it, not wanting the light to give me away, and finger the silver chain on my wrist instead. Finally, a shadow of movement stirs behind her curtain, and I loose a breath of relief knowing she got home safe.

This knowledge, plus her bracelet against my skin, settles my inner demon and allows me to wander home with a jaunt in my step and not even a lingering fancy about lighting anything on fire.

5

———

YOU DON'T EVEN LIVE HERE

August 12, 1979: I'm following in Mother's footsteps even though I never wanted to. She always insisted that we move every few years, convinced it would delay the urge to follow the stars and keep us safe from those who would seek to use us. I don't know if it helped, but I'm willing to try anything.

LOR

I can't get him out of my head. That human from the bar. The one who made me the gayest purple drink I've ever seen and was delighted beyond comprehension when I drank it. Irritation flashes in my gut and I roll my eyes. I can't believe it actually tasted good. I kind of want another, but hell will freeze over before I admit to it.

My thoughts trickle back to him and I pace circles around my living room. No one has caught my attention like this in ages. Perhaps ever. It doesn't make sense. I'm going to wear a path in the already worn carpet if I don't stop soon.

The cat seems to agree. It yowls and then darts for the

window, glaring at me to let it out. I don't blame it; I want out, too.

"Miserable creature," I grumble, closing the window behind it and drawing the sheer curtains before I resume my pointless circling.

My brain has been turning it over and over, but for the life of me I can't figure out why I'm so stuck on him. He's attractive, sure, with that silver lip ring and mischievous grin. The messy hair, painted nails, and the godsdamned eyeliner.

That was the first thing I noticed, and yet...

There's something off. He sets my instincts on alert for some reason, like something about him isn't as it seems. Something intriguing that pulls to my darker side, despite his outward charm and endless smiling.

I don't trust it.

And whatever this game is that he thinks we're playing... I'm not taking part. He's on his own.

With that final thought, I fling myself into bed.

SOMEONE'S WATCHING ME.

I can't shake the feeling over the next couple days, but despite my increasing paranoia and watchfulness, I don't spot anyone. There's no sign of someone lurking around, but the hair on my neck prickles multiple times a day, especially when I'm home alone at night. I keep the curtains drawn and have become even more of a recluse than normal, but it doesn't seem to help.

On top of that, I've lost one of my bracelets. I peer under the couch for the thousandth time today, but see only dust bunnies and shadows. I'm not sure when or where I lost it, but it makes my wrist feel uneven to have only two chains on it instead of my normal three. It was my prettiest one, too.

My hand sinks into the couch cushion as I push myself up off the floor. I go to take the cushions off it next, but the cat is perched on a pillow right in the middle.

It stares at me, not moving except for the very tip of its tail flicking back and forth. I narrow my eyes as we lock gazes. Apart from the tail flick, it doesn't move so much as a muscle twitch.

I give up first, huffing a breath. "Can I..." I trail off, gesturing at the couch.

Its ears flatten.

"Oookay, cat. Never mind," I say, rolling my eyes.

I've already checked under and between the cushions and pillows, anyway. I know the bracelet isn't there. At least it wasn't sentimental, so I can always replace it, assuming I end up *not* broke at some point in the future.

I sigh in defeat. The cat settles itself into a fluffy cat loaf, looking appropriately smug with the fact that it's in charge.

"You don't even live here."

A bigger tail flick, then it closes its eyes.

"*I* think it matters, you ungrateful beast," I mutter.

The cat slits its green eyes open and I back away. I've learned that look the hard way. It means go away, before the claws come out.

Why couldn't the neighborhood cat be cuddly? Or even just mildly friendly? Every so often I try to pet it, and while sometimes it allows a couple gentle pats, most often it bats me away with a screech and then proceeds to either hiss at or ignore me for the next two days.

Once it even pooped in my shoe. I don't know what I did to deserve that, but it was the most disgusting thing I've ever had to deal with. I almost gag just thinking about it.

And yet, for some reason, I continue to let the damn thing in and feed it. Regardless of how grouchy it is, I'm glad for the company. Many days, the cat is the only living being I talk to.

I flick the light on and plop down in a chair at my rickety kitchen table—instead of on the cat-owned couch—to do some more research. I found a moderate amount of stardust on my last outing, but not enough to make Ole Buddy Big Guy happy. Then again, there will never be enough to make that awful man happy. My gut clenches with a toxic cocktail of regret, anxiety, and shame when I think about the predicament my current life and financial situation is in.

I've only been sitting here for a half hour, updating myself on the various meteorite tracking sites, when I feel it. A strong enough pull that it can't be ignored.

I slam the laptop closed, and the cat cracks its eyes open to glare at me again. I snag my leather jacket and slip my feet into black riding boots.

"You staying? I'm not sure how long I'll be gone."

The cat stands and stretches with a yawn, then hops off the couch and meanders over to the door.

"Take your time, not like I'm in a rush or anything," I grumble, rubbing the aching pull in my chest.

I fill my pockets with necessities, grab my go-bag, then open the door to a wall of afternoon heat. The cat winds between my legs, rubbing its chin on my boot before it darts out ahead of me. I stare as its fluffy tail disappears down the stairs.

Was that affection?

I don't understand cats.

A few minutes later, I'm straddling my bike and it roars to life with a rumbling vibration between my legs. I don't know where I'm going, but the pull of the fallen star is unrelenting, strong enough that I don't need any research first. I follow it as best I can, getting a general sense of the direction I need to go and winding my way out of the neighborhood, out of Chicago, away from the water.

All I know is I'm heading west.

I open the throttle once I'm outside the city, the steady purr of the engine lulls the constant anxiety that lives under my skin. Acting on the star-chaser urges by following the pull inside me has dulled the ache in my chest. It's placated for now, so I can relax a fraction. I love the feeling of flying free, shooting away from my life and out into the wild world.

I just wish it was reality instead of an illusion.

Perhaps it could be a reality someday. If I work hard enough, find enough stardust to earn more money, I might be able to escape. My overlord mob boss would never let me go willingly, but if I can save up enough, I might be able to get out of Chicago without him noticing until it's too late. I could find a new place to settle down. Start over where I'll be free, maybe even happy.

The hair on the back of my arms starts to prickle, snapping me out of my silly daydreams. Someone's following me again. Is it the Boss Man? Is that what's been going on? Does he somehow know my dream of disappearing, so he's been tailing me?

Can't say I blame him, if so. He's certainly not an idiot, but his goons normally are. When he's put a tail on me in the past, it has not been subtle, and I've been able to shake it easily.

This time, I'm out on the wide open road with fields all around me. I don't see anyone in my mirrors, so I risk a glance behind. There might be another motorcycle a ways back, but it's hard to tell. I pass a few cars, and a few pass me while I drive through the afternoon and into the evening, crossing the invisible border from Illinois into Iowa. The sensation hasn't let up, and as the sky darkens, a single light shines behind me, confirming there's another biker on the road.

It's probably a coincidence and I'm being paranoid. This is the most direct highway west, and it makes sense I wouldn't be the only driver on it.

When I pull up to a gas station, every sense is on alert. My heart races, adrenaline pumping through me as my feet meet the pavement. I leave my helmet on, but raise the visor so I can hear and see better, taking in every detail around me from the chipped paint on the curb, to the peeling stickers on the pump, and the sole pickup truck parked next to the building. An empty beer can rattles across the parking lot with a stray breeze and the overhead lights buzz, grating against my tired ears.

The other bike rumbles into the lot a few minutes later, and fuels up at the station across from me. The biker doesn't take off their helmet or gloves, but they turn and give me a chin jerk nod as they fill their tank. I offer a narrow-eyed glare in response, then pointedly turn away. I'm not trusting anyone, no matter how friendly they may appear.

I keep a wary eye out, watching from the periphery and reminding myself that just because they followed me into this station doesn't mean they're *following me.* This might be the only gas station for miles, I have no idea.

The other biker strides into the store, and I take the opportunity to leave them in the dust. I kick my bike into gear and take off as quick as I can, finally breathing a sigh of relief as I leave them behind and my paranoia settles.

I knock my visor back down and fall into the peace of driving at night. The stars twinkle above me, their song trickling through me, and my heart aches with a homesick longing I'll never be able to fill.

It's impossible to be reunited with my ancestors. My family comes from the stars, though the how and when of it has been lost to time, along with the world's acknowledgement of us. Everyone knows about vampires, demons, witches, and even shifters, but for the most part they can be ignored, since there are so many protective regulations and laws in place. To the few people who *have* heard of my kind, for most it's folklore. A magical bedtime story, but nothing real.

I scoff. If only they knew the truth.

While the world at large might not know about star-chasers, I know all I need to. Between my mother's rote warnings and my grandmother's journal, I've learned every hard lesson there is. Two of which are all but embedded in my DNA at this point: Don't trust anyone. All star-chasers go mad.

Unfortunately, I learned even more at the hands of my blackmailer. He's the one holding my leash, and he's also the one who taught me what stardust can do. I knew some people valued it, but I didn't know why. Turns out it doesn't affect humans, but when used by supernatural creatures... that's a different story.

My evil overlord reveled in demonstrating how powerful controlling the only stardust supply in Chicago made him. Stardust makes vampires stronger and faster for a short period of time. Appropriately, they call it "juice." It's got a bad crash afterwards, though, and they often end up knocked out for an equal amount of time.

For shifters, it's "blitz," giving them a euphoric high when ingested. Demons can use it to make their natural magical abilities more potent, normally by rubbing an infused lotion or oil on their temples and neck. I'm not sure what they call it, as I've thankfully never met a demon, nor have I heard many people speak about them. I think they're mostly imprisoned or work for the government.

And witches can use stardust for all sorts of nefarious purposes. None of the common folks know that what they're actually using is the remains of my ancestors, scavenged from fallen stars. Of course, once hooked on it, those people will do whatever they need to in order to get more.

Even kill each other.

I shudder as the gruesome memories flash through my mind. The 'games' the mob boss makes me watch when I don't fulfill my quota, or when he thinks I need a reminder of his power and control. I shake my head, envisioning the blood and desperation, the screams and the deathly quiet all scattering into the night around me—left far behind as my bike takes me away from it all.

The emotional rush of being on my motorcycle with the air whipping by and the illusion of freedom, in combination with escaping a probably made-up pursuer, has my heart beating erratically. Add to that the apprehension growing in my chest as I sense my destination getting closer has my palms sweating in my gloves and my stomach twisted in knots. The call of the fallen star is getting stronger with every mile that passes.

I dread what I'll find, knowing however much stardust I collect, whatever magical remains of my ancestors I discover, will have to be sold to a horrible man so I can continue living a pathetic life.

It's despicable.

It's my only option.

I hate myself for it.

6

———

SO CLOSE, YET SO FAR

Ro

There's a manic grin on my face. It's the main reason I didn't take my helmet off when I went inside the gas station. I could tell Alorra was on edge as soon as I pulled into the spot across from her. Her shoulders were up by her ears, and I was afraid her grip was going to break the pump. I don't want her to be afraid of me, but I can't deny that the demon loves the chase. The glare she shot me when I tried to put her at ease was adorable, although I think she was trying to put me off.

I shrug, whistling as I walk back out of the store. It's hard to whistle with a helmet on, but I manage well enough. I snagged some peach rings and watched through the window as she took off into the night, the headlight from her solid black bike spearing the darkness in front of her. I don't mind if she has a head start. I'll catch up soon enough.

There's an undeniable bounce to my step as I skip over to my bike—black with purple accents—and tear out of the lot after her. It doesn't take long before I see her tail light ahead of me. I turn my lights off, not caring even a tiny bit how dangerous it is. I don't want to scare her off again, and I doubt she can hear my bike over the sound of her own.

It's so dark out that as I get closer, her braided silver hair reflects the light of the moon and stars as it whips behind her. It's like a beacon, a falling star I'd follow to the ends of the earth, if only it would grant my one wish of catching her.

It takes me by surprise when she veers into a hard turn down a dirt road. A cloud of dust billows in her wake, obscuring my view of her and the road. I scramble to adjust my speed and maintain control as I follow her. This woman just keeps getting more and more interesting. I've never been out this way before, and I wonder where she's taking us. Does she have an isolated cabin out here? Maybe she likes camping. Or what if she's involved in something nefarious?

The demon inside me perks up, liking the sounds of that one. It feels like a pinwheel rolling down my back, prickles of anxious anticipation raising goosebumps on my skin and tripping my heart.

She pulls off into what looks like a small canyon, the landscape out of place in an area surrounded by farm fields. I park my bike out of sight and try to follow her as quietly as I can, crouched low behind boulders and a rim of fresh turned earth as I skirt around the outside of it.

I cringe at the sensation of my inner demon purring in my chest, unreasonably pleased to be doing something this unlawful and unethical. It's confusing, because the happier my demon is, the more shame I feel. Succumbing to my demonic instincts means I'm not on the path toward being a good person. And if I'm not a good person, there's only one other thing I can be.

It's better than setting fires or stealing things. At least this way I'm not hurting anyone.

I'd never hurt Alorra, I'm simply fascinated by her. I'm

sure there's some explanation for why, I just haven't found it yet.

On all fours, I slowly creep up the ridge of dirt, choosing a path further down from where she did in case she comes back that way. The earth is cool beneath my hands, the warmth from the sun having leeched out hours ago, and I wince when my knee lands on a sharp rock. None of it deters me—the dirt or the rocks or the darkness or the cold—and when I reach the top, I peek over it to see her climbing down the other side.

She hops from boulder to boulder, then slides down a few feet of loose dirt with one foot in front of the other, her arms out for balance. I think I have hearts in my eyes. I had no idea she was so athletic, and her silhouette in that tight leather riding gear... Well, it's doing something to me.

I settle into a nook on the top edge of what I'm now noticing is a perfectly round canyon. My eyebrows draw together as I take it in. It looks like an impact site of some sort, but I can't see well enough to tell what might be in the middle. Alorra jogs to a central point and crouches, then touches one hand to her chest. She stays in that position for long moments, long enough that I start to become concerned.

My inner demon goes on alert, his hackles rising at the thought of something being wrong. Is she okay? Is there something bad, tragic, horrifying there that she can't handle? Does this spot mean something to her? Is she having a heart attack or a seizure or something?

I'm about to leap over the edge and sprint to her rescue when she moves again. I duck back down, peering into the dark as she slings the bag off her shoulder and unrolls something. Then she pulls out what must be a shovel, because that's the only thing that makes sense based on the movements I can see. She's shoveling dirt and scooping rocks into the cloth bag she unrolled.

I shake my head. Maybe I'm not the only one here who is

mentally unwell, but who am I to judge? I let out a quiet snort, then carefully pick my way along the unstable rim to try to get a better look at what she's doing. I drop to the ground again when she stands and turns, her face angled to the ground as she seems to search for something. When she doesn't find it, she places her hand on her chest again and turns her face up to the sky, then starts walking. Without watching where she's going—while in a canyon full of loose rocks and dirt and boulders.

Okay yeah, this woman is definitely not well.

I'm about to run to her rescue—again—when she halts in place and drops to a crouch—again. This woman is absolutely confounding, and the more I watch, the more I want to know. What could she possibly be collecting? I would guess maybe bits of meteorite, given we're at an impact site and she's picking up rocks, but how can she tell with it being so dark? Maybe she's a witch? And the weird movements... Is she performing some sort of ritual, or casting a spell?

I know nothing about witches, but it seems the most likely guess.

Alorra repeats this process a number of times. Standing, walking with her eyes closed and face to the sky, following some unseen, unfathomable path before collecting more dirt and rocks into her bag. It has to be getting heavy, but she doesn't stop for what must be close to an hour. Long enough that my legs are cramping and my brain has run through every increasingly far-fetched scenario I can possibly think of for what she might be up to.

When she finally ties the bag closed and puts away her tools, I breathe a sigh of relief. But then she turns toward me, and I realize I moved into the path she took to get down there in the first place, despite having tried to avoid exactly that. My eyes flare wide while my inner demon feels like it's pulling me in two directions. One side wants to confront her, the other wants to hide so I can keep following her, and then there's what *I* want which is to just not get caught.

Shit, shit, shit.

My head whips around, looking for an easy hiding spot, but there's only bare earth on this side. I can't stand or she'll see me, so I scramble on my hands and knees, wincing with each sharp rock and stick that stabs my kneecaps, until I'm far enough down the outside of the rim to stand.

Of course, as soon as I do, my legs cramp and my feet slide out from under me. I tumble down the hill and a shrill, involuntary shriek of alarm splits the quiet night. Then I land hard on my back and the breath is punched from my lungs.

Shit on a witch's stick.

I wheeze, trying to draw in air but not succeeding. The stars spin above me and I don't feel real, like maybe my body isn't on this plane anymore. Even my brain stops working for an endless moment as the universe pauses, admiring my monumental fuck-up.

Next thing I know, there's a flashlight beam blinding me as Alorra crests the ridge and picks her way down the other side. I try to sit up, but grimace when my entire body feels like one massive bruise, so instead I lay there and wait. She steps gracefully over the loose rocks around me until her booted feet stop next to my head.

Scary, sexy booted feet.

I raise a hand to block the light from my eyes and attempt to look up at her, but all I can see is a glint of metal from her other hand. I wouldn't blame her for stabbing me, but I really like this shirt, so I hope she doesn't. Maybe it's the shovel she was using earlier?

"Hey!" I say, donning my most charming grin. The one that always gets me laid and will hopefully get me out of this situation with minimal damage.

I hold both hands up in a surrender pose as I struggle to

my knees, my back screaming when I straighten it. She bran-dishes what I can now see is definitely a knife.

"Don't move," she hisses.

"Whoa, whoa, whoa. Easy there, spitfire." I freeze, not moving a muscle as I regain feeling in my extremities.

Tension crackles through the air between us, and it feels like even the wind is holding its breath, waiting to see what she'll do. I'd prefer to be on my knees for her for a different reason, but this really isn't so terrible.

Only... She doesn't do anything.

I wince, now feeling too much as my knees protest the hard, uneven ground beneath them.

"Could you maybe not point your flashlight directly at my eyes?" I say, waving one hand a few inches in the hopes she'll direct it elsewhere before I'm too blinded to drive home.

She doesn't so much as twitch for an eternity, but eventu-ally she lowers the light, angling it at the dirt instead of my face. I blink, then close my eyes for a few moments, my head spinning and eyes smarting with the afterimage before I blink again and my sight starts to readjust.

"Wait," she says, some of the tension loosening from her shoulders as I blink up at her. "Bartender?"

"It's Ro, actually, but you can call me whatever you want."

Alorra blinks at me. I still have my hands in the air, and my face is level with her bare stomach. She's wearing a black crop top under her leather jacket. I want to lean forward and lick the pale skin peeking out at me.

"Why are you following me?" she demands. No fear, no uncertainty, just pure fire in her words. My inner demon wants to roll around in her attitude, and so do I.

My eyes flick back up to hers. They're glaring at me, dark with defiance, and I grin.

"What was that you were digging?" My curiosity gets the

better of me. It's no longer a want, it's a need. I need to know everything about her.

"Who are you?" she says.

"Have you always had silver hair?"

Her glare turns into an entire look, with narrowed eyes and a clenched jaw. She brandishes the knife and my smile cracks even wider. This is a fun game. I wonder what she'll want to know about me next.

If I know what she wants, I can bribe her with it later.

Or... wait. I don't think I do that anymore. Bribes and manipulation are bad. Good people don't do bad things. So, no more manipulation? *No more fires. No more stealing. Absolutely no killing.* Although, I don't think I'm in danger of any of those right now, for perhaps the first time in my life.

I'm distracting myself when there's a perfect reason to focus right in front of me.

"You gonna use that?" I ask, angling my chin at the knife, and attempting to contain the delight fizzing through my veins. She's a fierce goddess standing above me. Eyes blazing, fists clenched, loose tendrils of hair dancing in the wind. Soft and strong at the same time, all powerful in her absolute control of this situation.

Alorra clicks her tongue, then clicks the flashlight off. She spins on her heel and stomps away, little clods of dirt rolling away from her with each step as her hair and skin seem to brighten under the sole light of the moon and stars.

I take her not stabbing me as permission to continue as I was, so I scramble to my feet, and dart after her.

7

NEVER NEGOTIATE WITH A DEMON

January 26, 1981: I had a nightmare last night. A reliving of the last years of Mother's life. The way she withered away, mind and body. Bones sticking through skin, indecipherable nonsense on her tongue, decaying muscles reflecting the decaying of her thoughts. In my dreams she haunts me, showing me the end I'm destined for. The early death I've cursed my sweet Renée to live.

LOR

He's stumbling along behind me, noisy scuffs in the quiet of night. I can't believe he's here, the cute bartender. That must have been him following me all this time. My feet flatten the earth as I carve through the debris scattered by the impact of the fallen star. I think he said his name earlier, but I can't remember it beyond that it was short. My mind was too busy swirling with panic over the thought that someone was about to murder me. I might not know his name, but what I do know is that he's infuriating.

An infuriating flirt who doesn't understand the concept of boundaries, apparently.

He trips and I whirl around, wrath ready to lash out on my tongue, but it stalls behind my teeth when my gaze lands on his puppy-dog eyes. His face is turned up to me with raised eyebrows and a crooked grin. Those damning eyes are wide and bright despite the dark, made more stark by the eyeliner he always wears.

I scowl and wrinkle my nose. I am *not* going soft for the clumsy, hot bartender who followed me hours outside the city to the middle of nowhere.

"Tell me why you're here."

I try again to get him to spill his secrets. I'm afraid if he replies with more questions that my patience will run out and I might actually stab him. On that thought, I flip my knife closed and pocket it, confident I can land a throat punch and run if needed.

"I want to be," he says.

Yep, good thing I put my knife away. It's all I can do not to growl at him as I fist my hands at my sides.

"What does that mean?" I manage to get the words out, despite my clenched teeth.

He shrugs. "I'm curious about you."

I roll my lips between my teeth, sucking in a deep breath through my nose. If I was religious, I might pray for patience. Or for a higher being to smite him.

"Who are you?" I ask.

"You're not asking the right questions, love."

"Don't call me love."

He shrugs again. "Okay."

I pull back, having been about to let my anger out again

when he agreed instead of fighting me. That's not what I expected. I blink, then narrow my eyes on him.

"Just like that?"

"Sure," he replies, a lazy grin on his face that I'm half convinced is only there to disarm me.

I won't admit it's working.

"Okay then, stop following me."

"Ah, can't do that one, unfortunately."

I gape at him. This man makes less than zero sense.

"Why not?"

He waves a hand around, like that somehow answers my question. I shake my head and raise my eyebrows, my eyes wide with expectation as I make it clear that's not a good enough answer.

"I can wait here though, until you get out of sight if you want," he says.

Are we negotiating him following me? That's absurd.

"How do I know you'll do that?"

"You don't, but if it means you'll come into the club again tomorrow, I'll do it. I always keep my word."

I narrow my eyes at the hopeful glint in his.

"Are you... bargaining with me?"

His entire countenance lights up at the word 'bargaining' and it sends a warning prickle up the back of my neck, but his words deny it.

"I would never!" he says, placing a gloved hand against his chest as though to help convince me of his sincerity.

I scoff at his dramatics and hitch the bag of stardust higher on my shoulder. I stare at him, letting my eyes run over his face, across his dirt scuffed shirt and pants, down to his laced black boots. I search for any hint of a lie or deception, but to my consternation he continues to confound me.

I have no idea if he's being truthful or not.

I turn and continue to stomp my aggression into the dirt

as I make my way back to my bike. My mystery stalker scrambles to follow and I pinch my lips to prevent myself making any other sort of face.

When I reach my bike, I start packing everything away with vicious, jerking movements. The hand shovel, flashlight, and other tools get shoved and zipped into a saddlebag. I carefully fold the cloth bag of stardust into my backpack, which I zip and slip my arms through, then buckle across my chest. Even if I wasn't planning on selling it, the remains of the fallen stars would still be precious to me.

It's all I have of my true home.

My heart thumps a dull, mournful beat in my chest, but I'm distracted from the encroaching melancholy when the bartender rolls his own motorcycle out from behind a copse of trees.

Oh, hell no.

"What do you think you're doing?" I call out to him.

"I thought we were leaving!"

"*We* are not going anywhere."

"Ah, so you're taking my deal then?"

"What? No—" I cut off my protest when he shrugs and swings a leg over the seat of his bike, flipping his helmet in his hands as he prepares to put it on.

This time, I do growl. Never have I felt so many emotions all in one night. It's the worst sort of rollercoaster. I kind of want the numbness back.

Liar.

"Get off your stupid bike and come here. I don't want to shout."

To my surprise, he complies with a grin on his face as he saunters over.

"Yes, m'lady?"

"Ew, absolutely not." The response spews out of my mouth

before I have a chance to think on it. His smile grows even wider, but I ignore it. I think my eye might be twitching. In irritation, of course. It has nothing to do with how enthralling his easy joy is.

"What will it take to get you to stop following me?"

"Oh, I'm afraid that's not possible. Otherwise I would have done it already," he says, a contrite look on his face.

Is he being serious? I shake my head.

"Okay. Fine. You go first. Leave now, and I'll follow when I feel like you've gotten far enough away."

He glances at his bike, then looks back at me. His teeth fiddle with the lip ring on the side of his mouth as his dark eyes ping between mine.

"What?" I say, the 't' cutting off sharply as I start to lose patience.

"I mean..." he says, then shakes his head before continuing. "I *could* do that, but I'll be honest. I'm just gonna pull over and wait for you."

"Ugh!" I throw my hands in the air and whip around, storming away a few feet before I turn back to him. One side of his mouth is pulled down and his big eyes are full of remorse. It makes no sense, and yet... something draws me back to him.

"Right. I'll leave first then. You wait three hours, then you can leave."

"Then you'll come to the bar tomorrow?" he asks.

I slump with relief. "Yes."

"Ten minutes."

"I—" I blink at him. Did he say ten minutes? "What?" I ask.

"I'll give you a five minute head start."

"You just said ten!"

I'm fairly certain my eyes are bugging out of my head. My adrenaline is starting to spike again too, a heady rush infusing my veins, although it doesn't feel nearly as panicky as it did before.

"Ah, did I?" he says, holding his hands up in a 'what can you do?' gesture.

"Two hours," I reply, gritting my teeth.

"Ten minutes."

"You can't haggle the same thing."

"Okay. Eleven minutes."

"Oh holy *fucking* shit! You are impossible."

He grins with a mischievous glitter in his eye, and my lips twitch. The slightest upward tick, but I clench them back into a scowl before he can see.

"One hour."

"Thirty minutes."

I pause, eyeing him. Thirty minutes? That could be enough time if I really push it. I angle my head around him to check out his bike, taking in features that are comparable to my own. Nothing especially upgraded—or fast—from what I can see.

His grin reappears, looking slightly more wicked this time as he holds out a gloved hand. I stare at it a moment before searching his eyes again.

Guileless.

A guileless stalker.

I tip my head to the stars as I suck in a deep breath, certain I'm going to end up getting murdered, but what else can I do? I reach out and take his hand in mine, sealing our deal. He licks his lips then twirls the ring in his bottom one with his tongue as he slowly walks backwards away from me. His eyes never leave mine, and I get that same prickly feeling of being watched that I've been experiencing all week.

Now I know who it was.

His black-lined eyes don't leave me as I shoot across the field away from him, and my skin tingles with the memory of his gaze long after I've left his sights. I check my mirrors and look behind me every few minutes, but there's no sign of him. Did he really keep his side of the bargain? If so, that means I have to show up to the club tomorrow.

My lips tilt into a smile before I realize what's happening. I feel like a fool, a silly girl crushing on the wrong boy despite knowing it won't end well.

I guess that's the draw, though. The danger, the excitement, the lure of the forbidden. I've had plenty of danger in my life recently, what with my 'boss'—I sneer as I think of him—threatening me at every turn. I didn't take him seriously at first, but then he had one of his masked goons shoot someone right in front of me.

I had nightmares for months, and his tactics to keep me in line only got worse, even though I didn't need any more convincing.

I took him seriously after that. Although, I don't think he'd kill me since he needs me too much, but he wouldn't hesitate to hurt me. My skin crawls as I think of returning to the dingy warehouse, then my heart hurts when I contemplate turning over more stardust to him. He wanted double this time, and despite finding a good amount tonight, I'm still not there. It feels hopeless, and I doubt it'll ever be enough. No matter how much of the magical substance I bring, he will always demand more.

As long as there's a market for it, he'll want it. Stardust is the kind of thing only the higher ups in bigger crime organizations know about. Everyone else thinks it's a synthetic drug.

I need another lead, an extra one that will put me ahead. One I can cash in for more money if I ever want to earn enough to get out of here. My thoughts continue to tumble over each other as I streak through the night, back to my empty apartment with not even a cranky cat for company.

I DEBATE NOT GOING to Tempo for hours as I intermittently wear the same circle into the carpet that I was pacing last week. This time, the cat isn't here to glare me out of it, though. I didn't see even a hint of headlights behind me on my drive home last night, so the bartender must have kept his word. Which means I have to stick to mine, too.

A weight lifts off my chest with the decision. It's a reaction I don't look at too closely, for fear of what it might mean. I definitely don't *want* to see him again, but I also don't want to bring on any bad karma or whatever. So I figure I kind of have to go.

Really, I don't have a choice.

My thoughts circle as I walk the few blocks to the club, my boots scuffing against the sidewalk. I shove my hands in the pockets of my leather jacket, hunching against the wind and trying to convince myself this isn't a terrible idea. Sometimes I like people. This might even be… fun? I shiver in revulsion at the thought. I don't think I'd know fun if it slapped me in the face.

I *have* been looking for someone to hook up with, though. Perhaps he could scratch that itch? My steps slow as I contemplate it, imagining that wicked smile, his lip ring glinting in the low light as he stretches out on wrinkled sheets. Messy hair gripped in my fist, eyeliner smudged as he pants beneath me.

My breath hitches in my chest.

It's a tempting image.

But then I realize, if I hook up with him I can never go back to Tempo. I've been spending lonely nights there for years now, and I won't let one man steal my spot. No, a hookup is out of the question. I mentally brace myself to face his irritating cheerfulness again as I pull open the door and stride inside.

Sure enough, he bounds over to me before I've even reached the bar.

"You came!" he says.

"I did..."

My eyebrows twitch together as a new feeling tightens my muscles. I feel strangely cautious in the face of his positive energy. It's something I haven't experienced before, but that in itself isn't new with him, this mystery bartender-turned-stalker.

"Ro," he says, apparently taking my trailing off as an invitation to share his name again.

Right, Ro. That was his name.

"Is that... short for something?" I ask as I settle into a spot at the bar.

As soon as the words are out of my mouth, I mentally kick myself for letting my curiosity and interest in him get the better of me. His eyes brighten at the question and he answers it happily, providing his full name—Foras Astaroth Cromwell, such a strange name for a human—as well as a lengthy explanation of why his parents chose those names. It's far too much information, much more than I anticipated or cared to know, and it's unexpectedly bewitching.

I don't want to know that he's named after a goddess of lasciviousness and a powerful nude demon, or that one of his namesakes is known for discovering treasures and recovering lost things.

It's an overwhelming number of things to take in all at once, and I don't have the capacity to deal with that much energy right now. The way his eyes sparkle while talking about ancient gods above and below, his fingers glinting with rings as he waves them around, gesturing to emphasize his words. His expressive face and the slight bounce he can't seem to quell as he overshares.

It's far too endearing, and that simply adds to my overwhelm.

I can barely manage small talk on a good day, let alone a full family history with ethical considerations to boot. Not to mention that the only emotions I'm competent at dealing with are depression, anxiety, and numbness. All these other things he's been sparking in me...

I blink once, realizing it's been far too long since the last time I did so, and my eyes immediately tear up. An irritating and unnecessary reaction. Before he can see, I shove away from the counter, spin on my heel, and stride out the door.

The wind hits me and I flare open my jacket, letting it cool my overheated skin. The way I was reacting to him, wanting to lean in, to feel him speak against my lips and run his hands through my hair. To absorb his words until they sink beneath my skin into the heart of who I am.

Terrifying.

I spent hours barricading myself against him, and he blasted through all of my walls in mere seconds.

It's too much.

I don't know how to handle it. Besides that I can't afford to let anyone get that close to me. What am I supposed to say if he asks about my family? I can't tell him my mom is a starchaser so she never stays in one place for more than a few months, and she's well on her way to going mad. And oh, by the way, I'll be going mad if I live long enough, too.

I don't do relationships because no one can know about my curse. It would only bring them tragedy, as it does for me and everyone else in my family. No one can know I'm a starchaser, or about my involvement with the black market. Plus, that awful, murderous boss man would put anyone I'm close with in danger. They could be used against me, and I'd be even more trapped, or worse, they could get sucked into that world of evil right alongside me.

Ro wants to share about his name, his family, his life? Fine, he can share it with someone else.

I don't want to know, and I don't care.

8

EMOTIONAL ROLLER COASTER

Ro

My mouth falls open as Alorra breezes out the door. I've never had someone walk out on me like that, but I can't stop grinning anyway. No matter that she left mid-conversation, or that she only spoke a few words.

Because she asked me a question.

That means she's interested in me. I'm grinning like a fool at the door that swung closed behind her moments ago. This is the best day ever.

I spin on my heel and throw my hands in the air, doing a happy little celebration in the wake of her sudden departure. Of course, I wish she had stayed, but I understand that I can be a bit much sometimes. Perhaps I might have overshared a little, it wouldn't be the first time, but it's nothing we can't overcome.

I fiddle with the bracelet in my pocket, then shrug and pull it out. I doubt she's coming back tonight, so there's no reason to keep it hidden. I sling it over my wrist and fix the clasp so it dangles loosely, then spin it around once with my fingers.

It looks good on me, matches my rings and the silver crescent moon necklace I sometimes wear. I make a mental note to start wearing a leather cuff too, so I can hide the silver chain if needed.

I smile and saunter over to a waiting customer, clinging tight to the joy that she came tonight. She held up her side of our bargain, a fact that makes me giddy with a swirl of disbelief and hope and excitement. My flames itch to break out and dance across my fingers.

Even more, she voluntarily spoke to me and asked about my name. Nothing can quell this feeling. I could take on the world and die a happy demon.

The music beats in my chest as I bounce on my feet, the volume increasing as night takes hold. Overhead hex lights pulse a rainbow of colors in time with the music, and the growing crowd cheers when a song they like comes on.

Logically, I know she left. Yet my eyes keep searching for a twirl of silver hair, swaying hips clad in black, fierce eyes daring me to make a move. And every time I look, I come up empty. A shard of disappointment grows, morphing into frustration, inspiring reckless impulses that I desperately push away.

My thoughts twist with unfounded hurt at her absence as the demon inside me grows restless.

Five hours into my shift, my mood has taken a drastic turn. Although I didn't truly expect Alorra to return, a sliver of my heart hoped she might. The longer I go without seeing her, the more my demon wants to leave and seek her out. To follow in her footsteps as she went home, or took her motorcycle out, or went to another club and... no.

That's not a thought I want to indulge. Flames flicker at my fingertips for a different reason this time, ready to scald and destroy. I roll a small ball of fire across my knuckles before circling it in my fist to put it out.

No more fires. No more stealing. No killing.

I take a deep breath and survey the crowd of sweaty dancers, hands in the air, bodies bouncing with the beat. My mood continues to sour as the night wears on. People get more and more drunk, the dancing gets more salacious, the music starts to pound in an unpleasant way, and I get increasingly antsy.

I like my job for the most part, yet there's one insecurity that continues to plague me when this type of mood hits. There's nothing wrong with bartending, and the club is fun, but I do wish I could do more. As it is, my life feels meaningless at times. Like I'm not contributing anything, but just floating along day to day.

I want my parents to be proud of me. I want to make a positive impact on society, but what have I done to earn it? Nothing.

My demon is pushing at the edges of my control, wanting out, to find Alorra, to set fire to anyone who may have put their hands on her in the hours since she left here. To steal her away and hoard her for myself.

I debate calling my therapist, but it's well past midnight, and I know she won't answer. She gave me emergency numbers for exactly this type of situation—when things start spiraling and my thoughts feel out of control—so I consider calling one of those instead. Each time I feel close to breaking though, I catch a glimpse of the light sparkling off Alorra's silver bracelet, and I settle a bit.

My fingers are constantly fidgeting with it, circling and twisting and spinning it to remind myself I'm not alone. That I have a piece of her right here with me, and somehow that's enough to get me through the night.

In the following days, I try not to seek her out, I really do, but I can't keep myself away from her. My feet have a mind of their own as I watch and study her habits and routines, taking advantage of her opening the curtains some mornings and noting the shadowy movements behind them when she doesn't.

I learn when she wakes up—late morning to early afternoon—that she takes care of a stray tabby cat but doesn't eat much breakfast or lunch herself, that she often disappears for hours at a time on her motorcycle. I keep an eye on her apartment, and I try to trail her anytime she leaves, but I quickly learn I'm not that great at it.

Who knew stalking was so challenging? I lose track of her constantly in those early days of learning how to balance stealth and speed, and more than once my frustration gets the better of me, resulting in a few more flaming trashcans thanks to my demon throwing a fit.

I wish I didn't have these impulses, that I could just be a regular man, but my therapist tells me that kind of thought process will only make things worse. Instead, I'm supposed to acknowledge and reframe those thoughts. The best I can do right now is remind myself that I'm doing my best.

Unfortunately, I'm not always able to follow Alorra since I have to get to the bar for my shift, and it irks me that I can't decipher what she does for work. I think I'm close to figuring it out today, though.

Alorra takes her bike out, riding into one of the sketchier areas of Chicago, and I'm able to tail her the whole way. When she pulls off into an alley, I park the next block up and sneak back on foot to see her disappearing around a corner further in. My brows furrow as I look up and down the street. This is not a safe area, and I can't fathom what she might be doing here.

I pick up my pace as I stride down the alley after her, trying to exude confidence, and ignoring the stench rising from the overflowing trash bins. But when I peek around the corner she took, there's no sign of her. I step into a shady alcove, my heel catching on the cracked pavement as my eyes scan the space. Dilapidated brick buildings line one side, and what looks like an abandoned warehouse takes up the other. There's no one around, and no telling where Alorra might have gone.

I scowl and kick a rock with my boot. It clatters across the pavement, then ricochets against a metal trashcan, and I cringe as the sound echoes through the alley. I huff out a breath of frustration as I turn away, circling around the alley to inspect the rest of it for any clues, but finding none. It's like she disappeared into thin air.

I try to take a deep, calming breath, but the putrid air sticks in my throat, choking me. This is a miserable place, and Alorra shouldn't be anywhere near it. The sun beats down between the buildings, heating the concrete and making the awful smell even worse.

My frustration spikes and I throw out a hand, reacting without thinking as a line of flame shoots into the nearest dumpster and the contents light up.

I stare at the blaze, the mesmerizing dance of red and orange and yellow tongues as they lick up the side of a brick building. It doesn't catch, but I stand there until it starts to die down just in case, ensuring I haven't put anyone but myself in danger.

The flames are satisfying, like being cocooned in a comforting, weighted blanket, so long as I ignore the disappointment lurking deep in my bones at once again failing to control my urges.

Lor

"You've done well this time, Alorra," the man says.

I hate the way he says my name, like he's entitled to it. I don't reply, and he doesn't expect me to.

His eyes don't leave the stardust as he speaks, and the goon in a white lab coat he has weighing and measuring it barely glances at me either. The light is nearly blinding in this sterile section of the large concrete room, minimalistic with everything in its place. So at odds with the cluttered external appearance of the run down warehouse. I thought I was lost the first time I was told to report here, but inside is a different world.

One I wish I had never become a part of.

The stardust is handled carefully, with the workers wearing latex gloves and masks, and the space lined with plastic sheeting. I reflect that it's probably being given more care than anything else in their miserable, crime-ridden lives, and although part of me is glad they're handling it respectfully, the other part of me aches.

I only just found that stardust, so to have to give it up so soon, knowing it'll be lost forever as soon as it's turned into a magical drug, feels like it's tearing out a piece of my soul.

"I'll expect another delivery next week. This is better, but still not enough," he says.

"I'll try—" I start to say, but he interrupts me.

"You'll *do*." His voice is cold, nearly as icy as the cruel eyes the probably-mafia-boss turns on me.

"It depends on the stars, I can't control that—"

"The stars have been falling for millions of years. If you can't find it, that's your problem," his tone is dismissive.

"There's no way of finding stardust that has been buried, I've tried!"

"Then you better hope the stars start falling faster."

This strikes me as uniquely tragic, making my heart thump in my chest. But I hold my expression steady, giving no outward reaction to his sneering tone.

"Of course, *partner*," I reply.

His eyes narrow and one lip curls up in disdain. I push my

luck every time I call him that and we both know it, but I hold his gaze with my own. Defiant, I refuse to back down.

Without me, he has no stardust.

He turns away, barking at his men to finish up, then strides in the opposite direction I came in from. It's a false win. We both know who has the power in this relationship.

I take it as a dismissal, but the tension in my shoulders doesn't loosen as I twist away from the remains of my ancestors. I hold my head high, faking confidence as I slip through the plastic sheet and walk back the way I came. My boots scuff against the concrete floor, and I slam the warehouse door shut behind me.

I suspect he has people watching the alley, so I don't let my resolve crumble just yet, continuing to stalk away with a straight back. There's a dumpster smoldering like it was recently set on fire, and I glance up and down the alley, wary of anyone who might be ready for more violence. I see no one, but it has my hackles up anyway.

I'm extra cautious as I take the most direct path to my bike, then a meandering ride back to my part of the city.

I know Ro has been following me, having noticed him multiple times the last few days, but I've been strangely unbothered by his presence. That in itself is concerning, as I've always been a loner and have no interest in getting close to anyone. I've never much cared for socializing or friends apart from the occasional hookup, but for some reason his eyes on me don't feel wrong anymore.

It used to prickle, setting my nerves on edge, but now it sends a heated tingle down my spine when I catch him following or sense him watching me. It should bother me—having a stalker—but I suppose I've gotten used to it.

I sensed him earlier, when I made a quick stop downtown, and glanced at the reflection in a window across the street to see him not even twenty feet behind me. Remembering it makes my lips twitch into a small smile. It's like he wasn't even trying to be sneaky. When I turned to glance behind me, I saw him ducking around a corner seconds too late, and it was all I could do not to stop and scold him, to tell him how to at least be a tiny bit inconspicuous.

Ridiculous human.

He seems harmless, so I let it go, only ensuring he can't follow me when I have to check in with my contacts or deliver the stardust to avoid putting him in danger. I roll my eyes at how easy it is to lose him.

Turns out, Ro isn't that great at stalking. All I have to do is backtrack or loop around, force him to stall and get further behind, then take a couple sharp corners.

He does seem to be getting better, though. It took a little longer to ditch him today than it has previously, and I'm almost proud of the progress he's making. I shake my head at myself and let my thoughts trail into the wind, my bike taking me to Tempo without my consent.

I decide to allow it, giving myself a couple hours to relax before I go searching for more stardust tonight. I just need to get out of the city, away from the bustle and metal and concrete, even if I don't have a lead. I want to feel the wind in my hair, and the moon on my skin, and the peace of the stars in a midnight sky.

9

RIDICULOUS IDIOTS AND THE AUDACITY OF MEN

Ro

Work is slow tonight. I'm leaning against the bar with my chin in the palm of one hand, elbow propped on the counter. Out of sight beneath the bar, I'm snapping my fingers with my other hand, causing the hidden flame to pop into being and disappear with each snap.

I sigh, glancing around. There's no one for me to serve, making it increasingly difficult to keep my mind off Alorra. I roll the conjured flame across my knuckles, savoring the warmth I can feel but not see, then roll and bounce it between my fingers as my eyes start to droop with boredom.

My gaze has started to fuzz as I stare at the clock near the register, the neon numbers blurry, when a presence enters the bar.

I know that presence.

My focus snaps to attention. My spine cracks when I straighten too quickly, and my elbow slips off the bar. I clench my fist, dousing my fidget-flame, and my entire body is pulled toward her. Black jeans, kickass black boots, a dark top baring her stomach, flowing silver hair, delicate line tattoos curling over her fingers while swallows take flight behind her ear.

Alorra eyes me as she saunters up to the bar, tipping her chin higher but not giving any indication of how she feels about seeing me again. I grin in the face of her apathy; I know it's a mask. She gave herself away the first time when she asked about me, and again by showing up of her own free will tonight.

No bargain needed.

"Fancy seeing you here," I say, letting the words roll off my tongue.

She side-eyes me, leans against the bar, and looks out over the empty dance floor.

"Are you drinking tonight?" I ask.

She turns around to face me after a few moments and slides onto a bar stool. I don't miss the way her eyes flick up and down my form before she looks to the wall of drinks behind me.

"Sure," she replies.

"You want the purple drink from last time, what I'm assuming is your usual trio of shots, or something new?"

Alorra shrugs, a graceful rise and drop of one shoulder as she tilts her head, but I don't miss the glimmer that lights in her eyes at the question. I grin and make the same sparkly drink she pretended not to like last time. I love how the swirling cocktail glitter in the drink sets off the silver shimmer in her hair.

I hold the drink out, inviting her to take it from me. Her fingers brush mine and send a tingling zap up my arm. I might not wash that hand for the rest of the night now. She stares at me, and I wonder if she felt it too.

I wait until she takes a sip, looking for that approving sparkle in her eye before I speak again.

"So, I told you my name, I think it's only fair you return the favor, no?" I say.

I already know her name from her ID, but I don't know if she realizes that. Besides, I want her to tell me. It feels important for some reason.

She pauses sipping the drink to glare at me over the rim of the glass, and I put on my most endearing smile. If she's even the tiniest bit attracted to me, I'm hopeful it'll help my case of winning her over.

Alorra lowers the glass to the bar, rolling the stem between her fingers as she spins it. She angles her head, and her eyes run up and down my body again, this time leaving a trail of fire in their wake. I have to do a double take to ensure there's no actual fire, as the heat from her gaze feels remarkably similar to my own flames.

I straighten under her perusal, practically preening at the feeling of her gaze on my skin. My grin grows, turning into a cocky smirk when her eyes linger in multiple places. On my mouth, my arms, my hands, my crotch.

She purses her lips then jerks her eyes away as her cheeks tinge with the barest hint of a delightful blush.

"Fine," she says. "It's Alorra, but..."

Alorra trails off, eyeing me again. I might have already known how lovely her name is, but hearing her tell me herself has elation thrumming my heart into a rapid beat. My demon is also satisfied at having tricked her into sharing information she didn't know I already had.

My inner demon is ridiculous and an idiot. Does that make me a ridiculous idiot too?

"But?" My grin falters for a moment, but hitches back up when she replies.

"You can call me Lor," she mumbles the words into her cocktail as she raises it to her lips for another drink.

I didn't think my smile could get any bigger, but she just gave me a gift. A nickname.

A crack in her armor.

"Lor," I murmur, tasting the perfection of her name on my tongue.

She takes another sip of my new favorite drink, and a faint hum of satisfaction reaches my ears when she licks her lips.

I want to lick those lips. And more. My eyes are glued to them until she reaches up and snaps her fingers in my face. I jolt with surprise, then offer a sheepish grin. She rolls her eyes and some of the tension falls from her shoulders.

"So, Lor," I say, snagging a stool to sit on and folding my arms on the bar across from her.

She pauses, eyeing me warily. She's a skittish one, but I don't mind.

"Yes...?"

"Ro," I offer.

She rolls her eyes again and one corner of her mouth tugs up. Another win for me.

"Yes, Ro?"

"Do you like your drink?"

Lor blinks in surprise, then looks down at the dregs of her purple cocktail.

"It's decent," she says.

"Decent." I hum a noncommittal noise and she narrows her eyes. I'll get her to admit she likes it eventually. "Alright," I say with a decisive nod. "I'll accept decent for now."

She snorts and I huff a laugh in surprise. I didn't know she was capable of such an unrefined sound. Lor spins her drink as I happily bask in her presence.

"What do you do for work?" I say.

I'm hoping she'll open up and share more with me. Although I've enjoyed tailing her, I haven't been able to figure out what she does, and it's starting to drive me crazy. Is she an artist? A musician? In school? There's no way she does something boring like a desk job, it just wouldn't fit her.

"Do you interrogate all your patrons?" she says,

I huff out a disbelieving breath as I look around dramatically at the lack of other patrons, and she almost cracks a smile before tipping back the last sip of her drink.

"Even when this place is packed, I have eyes only for you."

I'm quite proud of that line, but I'm not surprised by her reaction.

Lor freezes for a moment, staring at me in disbelief before she deliberately places her empty glass back on the bar. Then she purses her lips, stands, and strides out the door.

I chuckle under my breath. I'm not bothered; this seems to be the norm for her and if she wants to hide from me, I'll let her think she can.

For now.

Besides, I caught the surprised look in her eye, the way her cheeks just started to flush as she froze for a heartbeat before jumping up and stomping her way to the door.

Finn walks up and slaps me on the back.

"Tough one man, better luck next time," he says.

"Nah, she's coming around," I reply.

I can be patient for her.

LOR

The absolute audacity of that man. That was the worst pickup line I've ever heard, so why on earth did it send my heart racing? I am *not* a horny teenager.

This is unacceptable.

I stalk out the door, wishing I could slam it behind me. I stomp over to my bike, pounding my feet into the pavement to rid the queasy, fluttery feeling of moths in my stomach, and scowling at the foreign sensation of a grin wanting to stretch across my face. The adorable, annoying cheer of that stupid bartender with his stupid sparkling eyes and infuriatingly sexy smile. No, wait.

"Ugh!" I shout my frustration to the sky before kicking my bike into gear, not bothering with a helmet. I need to feel the wind stinging my cheeks, the speed and rumble beneath me as I soar away from the troubles plaguing me.

Unfortunately, it's a stardust-less night, so I'm back on my bike again the next day after having been rudely awoken in the early afternoon by an aching pull in my veins. It was so urgent I didn't even have time to eat, barely managing to splash water on my face and rinse my mouth before I was stumbling into my boots and fumbling to lock the door behind me. It feels like my very soul is urging me to move, tugging me relentlessly onward.

I wouldn't be able to resist it even if I tried.

This is why everyone in my family goes mad, because it's uncontrollable, this curse. Those who don't understand it think it's a gift, to be able to sense fallen stars.

But it's not. It's the opposite.

I'm on a long stretch of highway leading south out of the city, and it's relatively empty considering the time of day. My brain is still foggy from sleep, and I'm so caught up in the pull that I don't notice another motorcycle on the road until they're right next to me.

I startle when the other biker pulls up alongside me, doing a double take and blinking to clear my vision. Then I recognize the black and purple bike, the matching black helmet with purple face shield, and the cocky, playful demeanor of the person riding it as belonging to Ro.

I shake my head, frustrated at the zip of excited adrenaline that prickles across my skin, and push the throttle. I lean into it, bowing over my handlebars as I floor it and the engine roars.

I hear his wild laugh as I zoom past him, or perhaps I just sense it, somehow knowing that would be his reaction.

My mirrors show him zig-zagging behind me, frolicking on his bike before he holds up a hand. I glance ahead, then back in the mirror, squinting to see what he's doing.

He's holding up three fingers, and he pumps his hand in the air once, now holding up only two. My breath catches in my chest. I look ahead, then back to the mirror. Ro motions again, now holding up one finger. Tingles of adrenaline spark as my heart skips and then races.

Ro slams his hand down and flattens his body to his bike. I don't react quickly enough, underestimating his burst of speed, and he catches me in seconds. He zooms ahead, and a whooping laugh reaches my ears.

I shake my head with a grin, knowing he can't see my expression. I eye him on his bike, the tight grip of his hands and the way his thighs hug the seat. My brain provides a drool-worthy visual of what he might look like without a shirt on, back and arm muscles rippling as he maneuvers around me.

It feels like my eyes are glued to him as he drops back, pulling up next to me again. I ignore him for a moment, forcing a neutral expression back on my face. When I glance to the left, he's pushed his face shield up, a smile in his eyes. They're dancing with mirth, and he does a little shimmy with his shoulders when we make eye contact. My gaze darts away, back to the road ahead as I pinch my lips, forcing them to remain in a straight line.

He slows, falling behind me again. I frown, eyebrows drawing together as I watch him increase the distance between us in my mirror. What is he doing?

I realize after a few minutes that he's simply back to following me. I guess he had his fun, and now... what? My curiosity peaks as my brain stumbles over the conundrum that is Ro—Foras Astaroth Cromwell. I can't believe I remembered that ridiculous name.

But why is he so interested in me? He can't know about my ability. Almost no one does with it being such a tightly guarded secret.

Outside of my absent mother, only the man who blackmails me is aware, having somehow figured it out. I've long accepted that I wasn't as careful as I should have been when I was so desperate for cash that I decided to wander to the seedier parts of town to sell the most precious thing I had. I've never felt so ashamed as I did that day, handing over some of the first stardust I'd ever collected on my own.

It's at this moment that I notice the renewed ache in my bones, and realize that cursed pull on my soul receded while I was playing with Ro.

I blink, glancing in my mirrors to ensure he's still behind me. How did he do that? Never before when I've been taken by the pull have I been able to ignore or shake it for any length of time.

He's an absolute mystery.

Ro's ability to distract me, to make me feel things I've never felt before and long thought myself incapable of feeling. Not to mention his bizarre fixation on me. He *must* have heard rumors. There are stories about my ancestors, the star-chasers, and he must have put two-and-two together while following me these last couple weeks. My heart plummets as my thoughts churn.

I mean honestly, what else would I be doing digging in the dirt in the middle of nowhere, especially that first night at a very obvious impact site?

I growl into my helmet, frustrated with my lack of self preservation. I *cannot* have given away my secret so easily for a second time. Even if he hasn't figured it out, I have no way of avoiding him following me now. My star-chaser curse won't let me deviate from the path, and Ro isn't going to stop following me. It's wide open fields with small patches of trees interspersed—not much room for losing a tail.

Curses tumble from my lips, but all I can do is keep going, so I push the throttle and hope I can ditch him with speed. I refuse to look behind me again, ignoring the infuriating man following me as I continue to follow the urge in my blood.

10

HOW NOT TO FLIRT WITH A DEMON

Ro

This is *so. Fun.*

She's hot as fuck on that motorcycle, now that I can see her in the light of day for once. It's making my pants a bit tight, nearing uncomfortable on my bike, but I don't care. I'm hooked, addicted even though I haven't tasted her yet. I'd follow my little flame, my shooting star, to the ends of the earth. Wherever she wants to lead me, I'll follow.

Though I am a bit confused about where she's taking us today.

She seems to really like... the middle of nowhere? But like, different nowheres.

Each time I've followed her, it's been to a new location, and a couple times, she's ended up digging in the dirt and carrying a bag of it back with her. I have no idea what that's about, and I puzzle it over in my head as I weave back and forth behind her.

Oh, oh! Maybe she's an archaeologist? A geologist!

My heart skips at having a solid lead on what her professional life might look like. I bet she's smart as a whip. I wouldn't have guessed she'd be the science-y type, she simply doesn't give off that vibe, but maybe she just really loves rocks.

My eyes roam, taking in the bland scenery around me. I've never been down this way before. We're hours south of Chicago, and yet she shows no signs of slowing. I hope she stops for gas soon, my stomach is protesting the long drive with no snack breaks. Regardless, I'm happy to be spending time with her.

Or... at least... near her?

I shrug. Either way, my demon hasn't been this calm in, well, ever. Since I started following her, my demon has been chill as heck. It's miraculous. I haven't even stolen anything since her bracelet, and I've only set a few fires, none of them destructive.

That's progress, no doubt.

It was fun playing with her for a bit there, and I kind of want to do it again. I wonder who would win in a race?

I scoff as soon as the thought crosses my mind. Because she would, *obviously*. I wouldn't be able to take my eyes off her.

Lor turns off the main road ahead of me and I whoop at the change, thrilling in another off-road adventure. I push the throttle, skidding over the packed dirt road to follow her. When the terrain gets too rough, she pulls over and parks. I've been keeping a slight distance, but it's closing quickly now that she's not moving.

She takes her helmet off and tips her head back, shaking her hair out as she rakes a hand through it. Her silver locks flow down her back in shimmering waves and I nearly crash at the sight. I jerk the handlebars and regain my center of gravity, narrowly avoiding a far-too-personal encounter with the rocky path.

Lor ignores me, not so much as glancing my direction, and I'm grateful she didn't notice my near catastrophe. She doesn't wait, and I don't expect, nor want, her to.

My mouth goes dry as I approach, pulling my bike up next to hers, although my gaze doesn't leave her form. She's already hiking away across a barren field, bordered by leafy green trees in the distance. I stagger off my bike, my boot catching on the seat as I try to hurry after her.

Lor walks for longer than I'd choose to, but this is her thing, and following is mine, so that's what we do.

"I know you're back there." Lor's sultry voice carries on the wind, and I grin at her back. I wonder if she knows how sexy she is.

"Pretend you don't!" I cup my hands around my mouth and raise my voice so she can hear me.

Lor turns around, walking confidently backwards, and I huff a laugh at her doing the opposite of what I said.

"Why?" she asks.

"It helps my demon urges."

If I didn't know better, I'd say she stumbles a step, but I'm probably imagining the momentary loss of control. She tilts her head, takes another step back. Her eyes devour me, inspecting me as she continues taking deliberate steps backward. I have no idea how she knows where she's going. Finally, she rolls her eyes and turns on her heel, picking her pace up again.

I've gained on her a bit during that strange walking-standoff, so I stop to enjoy the boring view for a few moments, turning away and letting her go on ahead again.

There's a bright yellow flower near the toe of my boot. I bend down to look at it, about the size of a quarter with stocky leaves and a yellow center. I pinch the stem and snap the flower off, then straighten and tuck it behind my ear. A spot of blurry yellow lines the corner of my vision, a cheerful little reminder of our adventure and all the treasures we can find.

When I turn back and see Lor only a little ways on, it's to her crouched down digging, filling up that cloth sack again.

I pat the flower to ensure it's secure behind my ear, then stick my hands in my pockets and start whistling a jaunty little tune as I saunter up to her. She only glances my way once, her hands pausing as she narrows her eyes at me before she continues bagging her dirt. I stop only a couple feet in front of her, just out of reach of her shovel, but close enough that my shadow falls over her.

"You look good on your knees," I purr, keeping my voice low. If the universe wants her to hear, she'll hear.

Her eyes dart up to mine.

"What did you just say?"

I allow a slow smirk to curl my lips as I drop to a crouch.

"Maybe I prefer you on *your* knees," she mutters.

My demon leaps with joy, my heart beating a frantic rhythm in my chest.

"I'm not at all opposed to that," I reply.

Lor glances at my mouth and I flick my tongue against my lip ring. Her lips pinch together, and I'm convinced it's an attempt at restraint. I've caught her eyeing my lips and piercings before; it's a common reaction. I tip my head, waiting for her to make her next move, but she doesn't.

Instead of getting flustered, Lor ignores the rest of my attempts at flirting, and it only serves to rile up the demon inside me. Her movements get faster as she shovels dirt into the bag, spinning and stepping carefully to a couple other locations to repeat the process before she practically speed-walks in the direction of her bike.

Lor glances behind her to see me looking around, bemused by the disheveled landscape she's left behind. Soon enough, though, I meet her wide eyes, and then I'm loping after her again.

She growls in frustration—an adorable attempt at intimidating me—when a twig snaps under my boot. It spurs on my demon, igniting the urge to follow, chase, possess. I tell myself to chill, but Lor increases her pace, and that has the opposite effect. My heart rate cranks up and a light sheen of sweat breaks out on my forehead.

I have no idea where her head is at, or mine for that matter. My speed increases to match hers, and a thrill of anticipation zips through my chest.

I grimace, fighting my instincts and rubbing my chest in an effort to quell the overwhelming impulses. They're getting too strong, exacerbated by my being in her presence and her actively trying to evade me.

Lor leaps onto her bike, barely securing her bag before revving the engine and taking off in a cloud of dust. I jump onto my own bike, my demon riding me hard. It's far too close to the surface at this point, making my movements and speed much more reckless than I'd normally give in to.

My demon keeps a steady pace behind her and I have to remind myself to blink, to breathe. My fists are clenched around the handlebars, my entire body rigid with anticipation, and my eyes fixed to her back. Her hair streams out behind her since she didn't take the time to secure it before trying to escape me, and it's a beacon too tempting to resist. My lips pull up in a snarl and I clench my teeth, desperate to rein it in.

I'm losing control.

I wrestle with my demon, and it's like I'm fighting myself. I try to turn the bike off the path, yelling inside my own head for my arms to twist, but nothing happens. I recite my mantra, telling myself over and over, "no more stealing, no more fires, no killing" but it doesn't do any good.

It's like one half of me is agreeing with those words, perfectly happy to follow that path, but another half of me is completely disconnected and doing whatever it wants. Unfortunately, that's the part that's in control.

I'm a prisoner in my own body.

My eyes dart around, frantically searching for any other outlet, but there's nothing I can safely light on fire out here and no one to steal from, apart from her.

Right as I'm preparing to attempt to throw myself from the seat to avoid whatever hell my demon is dragging me into, Lor brakes hard. Her bike swings around, skidding through the dirt and pluming dust into the air as she pulls to the side in a 180 and faces me.

My pulse hammers in my chest, her actions having startled my demon, further throwing my mind and body into chaos.

I slam the brakes, adding to the dust in the air and my back tire swings out, fishtailing for a moment before I come to a stop just feet from her. Lor yanks her helmet off and her grey eyes flash in the sun.

I had never put mine back on. I'm hoping it's still secured to the back of my seat or I'll have to get a new one. We stare at each other, both of us panting, our eyes locked. My demon struggles for control and I wrestle with it, locking up every muscle in my body.

Her face is flushed and there's a sheen of sweat on her brow. Lor's pulse jumps in her neck, pulling my gaze. I want to suck the delicate skin between my teeth and abuse it until she's a writhing, moaning mess beneath me.

Whoa.

I shake my head, averting my gaze and trying to get a grip. I release my bike and flex my hands in my gloves, then roll my shoulders while sucking in deep breaths to release some of the tension.

It's only been a few minutes, but it feels like hours since my demon decided to turn what was a fun game into a terrifying loss of control. I suck in a slow breath, holding it in my lungs as I fight for calm, then release it in a controlled stream.

When I look back up, Lor is off her bike, pacing back and

forth. Five steps, turn, five more steps, turn, glare at me, five steps. Another glare. I heave in another breath, sucking air into lungs that feel starved, and finally move.

I swing off my bike, and before my second boot hits the ground, Lor is shouting.

"*Stop* following me. Stop, just stop!" Her hands are clenched into fists at her sides, vibrating with concealed tension, and my chest constricts with regret. I speak before I can think better of it.

"I can't." My voice is hoarse, full of regret and shame, and I have to force the words out. "I've *tried*."

I rake both hands through my hair, tugging as my body movements mirror hers. We're both pacing, stomping with anger and frustration and fear. A bead of sweat trickles down the center of my back, and I try to take a calming breath. It shudders in and out of my lungs. I squeeze my eyes shut, clench my jaw, and turn my head to the sky.

I don't know what to do.

The thought derails me. It takes all the wind out of my sails, and the tension drains from my body. I slump to the ground, folding my arms over my knees and resting my head on my forearms.

I hear Lor's pacing stop, but she doesn't come any closer or say anything.

"I think even my therapist has given up on me," I say, my words devoid of emotion, spoken as a mumbled fact to the ground below me. My demon kicks inside my chest, an uncomfortable jolt of disappointment and shame.

Her boots crunch once, twice, three times as she steps toward me.

"Your..." she starts, then trails off.

I can feel her eyes on me, trying to pick me apart and figure me out. *Good luck.*

"You're in therapy?"

"Yes," I say, half drained, half exasperated.

"But..." Lor trails off again, and I finally raise my head to look at her.

She's more open than I've ever seen her before. Her eyes are wide, her head slightly tilted and brows furrowed with confusion rather than condemnation. She takes another step closer before lowering herself to the ground only a couple feet away. She blinks at me, then her eyes dart to the side, taking in the distant horizon before she looks back at me again.

"But you're a demon." Her tone is carefully restrained, but confusion and disbelief seep into it anyways.

"Yes."

She flinches at my brusque tone, and my insides pulse with disappointment again. It's not in my nature to be mean, and I don't intend to treat her poorly. But the last half hour has gone completely off the rails. I've never experienced anything like the emotional rollercoaster I just went though, and I don't know how to deal with the aftermath, this crash of it.

My therapist is going to have a field day helping me pick this one apart.

I sigh and swipe a hand down my face. I can do better than this. She's not running anymore, so my demon has settled. Maybe this is a chance to fix things.

"You have questions," I say. "Go ahead."

"Does it help?"

"Therapy?"

She nods and I look away, contemplating the question. June told me therapy wasn't a quick or easy fix, and I didn't expect it to be. It's only been a few months, and although I've learned a lot, putting things into practice is easier said than done.

"Hmm..." I reply, my gaze drifting back to hers. "Honestly? I think it's too early to tell. I'm hopeful it will, though."

Lor nods again, her expression morphing to thoughtful consideration as she sweeps her gaze across the landscape.

"Have you ever been to therapy?" I ask, cautious of the new, fragile peace between us.

"No." Lor draws in a deep breath, then continues. "No, but... I've thought about it. I just don't know... anything."

It's my turn to nod. I get that.

"It's intimidating."

"What does it help you with?" she asks.

A small smile tilts my lips as I look to the blue sky above us. That's a more complicated question than she realizes, and my demon is stirring up again, wanting more of her.

"I'm learning about myself, about my inner demon. How my thoughts and emotions work. I'm... trying to change how I handle things. Trying to be a better person, you know?"

I look back down to see her staring at me. A desperate sort of yearning filling her eyes, piercing my spirit. My heart thuds a heavy beat, and my skin prickles with awareness.

"Yeah, I think I need some of that," Lor breathes the words on a soft exhale, and I ache for the pain radiating from her.

"Can I touch you?" I blurt, then bite my lip ring, fidgeting with it.

Lor doesn't react as I feared she might, though. Her eyes narrow as they trace over my face, across my shoulders and down my tense arms, considering.

"Why?"

"It'll help..." I wave one hand around. "Settle my urges, I guess. My demon is... struggling." I bite out the words, hating to have to bare my vulnerability in this way, but there's no progress without change. June tells me being vulnerable is good, even if it doesn't feel that way at first.

Lor is understandably wary. She holds my gaze and her

eyes dig into me. I try to be as open as I can, willing her to see everything I am.

Finally, a decade later, she scoots closer, halving the distance between us, and holds out one hand. My heart flip-flops, skipping an unsteady beat as I take in the meaning behind her gesture.

This is a turning point, and I do not want to mess it up.

I reach out slowly, slotting my palm around hers and twining our fingers together. Lor inhales a soft gasp, but I was ready for the lightning between us.

11

DOOM AND GLOOM

*October 10, 1983: I fear I am in danger of
being discovered. Mother always warned
me: never tell. No one must ever know of the
curse in our blood, lest we be sent to the
asylum as happened to Aunt Mona. She
was declared insane, taken away in a
straight jacket. We never saw or spoke to her
again.*

Lor

The spark from his skin against mine sets all the hairs on my arm standing and spreads goosebumps down my neck. My eyes fly to his, but I see only soft acceptance there, no surprise. He was expecting that. Does he know something I don't?

Ro offers a tentative smile, and I think I give him one in reply. It feels foreign on my face, like I'm doing it wrong, and I quickly look away.

Silence falls between us, but it's not awkward or uncomfortable. The wind swishes across the field, insects buzz and the sharp call of a falcon rings out high above. His hand is warm against mine. It feels good, right, and also radiates warmth in a way that isn't entirely human. I've been trying to ignore the truth he dropped on me, but there's no more running from it.

Ro is a demon.

I'm not sure why that fact triggered me. It's not like I'm human either, although I am the most human of all the non-human creatures. I guess I had assumed he was safe, a regular human who wouldn't care about or even know the significance of stardust.

I've always heard demons were evil creatures. That they have no regard for the law, let alone morality, and they do whatever they please. Then I realize what this demon has been doing lately: stalking me, probably responsible for the random smoldering trashcans I've come across, and who knows what else. I have no doubt he's broken the law in other ways.

Now that he's told me, I can't unsee it. *Of course,* he's a demon.

But...

He's basically a puppy—a chaotic, far too enthusiastic puppy with poor decision-making skills—but still. He's been following me around and lapping up any scrap of attention I throw his way. It's bizarrely endearing, and somehow the frustration and anger I constantly carry around evaporate in his gentle, eager presence. It's like Ro fits the mold of a demon, and then reshapes it.

How is he possible?

I look over at him, seeing him already watching me, and stare into his hazel eyes. They're flecked with gold, and now I wonder if that's his inner demon magic that seems to make them glow. His eyes are captivating and far too expressive.

Dangerous.

Why is he interested in me? My instincts tell me I can trust him, but my history with those who are supposed to love and care for me have turned my heart black and bitter, surrounded with a wall of barbed wire. I trust no one, because everyone always leaves.

Besides, even if I did trust him, what am I going to do? Give him a life of caring for someone who is destined to go mad?

I scoff, and Ro's eyebrows shoot up. I shake my head, averting my gaze. I don't even know when it'll happen. It could be in two years or twenty, but at some point, my curse will ruin my life *and* that of anyone I'm close to.

Even more than it already has.

"Is everything okay?" Ro's voice interrupts my brooding.

I cringe, recognizing again that my lack of social skills have likely made things awkward, and wishing for the millionth time that I could be normal.

"Just... stuck in my head, I guess," I reply, not sure what else to say.

"I get that. Do distractions help? That always helps me," Ro says.

He looks eager and hopeful, with wide eyes and slightly raised eyebrows, body poised like he's ready to jump into battle against my thoughts. I shrug.

"Probably, yeah," I say. "But we're kinda stuck in the middle of nowhere."

"That's okay, I can distract you! What should we do?"

Ro lets his knees drop from his chest and straightens, stroking the thumb and pointer finger of one hand along his chin like a wanna-be evil villain that can't stop smiling. My lips twitch as I watch him look around at the sparse landscape.

"We could play I spy or charades, or if you don't want to do that, I can put on a little skit. I don't know any, but I'm sure I could make something up."

Ro starts to stand, but I tug the hand still clasped in mine.

"No." I huff out a tiny laugh, shocking both of us.

Ro freezes and stares at me. I can feel my face turning red, so I look away again.

"I mean," I mumble into my shoulder. "It's fine, you don't have to do all that."

He slowly lowers himself back to the ground, and I chance a look at him. His eyes are running over me, and it makes me wonder what he sees.

A broken girl? Someone lonely and sad? A lie?

All would be true.

"We could just talk?" Ro says, the words turning up at the end in question.

I nod, unable to speak around the lump in my throat.

Ro doesn't seem upset by my lack of verbal response, instead offering a tender smile before his grin turns mischievous and he launches into a story. He starts with his early experiments making cocktails, before he took any mixology classes, and how he once made a drink so terrible it gave Finn a headache that lasted days. Apparently, it was Ro's first experience with cleaning up vomit, too.

The dramatic full-body shudder he lets loose makes me smile again.

Ro shares stories about customers at the various bars he's worked at. Stories of drunken shifters, and silly humans, and tales of the most ridiculous drinks he's ever been asked to make. He requires little to no input from me, keeping up a constant flow of words that my brain soaks up like a sponge.

It's strange, the way his chatter doesn't bother me. His voice soothes an anxious part of my mind that is used to going, going, going. I place my free hand on the cloth bag containing the stardust, and the hum of its magic thrums against my palm. It warms me from the inside, bringing another layer of peace that I don't trust. The dichotomy sets me on edge; tranquility and distrust, serenity and apprehension.

We end up sitting together, holding hands, for far longer than I would have guessed possible for two people who aren't actually doing much of anything. Ro's thumb sweeps against the back of my hand every so often, sending tingles up my arm.

I ignore it, and he smiles.

He seems pleased to finally be cracking me open, somehow recognizing that even though I'm not sharing much verbally, this is still me letting him in. I don't know what to make of it all—of him, my reactions, my jumbled feelings and calmed thoughts.

"I should go," I say, suddenly needing out.

I drop his hand and pull away. I can't take anymore of whatever this is. It doesn't feel safe, though logic tells me it is. "It's getting late. So. I better get home."

Ro hops up, then holds out both hands. I hesitate before settling mine into his, and he practically throws me onto my feet in his enthusiasm to help me stand.

"Whoops. Sorry, Starfire," he says with a grin. "Got a little carried away."

Ro laughs like he told the world's funniest joke, but I don't crack a smile. My heart stumbles at the nickname. I've never had a nickname before, apart from Lor, which I always ask people to call me because I don't like Alorra.

I can't figure out how I feel about it. I'm staring, I know I'm staring, but my brain has reached its limit for the day.

I spin on my heel and re-strap my backpack around me.

"So..." Ro calls behind me. "Same time tomorrow?"

There's a grin in his voice, and I peek over my shoulder, unable to resist seeing it one last time. I don't contradict him, even though I should. There's a reason I'm not interested in a relationship, and especially not with someone who seems as kind and genuine as Ro.

My lifestyle, the life of crime and people I'm involved

with... They'd chew him up and spit him out before he even knew what happened. Not to mention my curse.

No, I won't subject an innocent—demon or not—to a doomed future with me.

His tongue laps at my nipple, teasing until it's a taut peak, and I moan through closed lips. Ro grins up at me and I bury my fist in his silky brown hair, pulling and tugging, trying to get him to go where I want. He nips at the curve of my breast before latching his lips around my nipple with a suck strong enough to arch my back. I groan, palming my other breast, and the vibration of his answering rumble sends heat flooding to my core.

Ro's form blurs in and out as he sucks and nips and licks his way down my body. I've been thinking about this for so long, I'm ready to come out of my skin with need. Ro's hands are nearly scorching as he spreads my thighs and settles his shoulders between them. He kisses up one thigh and I lose track of time, my mind fuzzy as it skips from one moment to the next, then he's sucking a hickey on the inside of my opposite thigh.

I squirm, attempting to thrust my hips, but they won't move, his arms pinning them down. He flashes me a wicked grin as he slowly—so torturously slow—lowers his head to my slick pussy. I try to move my hands, to spear them into his hair and yank him to where I want him to be, but my arms don't move.

Ro chuckles, his breath ghosting over me and sending tingles racing up and down my spine. His eyes glow a bright, molten gold as he looks up at me from between my legs.

My breath stutters in my chest and I groan again, so desperate to come that I nearly start begging. I'm chanting his name in my head, cursing him, but refusing to plead. My throat feels too tight, and I fear I might actually be saying his name aloud.

"Ro, Ro."

My voice is soft, but gaining intensity as his tongue teases my outer folds and his lips graze the crease of my inner thigh. I thrash against his hold, my patience snapping as I finally yell.

"Ro!"

I jolt up in bed, chest heaving, panicked at having been awoken by a shout, only to realize it was me.

I'm the one who shouted.

Because...

"No," I murmur, then my voice gains desperation again for an entirely different reason as the dream comes back to me. "Nooo, no, nonono!"

I bury my face in my hands, ignoring the sweat slicked hair sticking to my forehead and my thumping heart. There's *no way* I just had a fucking *sex dream* about *Ro*.

"Uhhgggggggg," I groan, falling back into my pillows as a scathing "mrow" replies.

I drop my hands and look to the side, where the cat sits on my window sill. It's clearly unimpressed with me—*same cat, same*—and places one paw on the window, demanding to be let out. I don't want to be here with me right now either.

It takes a few seconds to untangle my legs from the sheets, then I heave myself out of bed, crack the window for the cat, and make my way into the bathroom for a cold shower. I'm finally cooling down, refusing to finish what my dream, no— nightmare—started, when the doorbell rings. I roll my eyes, not bothering to hurry to answer it, and step under the cold water again.

When I finally turn it off and step out, the doorbell rings again. I ignore it still, having no interest in interacting with anyone if I don't have to. But a few minutes later, someone knocks. I've barely had time to throw some clothes on, but fuck it.

Exasperated and already done with this day, I stomp to the door, ready to lay into whatever evangelist or preacher thinks they have a right to my time.

Ro

Lor flings the door open and my jaw goes slack. Her eyes are spitting mad, luminescent grey in the soft light, but it's her sexy as hell outfit that scrambles my brain. She's wearing a black knit crop top, high neckline with no sleeves and no bra, hard nipples poking through the fabric like they're begging for my attention. Her stomach is on display with loose black sleep shorts that barely cover her ass, leaving miles of bare leg ending with bare feet tapping the floor in agitation.

And on top of it, her hair is dripping wet. It leaves trails of water down her neck, across her shoulders, there's even a glittering stripe that's made its way past her cropped top and down her stomach. I gulp, averting my eyes before my quick perusal turns to leering.

I bend down, swiping a hand out toward the ground, and then rub my chin as I stand back up.

Lor's fiery gaze flips to confused, and she stares at me for a moment before speaking.

"What are you doing?"

"Picking my jaw up off the floor," I reply.

Lor slams the door in my face and I bark a laugh. I caught her quick grin before she was able to hide it. It was small, but I've become an expert in reading her micro-expressions.

I bite my lip, trying to hold in my own grin as I knock again. Two quick taps.

Lor opens it immediately, her face composed into what

I'm sure she thinks is a neutral mask, but I can see her curiosity and the playful edge she won't let out. I lean against the doorframe, propping one forearm above me as I angle my head at her.

"You gonna invite me in?"

"No," she says.

"Why not?"

"I don't want you here."

Huh. My eyebrows pull down and the urge to grin falls. That's not what I expected.

I'm stumped. I can't tell if she's serious, but decide to take her at her word. I'll satisfy my demon by hanging around outside for a bit, like I usually do.

I drop my arm and step back with a nod, ready to leave her in peace, but then she speaks again.

"Fine," she huffs, rolling her eyes.

"No, I don't want to inconvenience you," I say. I also don't *really* want to be where I'm not wanted. I think that's a pretty basic thing, to want to be wanted. My demon might want to be near her, to follow and know and possess her, but I don't want to be anywhere I'm truly not welcome.

Her eyes soften, as does her voice.

"You're not an inconvenience," she says. "Please, come in."

Lor steps back, swinging the door open wide, and then turns around, expecting me to follow. I hesitate for a heartbeat, warring with myself. But then I remind myself that Lor isn't the type of person to do anything she doesn't want to do, so if she didn't want me here, she wouldn't have invited me in.

She had no problem telling me to get lost in the past.

I step inside and push the door closed behind me, my eyes sharpening on her ass as she saunters into the kitchen. She glances over her shoulder and smirks when she catches me looking, but I don't mind. I grin and shrug.

"What? You're hot," I say.

Lor rolls her eyes again—and again, I catch the hint of a smile as she turns away. Why does she always try to hide it?

"You can get yourself some coffee if you want," she says, gesturing to a cupboard on her left. I take the invitation to snoop, making myself at home as my demon purrs with contentment in my chest at being invited into her space.

12

———

BOUNDARIES? NEVER MET THEM.

*June 30, 1988: I'm so tired. My bones, my
blood, my very soul is tired.*

LOR

I can't believe Ro is in my apartment.

Of course, right as I'm recovering from the most unwelcome sex dream of my life, he has to show up on my doorstep like a godsdamned wet dream come to life. My eyes start at his feet and trail a path up his body as time slows.

High top canvas shoes, light blue jeans held together on one side of his hips with a silver chain, laced up like a shoelace. My eyes get stuck on the flash of skin beneath... Is he not wearing boxers?

I suck in a breath, my core clenching. A tight white tank bares an inch of skin above his pants and he has a loose, unbuttoned ombre rainbow tee on top. It hangs open, framing his lean, muscular chest. His wrists are covered in leather, beaded, and silver bracelets, and he has a single silver chain dangling from his neck with a crescent moon charm hanging to the middle of his sternum. His lip ring, the eyebrow piercing, the messy brown hair, his smoldering eyes—they all torture me.

It's really not fair.

My skin is extra sensitive, every nerve alight so it feels like there are bees in my veins when he's not touching me. Ever since he asked to hold my hand, all I want is his skin on mine again. My body yearns for it, like with every breath I'm being drawn closer, deeper into his orbit.

He snoops around my kitchen while I stare at him, and I find that I don't mind it. Even if he finds the stardust, he's seen me collecting it, so it wouldn't be a surprise to see what he hopefully assumes is a bag of dirt sitting around.

Ro finds the mug cupboard and pokes around, not seeming to find what he wants. He eventually pulls out a chipped purple one, the most colorful and least boring mug I own, then pours some coffee before opening the fridge.

"I don't have any creamer," I say, assuming that's what he's looking for.

He shrugs, closing the fridge, but I can see the slight disappointment in his expression. I click my tongue against my teeth, then angle around him to open a drawer he hasn't explored yet.

"Here," I say, tossing a few sugar packets at him. "Best I can do."

He beams at me.

I swear, a ray of sunlight shoots from his eyes, and it's obnoxious as heck. I pinch my lips, ignoring how it warms me from the inside as he tears open the first packet and stirs it in, a pleased little smile on his lips.

I let my own tilt up, happy to have done something to make him happy, even if I still refuse to admit that to either of us.

Then he rips and dumps a second packet in.

My smile falls when he grabs a third pack of sugar. There's no way... Yep.

"Are you for real?" I say, aghast at how sickly sweet that coffee is going to taste.

"What?"

Ro turns wide, innocent eyes on me as he pours the entire third sugar pack into his mug. He deliberately sets the empty paper on the counter, still holding eye contact.

"That's got to be a crime," I mutter.

Ro raises his eyebrows, briefly swirls a spoon through his mug of sugar, then looks directly at me again. He cups the mug in both palms, slowly raises it and takes a sip, then groans dramatically with pleasure.

My eyes flare wide, because that's far too close to the sound he made in my dream. I whip around, the muscles in my lower abdomen clenched tight and a groan of my own threatening low in my throat. I refuse to let him see how hot my face is.

I will not succumb to whatever charms this demon throws my way.

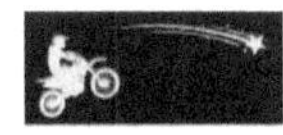

RO CONTINUES to randomly show up at my place over the next week. Always without warning, despite the fact that I caved a couple days ago and gave him my number so he would stop surprising me.

Instead, he simply texted me the next day asking what my favorite ice cream was. Then he showed up ten minutes later with a different flavor.

"Why did you ask what kind I liked if you weren't going to get it?"

"Ah, well I was, I even grabbed some. But then my demon threw a fit, so I had to go back and snag this one instead."

It's not hard to read between the lines. Snag clearly means steal, and I shake my head.

"I know, I know. I'm trying to do better! At least it wasn't anything big," Ro says, his shoulders slumping as he shuffles his way into my kitchen and sets the carton of strawberry ice cream on the counter.

I trail after him, my eyes glued to the way his pants hug his thighs as he walks. Then he clears his throat and I jolt, darting my gaze up to his to see his teeth biting at his lip ring as he half-smirks.

"See something you like?" he asks.

"Don't push it," I say, pulling out two spoons from the drawer near my hip, then grabbing the ice cream and pulling the top off. I hand him one spoon, and dig in with the other.

Strawberry isn't my favorite, but it's not terrible.

Ro is frozen with his hand up, fingers clenched around his spoon and eyes locked on my mouth as I slip my spoon out from between my lips. I'm starting to enjoy his attention being on me, something I never expected and will still vehemently deny if asked, but I decide to lean into it. I swipe my tongue out, slowly licking across my bottom lip.

His throat bobs with a hard swallow, and I lean forward over the counter, dipping my chin to look up at him through my eyelashes. Ro matches my movement, leaning toward me, and I toss his own question back at him.

"See something you like?" I whisper.

Ro throws his head back with a bark of laughter. I can't help smiling when I hear it. He's so easy to tease, taking it all in stride and never getting offended or upset.

"Yeah," Ro replies, lowering his voice as he meets my eyes, then lets his gaze pointedly dip down my body. "I see a lot that I like."

He keeps turning it back on me and I grit my teeth, somehow feeling both turned on and frustrated at the same time. Every time I think I get one up on him, he comes back harder. It's infuriating, but I can't be upset by his quick wit.

It's what makes him so fun to be around.

The tension builds each time he shows up, and I start to suspect he's outside my apartment more often than he lets on. My skin will start to tingle sometimes, and I swear I've seen deeper shadows in the trees across the street than is normal.

I think the cat knows too, as it hasn't been coming around quite as much as usual. I wonder if it's a sign I should be paying attention to, until one day Ro shows up at the same time as the cat.

I let the cat in first, cracking the window and waiting an eternity for it to decide to saunter inside. Then I rush to the front door and let Ro in. His signature grin is in place as he steps through the door, but when I angle sideways to let him pass, he freezes.

"Finally," he breathes.

I raise an eyebrow, looking between him and the cat. They seem to be having a stare-down, although Ro is doing it with excited glee, and the cat seems to be acting on reserved suspicion.

"I thought I'd never get to meet your cat," Ro says, turning bright hazel eyes on me.

"Oh, it's not my cat."

"What?"

Ro turns toward me fully, confused eyes darting between me and the cat, then to the food bowl on the kitchen floor. I caved and got it recently after getting tired of the cat batting random things off the counters in search of sustenance.

I wave my hand in the air.

"It just shows up sometimes and I let it in, but it's not mine."

"Riiiight," Ro says, turning back to the cat. He crouches

down, carefully lowering himself to the floor and holding out one hand.

"It tends to not—" I start to warn him of the cat's antisocial behaviors, when the traitor walks right up to Ro, takes one sniff of his hand, then bumps its head into his palm.

Ro's smile lights up the whole room, and he immediately starts chattering to the cat.

"Oh, you're just a little sweetie, aren't you?" he says.

I grumble a denial, but they both ignore me.

"Yes, oh you're so soft, and so pretty," Ro continues. "Handsome? Pretty?"

The cat twists between his ankles and rubs its chin along Ro's shin.

He turns to me. "Is it a boy or a girl?"

I shrug. "No idea."

Ro frowns, then turns back to the cat.

"Well, that's okay. It doesn't really matter anyway. You're purr-fect just as you are. Aren't you?" he says.

Oh my god. I refuse to laugh out loud. That can't even be called a joke, but inside I'm definitely chuckling.

Ro smirks at me like he knows.

"Just purrrrrr-fect," he continues, this time rolling the R in a way that hitches my breath. It makes me wish he'd do it again, but with his tongue on certain parts of me this time.

"Do they have a name at least?" he says.

I shuffle my feet and look away from the two of them as I slip by into the kitchen. I need to get my head on straight.

"Ah, well," I say, stalling and trying desperately to think of a good name for a cat. "I just call it... Cat?"

I can feel his flat stare burning a hole in my back and I wrinkle my nose. Since when do I care what other people think?

"Well, that's not going to work, is it pretty kitty?" Ro coos to the cat, and to my horror the cat flops into his lap and starts purring. Belly up, claws retracted, no teeth in sight.

I stare at them, and Ro grins up at me.

"Betrayed by my own cat," I grumble.

Unfortunately, Ro hears, and his grin turns wicked.

"I thought you said it wasn't yours," he says.

"Oh, fuck off."

I stomp away to flop on my sofa, secretly pleased that they get on so easily, but a bit jealous too. Why doesn't the cat snuggle with me like that? And why do I wish I was the one in Ro's lap instead?

The cat finally has enough of Ro's attention and wanders off, freeing Ro to pester me again.

"Are you pouting?" he asks, a hint of flirtatious delight in his tone.

"I don't pout." I bite my words off so they come out more sharp than I intended.

"Ah, of course," Ro says, placating.

I start to bristle, but he plops onto the couch next to me. A wave of his scent washes over me, something along the lines of a wood-burning stove, but with a more dangerous undertone. Welcoming in a daring way, so cozy you risk being smothered without realizing it.

I try to resist my instinct to suck it as deep into my lungs as I can. It's futile, as there's no escaping him. Especially because it's not a big couch, a loveseat at best, which means we're now shoulder to shoulder, hip to hip, thigh to thigh. His warmth presses into me and I stiffen. This is more physical contact than I've had in ages, considering the dry spell I've been going through.

Not because of him. I just haven't found anyone I'm interested in enough to sleep with lately.

I shift, trying to put distance between us, but all it does is sink me further into his side. Ro angles his body so I'm leaning into the cushion by his shoulder, then snags my legs under the knees and throws them over his lap.

I gasp. It slips out despite my mortification, but Ro doesn't react.

No making fun of me, no smirk, nothing. He runs his fingers lightly down my legs, from my knees to my ankles. His eyes follow the path his hands take, and he wraps his fingers around my ankles, squeezing once before loosening and coasting his palms back up. He brushes over my knees, leaving one hand there while the other grazes the top, then outside of my thigh.

My breaths are shallow, with every inch of my awareness focused on his lingering touch.

Ro's fingers flex on my hip, and he slows even more as he lightens the contact. His eyes are hooded, still fixed on his hand as he touches me. He pauses for the longest second as his eyes dart up to mine.

I'm frozen. I don't think I'm even breathing as I wait for his caress to continue.

He searches my eyes, and I stare back at him, waiting.
Waiting.
Finally, his eyes flick back down, and I follow his gaze, watching as he moves his hand up again. His palm sears into the bare skin at my waist, and tension throbs through me.

I think we both suck in a breath at the contact, but I can't be sure; too much of my focus has narrowed in on the heat of his palm.

Our eyes fly back to each other and when our gazes collide, every thought of denial dies a sudden, scorched death at the heat in his gaze. He is pure want, evident in the rigid lines of his body. His neck is taut, the tendons standing out in sharp relief where they meet his shoulders. His hands keep clenching and unclenching where they grip my calf and waist. The muscles and veins in his forearm flex with every movement, and each breath he sucks in is labored.

"Ro," I whisper, his name leaving my lips without my permission as my eyes fix on his mouth.

He shudders, his lips parting. That damned lip ring taunts me, and in that moment, I decide it's *mine*.

Mine to lick.

Mine to fiddle with.

Mine to bite and tease.

I crash my mouth to his, ignoring his surprised grunt as I throw myself at him.

13

"JUST THIS ONCE"

Ro

I topple backwards with a soft oomph, angling our bodies as I fall back on the small sofa so Lor's body covers mine. I'm leaning against the low armrest, partially reclined with my legs bent and feet on the floor, and the most heavenly weight straddling my thighs.

Her lips are soft but demanding when they meet mine, somehow more perfect than I dreamed they'd be. My hands clench on her waist, pulling her into me as I hum with satisfaction into her mouth. Lor's tongue licks my lips and I part them for her, only for her to pull back slightly.

Before I can react, her tongue swipes out again, this time licking the side of my mouth, right over my lip ring. My lips quirk into a smug smile, but it quickly falls when she doesn't stop. Her lips close over my bottom one, and her teeth tug while her tongue plays with my ring. Is this what she's thinking about every time I notice her staring at it?

She sucks on my lower lip, slowly pulling away until she lets it go with a pop. I lunge after her, taking her lips with mine this time and demanding access to her mouth in return as heat flares through me. Her tongue battles mine, teeth nipping as our mouths fight for dominance, and I flip our positions, turning her onto her back under me. I yank her hips into mine and her legs circle me, holding me to her or her to me—I can't be sure, but I'm not about to complain.

This is as close to nirvana as I've ever been.

I snake a hand into her hair, then use my grip to tip her chin up, forcing her mouth to relinquish mine. She cuts off what I'm sure was about to be a whimpered protest, but I ignore it, turning my attention to tracing her jaw with my tongue. I lick and kiss down her neck, sucking over her pulse point and demanding it leaves a mark for everyone to see.

"Ro," Lor says, breathless and shuddering.

My name has never sounded so good and the last thing I want to do is stop, but I sense the question in her tone. I lick up her throat and nip her earlobe, sending another cascade of shivers down her body before I pull back.

I hate the inches between us, and my demon wants nothing more than to *take*. That's not who I want to be though, so I force the urge down, quelling it with the uncertain, skittish look on Lor's face.

I've never known her to be unsure of anything, and it's enough to sound alarm bells in my head.

"Lor?" I whisper, backing off to give her space. "What is it? Did I go too far?"

Her hands follow my body as I pull away, giving me a moment of hope, but then she seems to notice the subconscious action and hugs her arms around her middle instead. I bite my lip to keep my protest inside. I want her wrapped around me again, but if that's not what she wants, I need to respect it.

"Please," I say, trying to keep the desperation from my voice. "Talk to me?"

"I..." Lor shakes her head, biting her lip as she turns her face away.

I practice the deep breathing my therapist taught me. Four in, four hold, six out, four hold.

Lor sucks in a breath and turns back to me. Her eyes search mine, flicking back and forth, then she runs her gaze down to where my hands are curled into the hem of my own shirt, doing everything I can not to reach for her.

"We don't have to go any further," I say. "We don't even have to do that ever again, if you don't want to."

Her body stiffens and my heart falls, but then she shakes her head.

"No," she says, her voice stronger than it was before. She straightens her back, sitting up and settling herself sideways on the cushion to face me. "No, that's not what I want."

"What do you want?"

I refuse to let the tiny flame of hope gain purchase until she tells me what the actual fuck is going on in that gorgeous, confusing head of hers.

"I want you," she breathes, and I swear my heart stops.

I blink at her, letting the words sink into my skin.

"But?" I say.

Lor gulps, swallowing hard but not looking away this time.

"But... it can't be anything," she says with a small shake of her head.

I tilt my chin as my brows furrow in confusion, prompting her to explain. Lor waves a hand between us.

"This. *Us,*" she says. "We can't be anything to each other. If we do this, it's just a hookup. Nothing more."

I hate it, but if that's what she needs to hear, I'll let it slide —for now.

"Ah," I say, then force my signature cocky grin into place.

"So, what I'm hearing is... We should do it just this once to get it out of our systems?"

Lor's shoulders slump with relief.

"Yes," she replies. "Exactly that."

"Sure, Lor." I click my tongue against my teeth. "Whatever you need to tell yourself. Just as long as you don't expect me to stop showing up and bringing you ice cream and going on rides together," I say with a wink, ensuring she knows she won't be rid of me that easily.

Lor scoffs. "I think you mean invading my space, stealing the wrong kind of ice cream, and stalking me."

I grin. *Oh, how good it feels to be seen.*

Lor rolls her eyes, twisting her mouth to hold in a laugh I'm dying to hear.

Then our gazes connect again and I let the smile slip from my face as I take her in. Tangled silver hair and shirt askew with kiss-swollen lips and a hickey on her neck. She's divine perfection, and I have *one shot* with her. To convince her we're more than "just this once."

My demon perks up, ready to win over our goddess, and I let my demonic urges to the forefront, allowing them to peek out more than usual. Lor's eyes widen at the look on my face as I lean over her, invading her space again.

I run my nose up her neck, closing my eyes and inhaling her clean, lightly floral scent deep into my lungs, leaving a trail of goosebumps along her collarbone. Then I stand, ignore her surprised shriek when I scoop her into my arms, and march to her bedroom.

Lor wraps her legs around my waist as I carry her, and her mouth latches onto my neck. She tortures me with her tongue, the most delicious curl of heat building in my abdomen from her teasing. I grunt when she nips my jaw, then feel the satisfied smirk of her lips against my neck. She wants to play?

Excellent.

I toss her onto the bed, admiring her boobs bouncing in her tight crop top, then I quickly follow. I snag her thin shorts with one finger and call to my power, singing a line straight down and tearing the remnants from her skin. Lor's shriek is one of outrage this time.

"What the fuck did you just do?" she yells, her eyes burning with indignation and no small amount of desire.

I cackle. She's perfect.

Lor's lip lifts in a snarl and she narrows her eyes, but I'm faster. I cover her body with mine and steal her lips in another kiss. The rigid set of her muscles softens beneath me, though she spears a hand into my hair and fists it. I welcome the sting, and I don't hide it as an appreciative moan rumbles up my throat.

"Heathen," Lor says, her lips whispering against mine.

"Demon," I correct, pulling back to take in the gorgeous, disheveled state of her beneath me.

Her lips are parted, and red marks line her throat and collarbone. Her hair is a riot of silver across the sheets, and her breasts heave with every breath she sucks in. I trail the back of my knuckles along the curve of her jaw and she shivers, a hint of insecurity stealing into her gaze.

I can't have that. Insecurity has no place here inside my stunning creature.

"You're more beautiful than I have words for," I say.

Lor scoffs and turns her head away, but I catch the faint pink creeping into her cheeks. I trace my fingers down her neck, across her chest to the neckline of her shirt. I start to heat my finger again as I pull at it, ready to burn her tiny top off like I did her shorts, when she swats my hand away.

"Nuh-uh," she says, a scowl thinning her pretty lips. "No ripping. I like this top."

Great, now my demon wants to steal it for himself.

I move both hands to the hem and slip it over her head,

then shove the urge to pocket it into the recesses of my mind. Her breasts spill free; she wasn't wearing a bra, and now she's clad in only tiny black panties.

My dick strains against the seam of my pants, begging to set free, but I hold back. If she's being truthful about only once, I'm going to make the most of it. This will be the best sex of her life.

Lor reaches for my pants, but I back up. I slide her up the bed as I lower myself down her body, dropping kisses and sucking a mark into the side of one breast before rolling my tongue around her nipple. Lor's hands tangle in my hair again as she gasps, arching into my mouth. I grin against her, plumping her other breast in my palm as I tease. I want to taste every inch of this woman for as long as she'll let me.

I turn my head and snag the inside of her wrist with my lips, sucking and licking that too as I make my way down to her navel.

"Fuck," Lor hisses, her muscles tensing beneath me.

I drag my nose along the crease where her thigh meets her lower stomach, then slip her panties down her legs. Her skin is the softest I've ever felt, and I never want to stop touching her. Her hands fist in the sheets, one next to her head and the other by her hip, like she wants to reach for me again but won't let herself.

We'll just have to see about that.

I lick and nip at her inner thigh, first one, then the other, ghosting my breath over her pussy in between. She's wet already, and her hips quiver as I get closer to where she wants me. I sling her legs over my shoulders, then return to sucking a bruising mark into the crease of her thigh, and it's at that point that she loses it.

"Godsdamnit, Ro." Lor growls the words, her voice husky with desire.

I flick my eyes up to hers, then slowly raise my head just

enough that she can see me bite my lip ring, then lick my lips. Her eyes lock onto my mouth and I drop my gaze back to the prize in front of me.

I let out a slow breath, knowing she can feel it, and her hips buck up toward me. That must have been the last straw, because next thing I know, both of her hands are fisted in my hair again and she's pulling me down into her. Lor raises her hips to meet my face halfway as she buries me in her pussy, and I've never been so turned on in my life.

I groan at the first true taste of her, and my eyes roll back, the salty musk assaulting my tongue as I dive in. I spread her open with my fingers, spear her with my tongue, then lap up every inch of her I can reach. Lor cants her hips and pulls me in tighter, a crack of desperation breaking from her throat. I suck on her folds, fuck her with my tongue, then close my mouth around her clit.

Lor's breath hitches and her hands spasm in my hair. I hold in my grin as I back off, lessening the intensity—much to her dismay.

"What the fuck," Lor pants between each word.

She wrenches her hand in my hair, attempting to move me faster, harder, back where she wants, and I grin as I leisurely lick a stripe from her opening to her clit, then circle it with what I know is not enough pressure to get her off.

"Asshole," Lor says, her head thumping back onto the pillow as she gives in.

"Demon," I correct again, and she huffs what might be a laugh. I hope so; I think I'm funny, and I'd love it if she thought so too. Maybe not while I'm pleasuring her, though. I frown at the thought and refocus on my goal: To drive Lor wild with want.

I continue to circle and lick, suck and kiss, nip and explore and eat my goddamn heart out. Lor responds beautifully once she lets go. Her shudders and whimpers drive me on as desire and satisfaction blaze through me. I bring her closer and closer to the edge, but I refuse to push her over yet.

Realizing I haven't explored inside her enough, I swipe two fingers through her wetness and then slowly press them into her. Lor tips her chin up and sucks in a deep breath as I rub against her front walls. She's so swollen, hard and straining on the inside, ready to explode.

I rub back and forth, lightly at first, then slowly increasing the pressure. Lor's chest heaves and one of her hands leaves my head to clench on her breast.

My movements falter, my eyes pinned to that hand as my jaw goes slack for a moment. Her fingers pinching her nipple between them as she crushes the soft mound with her palm makes my dick weep in my pants. My hips grind against the bed, seeking relief, and I suck in a breath as need swamps me.

I swallow hard, then yank my attention back to her pussy. My fingers curl and work in a steady rhythm, building her up one final time. Her inner muscles clench and release, her hips attempt to buck into me, but I hold her steady.

When I latch onto her clit, sucking and running the flat of my tongue over the sensitive nerves, she stops breathing. Her entire body tenses, arching on the bed as a low, whimpered gasp escapes her lips.

She convulses around my fingers, wave after wave of muscles tensing and releasing as her clit throbs against my tongue. I groan as I hold back my own pleasure, stilling my hips where they were bucking against the bed.

And then Lor's body shakes and she crashes back to the mattress. I slowly lighten the pressure of my fingers and mouth, allowing her to finally take the lead and ride out the rest of her orgasm, using me as she sees fit.

She's a goddess, a being not of this world. Her skin is nearly luminescent, lined with a thin sheen of sweat as her muscles tremble with aftershocks. I lick up the sides of her pussy, kissing her outer lips and tasting her pleasure.

Lor shudders again, then pushes against my forehead, but I can't help it. I don't want to be done tasting her.

"Ro, no," Lor says in protest. Her voice crackles, broken and hoarse. It's the sexiest thing I've ever heard. I pull back and pout, sticking out my lower lip.

"One more?" I ask, widening my eyes and giving her my best impression of hopeful pleading.

"No, no more!" Lor says, swatting at my forehead with a delirious laugh, and my heart stalls.

She's *laughing*.

Screw the sexy voice, *this* is the best thing I've ever heard.

14

PRETENDING TO BE UNIMPRESSED

*February 1, 1990: I think it's happening.
Mother said it would be so. That star-
chasers always go mad, in the end. I feel it,
my mind slipping away. There are times I
don't know where I am, who I am, what
I'm doing. Times when the only thought in
my head is to get to them, free them, rescue
them. I fear I'm losing touch with reality,
and there's nothing I can do to stop it.*

LOR

It takes far too long for me to catch my breath. That
orgasm was like nothing I've experienced before. I thought I
passed out for a moment, but the blackness cleared quickly,
and now I'm left with quivering legs and a tremor in my pussy
that won't stop. I've had some good hookups before, but
nothing has come close to whatever *that* was.

I realize my eyes are closed, and I force them open, only to
see Ro's eyes practically glowing as he watches me, still
between my legs. He looks almost as undone as I feel.

"What?" I ask. I hold in an eye-roll at how hoarse and breathy my voice is. I bet he loves knowing how wrecked I am after that performance.

"Nothing," Ro says, averting his gaze.

I narrow my eyes at him, but he shrugs it off and grins, then shuffles up the bed next to me.

"That was hot as fuck," he says.

I let out a low chuckle, and he beams like he won a prize. I shake my head and he nuzzles into me, biting his lip with his eyes on my mouth.

I lick my lips, then let my gaze trail down his body. He took his shirt off at some point, and I'm not at all surprised to find more tattoos on the exposed skin. Fine lines that follow the curves of his hip bones and disappear around to his back. More dark lines angle along his lower ribs and waist, guiding my eyes up and around.

I am surprised by the pierced nipples, although I shouldn't be based on the number of piercings he has in other places. I trace the metal bars with one finger, and he shivers beneath my touch. It's then I wonder what *else* might be pierced.

My gaze darts down to the bulge in his pants, then goes back to my finger on the bar through his nipple, and finally up to his face. Ro must read the thoughts going through my head, because he lets out a huff of laughter before speaking.

"Don't get your hopes up," he says. "I'm not that much of a masochist."

One side of my mouth quirks up and I shrug one shoulder. I'm not bothered either way, but it would have been a new experience for me. Still, I'm not going to let an opportunity pass me by.

"No?" I say, turning my voice as sweet as I can. "Prove it."

Ro's gaze heats at my words, and he levers himself up on one arm, staring down at me before he grins and hops off the bed.

"You asking for a show, darling?"

I run my eyes up and down his lean form.

"I certainly wouldn't say no, if you're offering."

Ro grins, then bites his lip. He must know that drives me wild, because he's been doing it a lot more lately. I'm quickly distracted when he slowly peels off his pants, leaving him in tight black boxers with a clear outline of his cock. He turns around, flexing his back and arms, then peeks over his shoulders and winks at me.

I laugh the most unattractive, guffawing laugh I've ever heard, then promptly slap my hand over my mouth. My eyes flare with mortification, sure I must have just turned him off quicker than his own grandma would.

But as usual, nothing with Ro goes as expected.

"Not the reaction I was hoping for," he says, turning back around with a rueful grin. "But I'll take it anyway."

Ro waggles his eyebrows and I drop my hand, pinching my mouth to stop the smile from spreading, but it falls open a moment later when he runs his hands down his chest and abs to the waistband of his boxers. He teases, inching it down, then swaying his hips and moving his hands back up. What little patience I possess was already used up when he edged me mercilessly earlier, so I hold no shame for not wanting to wait again now.

"I don't know if I want to murder you or fuck you," I mutter under my breath as I lunge forward, grabbing his boxers at his hips and yanking them down. I should rip them apart like he did to my poor shorts.

His dick nearly smacks me in the face as it bounces free, and I stifle a squeak of surprise as I lean back to take him in. Ro grins down at me.

"Oh, if you wanted those off, you could have just asked."

I ignore the infuriating gall of this man and choose to admire his body instead. His arms and legs are well muscled but not obscene, probably from hours on his feet back and forth behind the bar. His chest is defined, but not in a gym rat way. He's lean enough that the V leading to his cock is prominent, and my mouth waters as I follow the line of him down to his cock. It's an average length, but more girthy than I'm used to.

My pussy clenches as I imagine how he'll stretch me, what it'll feel like having him fill me to the brim.

"Like what you see?" Ro asks.

The smirk is audible in his tone, so I shrug and scoot back on the bed.

"It'll do," I say, meeting his eyes.

Ro laughs and leaps onto the bed after me. "I know what that means in Lor-language. That's high praise coming from you. You love it, don't you?"

My face flushes and I open my mouth to deny it, but nothing comes out. I snap it closed, then narrow my eyes and wrap one hand around his cock.

"Keep talking, smartass," I say, squeezing my hand. "See what happens."

Ro slowly leans forward, closing the space between us as his eyes darken. Then he whispers against my mouth.

"Demon."

My lips twitch up at the corners, but he's already moving, crashing his mouth against mine again, and I open to let him in. When we're both out of breath, he pulls back and runs his fingers through my hair, scratching along my scalp. I practically melt into his touch, not fully registering his words as my eyes flutter closed and I tilt into his hand.

"Tell me what you want, Lor. How do you like it?"

"I..." I blink my eyes back open as my brain catches up with the situation. My gaze dips between us. "I'm happy to return the favor."

Ro hums a low note in his throat and I look up to see him slowly shake his head.

"No, I don't think so," he says. "If this is the only chance I have to fuck you, I'm not wasting it."

"You don't want my mouth on you? Fine," I say, pretending haughty disinterest.

"Well, hold up a second," Ro says, quickly backpedaling. "I never said that."

I cock an eyebrow and he grins. "There's always next time."

I've had enough of his bullshit. I sit up and push against his shoulders as I swing one leg over his hips and reach for the box I keep in my nightstand drawer. I tear open a condom, slick it over his dick, and glance up to see him watching my fingers as they move over him. He gulps and I wait a moment, pausing until he makes eye contact. He fixes his cocky smirk into place and tips his chin up.

I take that as permission, so I close my fist around him and move forward until his hard cock is beneath me. Ro's hands fly to my hips, the heat of his palms sending tingles across my skin. I run his tip up and down my pussy, spreading the lingering wetness, then riding my clit along the hard shaft. Finally, I notch him at my entrance, tip my head back, and suck in a deep breath before sinking down.

Only the first inch, the swollen head of his cock enters me, and it's already enough to have me panting.

"Eyes on me."

Ro's strained voice cuts through the pulse pounding in my ears and I wrench my eyes open. I hadn't realized that they were closed, I was so focused on the stretch as he fills me. My gaze meets his and my breath hitches in my chest. His eyes are banked coals, glowing hazel, so full of heat and raw desire it takes my breath away.

Ro taps my hip with one finger, the rest still gripping me,

holding me steady above him. It brings me back to the moment, and I suck in another deep breath.

I clench and then release my inner muscles, allowing myself to sink lower, taking another couple inches. He's rubbing against spots I didn't know were possible to reach with a dick, but his width has me imagining how obscenely stretched I must be. I try to steady my breathing, but I'm so full already, I don't know if I can take any more.

I attempt to push down again, but I don't move. I look down, putting more weight on it, but again, I'm speared on his dick and apparently stuck with only a couple inches inside. An involuntary, panicked whimper escapes my throat and my eyes shoot up to meet Ro's gaze.

His eyes soften, and I don't contemplate how desperate I must appear for that look to cross his face, because it achieves the only thing I want right now.

Ro tightens his grip on me and pushes up with his hips while simultaneously pulling me down onto him. A slow, steady glide as he fills me inch by inch. I stop breathing, the air getting trapped in my lungs as sensation sparks along my nerves.

Never has sex felt this way.

I've played with women and men, nonbinary and gender-fluid folks, all kinds of toys. But nothing has felt like *this.*

I nearly sob when my inner thighs meet his hips and he's fully seated in me. My mind is spinning, the feeling of him filling me overwhelming. Ro takes a shuddering breath and squeezes my hips, holding us both steady.

"Fuck, Starfire," he says, voice gravelly with desire. "You feel even better than I imagined."

He's imagined this. He called me... star... wait, what did he just say?

The blood starts to drain from my face, but it's immediately pushed from my mind when he rocks my hips against him, lighting a fire inside me. I gasp and arch my back, rocking myself again. Ro releases my hip with one hand to reach up and palm my breast.

It feels heavenly, having his warm hand cover my entire breast, the nipple trapped between two of his fingers as he squeezes and fondles it.

"God, that feels good," I say with a moan.

Before I know it, I'm moving. Lifting and falling, grinding my clit against the thumb he angles between us, circling my hips, fucking him until the sparks spread. Ro pinches my nipple, rolls it between his fingers, tugs on it.

"Ah," I gasp. "Fuck, Ro."

"Yes, Lor," he says. "Keep going, take what you need."

I speed up, his hand on my hip helping me set the pace and keep me steady as he continues to pluck at my nipple and soothe it with a warm palm.

"I, Ro, I..." I trail off, no idea what I'm trying to say, just that I want more of him.

"I know, Lor," he says. His voice is lower than I've ever heard it, hoarse and drenched with desire. "You're perfect, doing so good. Fuck, Lor. So hot and wet, so fucking tight on my cock."

His dirty words spur me on, and my inner muscles twitch and clench.

"I'm close," I say, panting as I claw at him. I wrap one hand around his wrist, the one torturing my nipple, and splay the other on his thigh behind me for leverage. My hips swivel and buck as I chase the high just out of reach.

"Fuck, Ro," I keen, desperate to come.

"Such a good fucking girl, riding my dick like you own it," Ro says.

My pussy clenches again and my hips stutter. Ro takes over, holding me steady and pounding up into me. I throw my head back as sparks tingle up and down my spine, heat pooling in my lower belly. Ro releases my nipple and moves his hand between us. My grip moves to his forearm, anchoring myself to him as he slots his fingers around my clit.

"You gonna come for me?" Ro grinds out, and I nod frantically. "That's right. Drench my cock, milk me dry."

"Don't stop, don't stop," I chant, and he doesn't. That perfect rhythm is relentless. It sends me higher, heat and tension building until I fear I'll die before it can snap. Then Ro's fingers close around my clit and he pinches, rubbing it between them.

My lungs stop working, and I throw my head back as time stands still. Waves of bliss crash over me, and I'm no longer connected to my body. I exist outside of this plane, in a place of euphoria as my clit throbs and Ro continues to hammer into me.

As I rejoin my body, shudders cascade through me, my pussy still clenching around him. Ro becomes impossibly harder inside me, then his thrusts falter and his dick pulses. I can feel it at my entrance and deep inside me as his own orgasm rips through him.

My body turns boneless and I collapse to his chest, both of us trying to catch our breath.

"Holy shit," I say.

"Holy fucking shit," Ro replies.

I huff out a breath, almost a laugh, and roll my languid body off him. Ro lets out a sound of discontent, but I can't bring myself to open my eyes to see what he's grumbling about. Then we simply breathe, chests rising and falling side by side. It's a moment of mutual satisfaction, which I've experienced plenty of times before, but somehow this feels deeper —significant even—and I wrinkle my nose, mentally turning away and focusing on how tranquil my body feels instead.

Ro rummages around for a moment, I suspect taking care

of the condom, and next thing I know he's snuggling up beside me.

I stiffen, not normally one for cuddles, but Ro nuzzles his face into my hair and releases a happy sigh. It brings a small smile to my face, and I relax a little, allowing him to pull my body against his. He turns me onto my side, fussing and adjusting us until he's comfortable spooning against me.

I'm surrounded by him, his fiery scent, the unnatural warmth of his body, and his soft breaths tickling the back of my neck as he relaxes into me.

15

———

CURSES AND LIES

*July 15, 1991: My soul... I fear for it. For
myself. My soul is so lonely. Nothing fills
the void.*

LOR

A relentless, angry meowing rouses us from our sex-drunk
stupors an indiscernible amount of time later. I groan and
stretch as Ro does the same beside me, then I get up to open
the door. The cat isn't going to stop yelling until it gets its way,
so I might as well let it in.

"Oh, hello Kahlo," Ro says, sauntering over to crouch
down by the cat.

I do a double take. Kahlo? When did that happen?

"Did you name my cat?"

"Thought they weren't your cat."

Ro smirks and the cat, Kahlo apparently, presses into his
palm. I narrow my eyes, a daring thread of betrayal stinging my
chest.

"Fine, they're my cat."

I jerk my shirt over my head and search for my shorts

before remembering Ro literally tore them off of me. Arousal zings between my legs at the memory and I huff. Too many emotions.

"I can't believe you ruined my shorts."

Ro stands and picks up his own shirt. "I can buy you a new pair, if you want."

He's still smirking. A proud, crooked tilt to his lips. He can't tell how much that turned me on, can he? I glance down at my hard nipples and wrinkle my nose. He probably can.

I slip past him, aiming for the kitchen for some water as he meanders after me. I need to cool down and get a grip on this situation. Mostly, I need to get Ro out of my apartment so I can process what exactly just happened. And figure out how to eliminate the desire to do it again... That was supposed to get it out of my system, so why do I want him even more now?

"Come on, Kahlo." Ro sits on the couch and pats his leg, and the cat comes trotting down the hallway to jump up on his lap.

Ro grins in delight, then turns his happy face up to me.

"Looks like you have a cat named Kahlo now."

I bite the inside of my cheek. It's impossible to be grumpy around Ro, he's just so goddamn cheerful about everything. I give in and let one side of my mouth tip up in response.

"I guess I do."

THE DAYS PASS MUCH the same after that, minus the mind blowing sex. I ignore the urge to jump on Ro's dick every time he shows up unannounced, and every time he follows me on his bike, and every time he grins at me from behind the bar.

All of which only serves to make me more and more cranky.

Ro seems perfectly happy to just be around me, and I can't

tell if he truly feels that way, or if he still feels the tension between us, too. I hate thinking that it might just be me, but I need to remember this distance is for the best.

He's too *good* to get caught up in the dark underworld that is my life.

I'm currently sitting on my bed, reminding myself why a relationship is a bad idea, and it's really putting a damper on my already abysmal mood. I'm flipping through my grandmother's journal, reading about her experience as a star-chaser. She died at fifty, when my mom, Renée, was only twenty-two. My mom had me later that same year, so I never met my grandmother. As usual in our family, the men are absent, so there are no known fathers or grandfathers in my history.

My grandma's journal entries are depressing but enlightening, and they're a good reminder of what my future holds. Eventual madness, insanity, losing my mind... Whatever you want to call it.

I used to hope there was a way to avoid it, but I've given up on that childish dream. It's one of the only things my mom was consistent on. She may not have really been there for me growing up, constantly moving us around and using drugs to cope with her curse, but she was adamant about this.

All Seren's go mad.

We also tend to die young, and the thought lights a brief flare of concern for my mom. She's fifty-one this year, and I haven't heard from her in months. That's not unusual for us, though, so I hope she's alright. As alright as any of the women in our family can be, anyway.

I'm flipping through the pages, skimming the later journal entries that get progressively more indecipherable as the madness sets in, when Ro's signature cheerful knock sounds on my door. A quick double tap, pause, single knock, pause, double tap.

I flip the journal closed, letting it slide from my lap as I stand to let him in. Kahlo comes running down the hallway after me, and I roll my eyes at the little beast. The traitor definitely likes him better than me. I open the door, my chest feeling lighter as soon as Ro bounces into my apartment.

"Hey, Starfire," he says, and my face heats at the strange endearment. Then he turns to the cat. "Kahlo!"

He drops to the floor and Kahlo instantly starts purring, rubbing their chin along Ro's arm and knee.

I close the door behind him and turn to the kitchen, then stare at my too-empty pantry. I don't have many options, but I haven't eaten yet today, so I need something. Ro wanders up behind me and drops his chin on my shoulder. His breath feathers over my neck, and I suppress a shiver.

"Oooh, mac and cheese!" he says. "I haven't had that in ages."

Ro reaches around, one arm on either side of my body as he leans into my back to rummage through the pantry. His warmth sinks into me, and I've never been so aware of the contrast as my muscles turn to jelly while my nerves alight against him. Ro pulls the box of macaroni from the cupboard, then starts opening and closing others as if he hasn't already explored every inch of my kitchen and doesn't know exactly where my single pot is.

I put my hands on my hips and wait. Sure enough, he glances at me, mischief dancing in his eyes as he pulls open another incorrect cupboard.

Then he starts whistling.

I twist my mouth to the side to hold in my smile as he finally pulls out the correct pot and fills it with water. He sets it on the stove, then spins around to face me.

"Oh! I almost forgot!" he says, shoving a hand in his front pocket.

I raise my eyebrows and his grin somehow spreads wider when he pulls out a bright pink cat toy.

"I got Kahlo a new toy!"

I hate the way my chest clenches and heart skips at how excited he is to play with kind-of-my cat.

"Kahlo, ps-ps-ps," Ro says, dropping to the floor and crawling to peek around the corner.

Now my heart is pounding for a whole different reason. What would he look like crawling to me? With no—nope.

Not going there.

I mentally kick myself and turn around, refusing to take in the cuteness that is Ro, an actual demon, playing with my demonic cat. That *must* be why they get along so well, there's no other explanation.

Soon I'm stirring butter and powdered cheese into the noodles, then looking around for Ro.

"Ro?" I call, taking the pot off the heat before stepping into the hallway.

My bedroom door is open, and I roll my eyes. He's probably poking through my dresser or something. I step into the room, and my stomach drops when I see him sitting on my bed with my grandmother's journal.

"Ro!" I sprint to his side and snatch the journal from his hands, snapping it closed. Terror pounds through me. Did he read it? Does he know my secret? Is he going to try to use me, too? Or... leave?

"What are you doing?" I yell, my voice unnaturally loud in the small space. I back away, chest heaving as I stare at him.

Ro holds his hands up, eyes wide as he leans away from my outburst.

"Whoa, I, uh, I'm sorry," he says, stammering. "I wasn't doing anything."

"You had my journal!" I clutch the journal to my stomach and his eyes drop to it, then return to mine. He looks taken aback by my reaction, but what did he expect? Journals are private, even a demon should know that's not okay.

"I didn't realize it was your journal, I won't look again."

He sounds contrite, his voice smaller than I've ever heard it, and full of remorse.

I eye him, taking in his tense shoulders, the wide eyes and shallow breaths. Either he saw and is ready to bolt, or he didn't and is scared I'll kick him out. I take a slow breath, trying to calm my racing heart.

I need to know.

"What did you see?" I ask, trying for a neutral tone.

"Nothing, I swear, I was just flipping through. I didn't read a word of it."

I pinch my lips as I stare at him, wishing I could tell if he was being truthful or not. Ro slumps under my glare, deflating as he sinks to the floor and leans against the side of the bed.

"I won't touch it again. I'd never read your personal journal. I know I'm not the best at boundaries, but this is one I wouldn't cross. It just looked like an old book, I..." he trails off, looking down at his hands. His knuckles are white where he's clenching them together. "I didn't know. I'm sorry."

I let the silence sit as my anger and fear dissipate. He's not running, so... What does that mean? Did he really not read it? I slide down to the floor, sitting against the wall a few feet away from him.

"It's not my journal, it's my grandmother's," I say quietly.

Ro glances up at me, sorrowful eyes framed by long lashes made more dramatic by the dark eyeliner he wears. He nods, but doesn't reply. Despite the disruption he's been in my life, my heart pangs when I think about losing him. It couldn't hurt to give him a second chance, could it?

My thoughts tumble from one to the next as I try to pull apart his essence, figure out what to do, how best to protect myself. Let him in, and risk my life and his? Or force him to go, risking my heart and budding happiness instead?

His gaze drops from mine, resigned, and the threat of losing more than just his eyes on me pushes me over the edge.

"You still hungry?" I say. "Mac is done."

"Yeah!" Ro's head shoots up, and he offers me a tentative grin.

I try to return it, but it feels unsteady on my face. I stand and offer him a hand up. His smile turns softer, more genuine as he takes my hand

Before I know it, he's back to his usual bubbly self. Despite my reaction and whatever damning evidence he may have seen in the journal, he doesn't treat me any differently. I dare to hope he may have been telling the truth, that he really didn't read anything. I'm rinsing my bowl, considering that possibility, when it happens.

A lurch in my gut that turns to a relentless pull. It's undeniable, stronger than usual, and I drop the bowl with a clatter.

"Hey, you okay?"

Ro appears over my shoulder, reaching around me to pick the bowl up from the sink and place it in the dishwasher. I cringe and take a breath, hating for him to see me so vulnerable, then nod. My thoughts are spinning as I try to tell the curse in my blood that I'll go—to get it to lessen for just a moment so I can grab what I need.

"Yeah. But, um. I have to go," I say to Ro. I'm short of breath and a light sweat breaks out on my forehead.

"Okay," he says, placing his bowl next to mine in the top rack. It gives me a moment to compose myself before he turns around and asks with far too much excitement, "Are we going on a ride?"

"We?" I'm distracted, searching for my keys as I stuff my fabric stardust bag into my backpack.

"Well, it doesn't have to be together if you don't want it to be, but you know I'll be behind you either way." Ro winks as he says it and I freeze, one hand shoved deep into my backpack.

My cheeks flush as my mind screeches to a halt. What did he just say? What is he talking about? My eyes are stuck on his cheeky grin, the wink throwing me off, and now he's tonguing his lip ring again.

"Get your head out of the gutter, Starfire," Ro says. "Although, I'm not opposed to being behind you in that way, either."

I blink, then my face blazes even hotter. I'm sure my neck is splotchy at this point, and I refuse to continue whatever nonsense is happening right now. I spin on my heel and wrench the door open, stomping out to my bike as Ro cackles behind me.

I can't stop thinking about his offer, if that's what it even was. I know I said just once, but the fact that he's here, behind me, and apparently still wants me too, is lighting my nerves on fire.

If only it weren't for this aching pull. And the uncertainty of what he might have read.

As I speed down the highway, it feels like my soul is being ripped away, with my body trailing behind it like a shadow. I'm frantic, ready to sprint to the impact site, but I'm not there yet. I take deep breaths, telling myself I'll be there soon, trying to calm the incessant ache that's threatening to turn my sight fuzzy.

16

CROP CIRCLE VS CORN MAZE

Ro

I weave back and forth on my bike, a silly grin plastered to my face under my helmet as I shoot down the highway after Lor. She didn't put her hair up, so it streams behind her, a beam of silver shimmering in the sun. She's bent low over her bike, back straight and ass perched on the seat in a way that looks so bite-able my mouth waters. I have no idea where we're going, as usual, but it doesn't bother me. I've loved spending so much time with her lately.

One time, my ass.

I snort at the thought. That woman will never be out of my system, and I can tell she still feels the tension between us, too. It's obvious in the way her gaze tracks me, the shivers and goosebumps that spread over her skin anytime I'm near, how her breath hitches when I stretch, and her eyes stick on my lip ring. She's good for my ego, that's for sure. Not that it needs any boosting.

Unsurprisingly, Lor turns off the highway onto a random side road and we zig-zag our way through the countryside. Fields of corn beyond deep ditches line either side of the road, and the sun is high above us. Lor eventually pulls over, nothing special in sight, and I pull up next to her.

She looks tense, her body stiff as she pulls off her helmet. We're in the middle of a random stretch of road, and her top lip pulls into a grimace when she turns and inspects the corn taller than we are. This is where she needed to go?

I'm confused, but I'm down for anything if Lor is involved.

"So. Corn, or corn?" I ask, pointing one finger across the road in front of us and jerking my other thumb over my shoulder.

"Funny," Lor grates between clenched teeth.

Her spine is rigid and her breathing seems shallow. I narrow my eyes as she carefully steps partway down the ditch before leaping across the more narrow bottom. Next thing I know, she's disappearing between the stalks, and my demon is perking up in my chest at the prospect of chasing her through a cornfield.

I let out a jubilant shout and leap across the ditch, then into the line of corn. My demon is intent on stalking his prey as I follow the glimpses of swaying hips weaving between tall plants a dozen feet in front of me.

I'm starting to get concerned, wondering how far we're going and if she actually has a destination in mind, when I step into what has *got* to be a crop circle.

"Oh, hell yeah," I say.

I raise one hand to shade my eyes as I dart my gaze around, taking in the cylindrical shape of smashed greenery and displaced dirt. We're surrounded on all sides by tall, happy corn waving in the breeze, and then there's this crop-circle-alien-crash-site business stretching out in front of me. Lor is already picking her way across the ground up earth, inspecting the dirt as she goes.

"Are we hunting aliens?" I call over to Lor, excitement clear in my voice as I spring after her.

Lor freezes, then straightens and turns back to me.

"What?"

"Aliens!" I say, raising my voice so she can hear over the wind swishing through the corn.

Lor stares at me for a moment, then shakes her head as she crouches back down. It looks more like a 'you're ridiculous' head shake than a 'no' head shake, though.

I shrug.

Whatever, she can keep her secrets. I'd let her have all the glory if we do find evidence of aliens, I'm just happy to be along for the ride. I start scanning the ground, choosing a spot away from her so we can cover more of it together, but I don't see any footprints other than my own. There's no burn marks from a landing craft or lasers or anything, but then if they had technology to land here, I guess they'd be beyond leaving signs that obvious.

A glimmer catches my eye and I swoop down to check it out, but it's just a sparkly rock. It's pretty though, so I pocket it, then continue my slow search, eyes scanning back and forth as I carefully step around the alien landing zone.

I jump when my mom's ringtone belts from my pocket, and flit my eyes to Lor as I pull it out. She glances up at me in confusion, but goes back to shoveling dirt into her sack without comment.

Hmm, are we not looking for aliens? Or did she find a clue in the dirt?

"Hey, Mom," I say, answering the video call.

"Foras Astaroth Cromwell."

"Wait, what? I didn't do anything!"

"It has been far too long since you've called your mother," she scolds.

"I'm pretty sure I called you two days ago."

"Oh," she says, then looks off screen when I hear my dad in the background confirming that we did, in fact, talk two days ago. "Right, well. Hello, darling!"

"Hi, Mom." I roll my eyes, but grin regardless.

"What on earth are you doing in a cornfield, dear?"

"Oh! We're alien hunting!"

My dad's face pops into the screen next to hers and I spin around, showing them the landing site and Lor a dozen strides behind me.

"Either that or we're researching crop circles. I haven't quite figured it out yet."

"Well that sounds wonderful," my mom says. "And who is this we? The lovely lady I see back there?"

"That's Lor," I say, turning to her. "Hey, Lor!"

She looks up and I hold my phone higher, pointing to it with the other hand for good measure.

"It's my parents, wave!"

She squints at me, then raises her hand to shield her eyes. I consider that good enough, and my parents seem to as well, calling hello to her even though she can't hear them so far away. Corn stalks are surprisingly loud when it's breezy.

"Is this the lady you've been stuck on?" my dad asks.

I flush and nod, rubbing a hand against the back of my neck.

"A corn maze wouldn't be my first choice, but to each their own," my mom interjects.

"It's not a corn—"

"I hope you brought protection, dear. We can tell you're smitten, so you better be treating her right. Don't forget that aftercare is important, even if you are in a corn maze."

"We're not—"

"Your mother's right," Dad interrupts, but then my mom cuts him off, pushing further into the frame.

"We'll let you get back to it!" she says with a wild cackle, then turns to my dad. He immediately crashes his lips to hers, and she drops the phone. I hang up before I get an eyeful of something I don't want to see.

"Wow," Lor says from right behind me, making me jump. "Your parents are a trip. I can see where you get it from."

"Ah, yeah," I say, a rueful tilt to my lips as I wonder how much to say, and what all she heard. I ruffle my hand through the back of my perpetually messy hair as I continue. "They're both demons too, but, uh.."

Lor cocks her head, her eyebrows raised. She's actually interested? My heart skips and I dive in.

"Yeah, they're sex demons."

Lor blinks once, twice, then stares at me.

"Sex demons." Her voice is skeptical, so I continue before she decides to write me off as a liar or something. Stealing, yes. Fires, sure. Lying? Not if I can help it.

"Yeah, but I'm not. A sex demon, that is. I didn't inherit those particular urges. Not that I don't like sex! Obviously, I mean, of course I like sex," I say, my entire face and neck flushing. I try to pass it off as heat from the sun by fanning my face with my hand, but I don't think it works. I have never been this flustered around someone before; normally, I'm a pretty smooth talker.

A slow, devious smile blooms across Lor's lips, and I back away from her a couple steps. At the same time, my dick starts to lengthen. I hope she doesn't notice the half-chub in my pants, but her eyes are darting between mine, so I think it's safe for now.

"You're nervous."

"I—no," I stammer.

"You are. Why are you nervous talking about sex?"

"I'm not! I love se—*talking!* Talking... about sex. Why— why wouldn't I?"

Lor is nodding, sinful smile nowhere to be seen, and

taking slow, deliberate steps toward me. My eyes widen with each step.

She drops her bag to the ground and raises one hand, reaching out to place her pointer and middle finger in the center of my chest. My heart is pounding so hard it feels like it's trying to escape. Her nails are painted a deep, rich purple, almost black, and she walks her fingers up my chest to the hollow of my throat as she speaks, her voice low and seductive.

"You need to get it out of your system again?" she asks.

My now fully hard dick twitches in my pants and I gulp, my chin tilted up to get away from her dangerous fingers. But all she does is scratch them lightly along my jaw before threading them through my hair at the nape of my neck and tilting her head.

Waiting for an answer, I realize.

I jerk my head in a nod, and one corner of her lips turns up.

"Use your words," she practically purrs, and my cock gives another valiant attempt to free itself.

"Yes," I rasp, "Yes, I want you. I need you, Lor."

She hums low in her throat, then the hand in my hair fists and pulls my mouth down to hers. I meet her readily, my lips already parted, tongue ready to dance with hers as she pulls me closer. I drop my phone to the dirt and my hands find her hips, then the bare skin of her waist. How is she so fucking silky?

Lor nips my bottom lip and then soothes it with her tongue. I groan into her mouth, pulling her tighter against me and shoving one thigh between her legs. Soft and warm, her tongue slicks against mine and I lose myself to her drugging kiss.

Too soon, we part for breath, and she looks around. I'm panting, light-headed, but who needs oxygen when Lor is an option?

"Not here," she says, and I let out the saddest whimper I've ever heard.

I'm not even ashamed, because it makes Lor smile again. She pats my cheek, then turns and swipes up her bag before sauntering back toward the corn. My eyes are glued to her ass, so perky and round in those tight black pants. I should have grabbed it while I had the chance.

My mind flies into overdrive as I picture it. How her cheeks would fill my palms, if her skin is as soft there as it is at her waist. I don't realize she's stopped walking until she snaps her fingers.

My gaze flashes to her face and she has one eyebrow raised. I grin and shrug.

"You've got an incredible ass."

She huffs, then keeps walking, calling out as she steps into the corn. "You coming?"

"Not yet," I say, then laugh to myself.

Hopefully soon.

Lor is fidgety when we get back to her place. I haven't known her to be so restless before. Normally, I'm the one who can't sit still, too full of energy. She sets her bag on the counter in the kitchen, but then keeps glancing at it like she's worried it'll disappear. The mood from earlier is over, obviously, and I'm curious where her mind has gone.

I flop onto her couch, and she eventually sits in the armchair near me, bringing the bag of dirt with her, and carefully placing it out of sight next to her chair. Despite having settled, she seems skittish still, like a deer ready to run at the slightest hint of danger.

I scoot to the edge of the couch and lean forward to place a hand on her arm, gentle so she can easily pull away if she wants, but with enough pressure for her to know I'm serious.

"Lor, what's going on?" I ask. When she doesn't reply, but glances at her bag, I continue. "Why were we really out there?"

She doesn't answer, instead looking down at her hands where her fingers are wringing together, knuckles white with tension. The fact she's still sitting here, hasn't run away or kicked me out, is significant. Her eyes keep flicking to the side of her chair and then back to her lap.

"It wasn't aliens, was it?" I try to lighten my tone, but she doesn't smile like I hope she will.

Lor sucks in a deep breath, her entire body expanding with it, then raises her grey eyes to mine. She stares into me, and I wish I knew what she was looking for. Whatever it is, I'll give it to her. I'd give her anything, do anything, if only she would trust me and let me in. She gives an almost imperceptible nod as she lets out the long breath she took.

"What did you see in my grandmother's journal?"

I blink in surprise. That was not what I was expecting her to say.

"Uh, nothing?"

Her walls immediately start to go up again, her eyes going distant and shoulders tensing.

"I mean, I saw writing," I hurry to say, and her defenses seem to pause. "But I didn't make out any of the words. I wasn't really focused on it, just kind of... idly flipping through? Being nosy, I guess, but without the concentration to take anything in. I don't know. Why?"

Her gaze pierces me again, eyes wary, and it's all I can do not to shrink away from that hard stare. I want to prove myself to her though, so I meet her eyes and will her to understand that I'm an open book for her.

Anything she wants, it's hers.

Whatever she's looking for, she must find it, and I relax as she sits back in her seat. When she speaks, her voice is soft.

"My grandmother was a star-chaser," she says.

It takes a moment to settle into my brain what those words mean. Then a shiver runs down my back and the baby hairs on my arms stand on end.

"You mean like... the mythical star-chasers?"

Lor nods, biting her lip, and I stay quiet. I'm not sure what to say to that, and I don't want to say the wrong thing.

"Yeah, except, we're not myths."

Again, it takes a moment to register. *We.*

As in, her grandmother *and her.*

Okay, clearly she's choosing every single word with care right now. I already sensed this was important, but I sit up and give Lor more attention and focus than I've given anything in my life. I don't want to miss a word, and I don't want to break the tentative trust she's placing in me.

"Okay, so..." I lean sideways to eye the bag she sat next to her. "That means in the bag is..."

After a moment, Lor slowly nods.

"It's stardust," she confirms.

"And... your grandmother's journal?"

"She wrote about it. Her life as a star-chaser. What little of it she had, anyway."

Lor's body starts to close in on itself, deflating, and alarm prickles along the back of my neck. Maybe this is too much for her? It's clear she wasn't sure about talking about it in the first place, and I kind of forced her hand with my snooping.

I mentally kick myself, then fidget with her bracelet under the leather cuff I'm wearing to hide it. My fingers are begging for a flame, but now is not the time, and I won't risk burning any of Lor's few possessions.

"We don't have to talk about it any more if you don't want to."

"You can't tell anyone." Her voice is hard and I hold in a flinch of surprise.

I lean closer and reach out, pulling one of her hands into mine. Her fidgeting stills as she looks between our hands and my eyes. To my surprise, it also soothes my itch to play with fire.

"I won't, Lor. I won't speak a word of it."

After another eternity of willing her to believe me, she sucks in a breath and nods. The tension drains from her body and mine loosens with relief. She almost looks like she's going to laugh for a second until her eyes snag on my lip ring and she stills for a long moment, then launches herself into my arms.

17

———

SNEAKY DEMON

Ro

Lor allowed me to sleep at her place after we "got it out of our systems for good this time" last night. I snort at the memory of her insisting this would be it. Neither of us believed it, but I didn't argue. I want more than just her body, so I can be patient for her. I roll over in the scratchy sheets, wondering how she sleeps on these every night, then haul myself out of bed.

She's puttering around in the kitchen, and the sound of the the coffee maker spluttering is so domestic I want to do a little happy dance. Smiling already, I wander into the hallway in time to overhear Lor talking to the cat she refuses to claim, but is totally hers.

"Kahlo, how many times do I have to tell you?" Lor hisses in a whisper. "Get off the counter."

Kahlo hisses back, then there's a muffled crash.

"Oh my god, you're so dramatic," Lor whisper-yells.

I'd bet all my savings Kahlo just pushed something off the counter in retaliation for Lor's scolding. I fake a yawn, covering my mouth to hide my grin as I round the corner into the kitchen.

"Mornin!"

Lor jumps, turning her scathing glare on me from where she's crouched on the floor wiping up coffee grounds. I pretend it's a smile; someday we'll get there. She's only just learning how to, so I can't expect her to be smiling at me all the time yet.

"You're a morning person, aren't you?" Lor says as though it's an accusation.

I shrug, tipping my nose into the air as the coffee starts filling the pot. "Mmm, that smells amazing. Did you make enough for me?"

Lor stands, tosses out the paper towels she was using, then turns back to me. I rub my hand over my bare chest, noting how her gaze follows the movement. Her eyes snag on my nipple rings, then dart up to my lip ring. Girl loves some piercings, lucky for me.

My grin widens. How can I not feel smug when she's devouring me with those stunning grey eyes?

Unfortunately, she doesn't follow through on whatever tempting thoughts she's having.

"I have to go," Lor says.

It's only now that I notice she's fully dressed. Black pants and a midnight blue crop top hug her subtle curves. Her long hair is up in two messy buns, and her fingers are lined with rings. She glances at me as she strides around the kitchen, putting things away and setting her keys on the edge of the counter.

"But the coffee isn't done," I say.

"That's for you."

I gape at her. She made me coffee? And...

"You're... leaving me alone at your place?"

Lor shrugs, but doesn't meet my eyes. I sense her tension,

and decide not to push it. Her trust is a gift, and one I don't take lightly.

I clear my throat. "Thanks."

Lor nods on her way to the bathroom, and I'm left alone in the kitchen. Kahlo saunters back in and I smile, bending down to offer head and butt scritches as the coffee maker beeps.

Then I realize what that means, her leaving me here alone. *She's leaving.*

I jump into action, snagging my shirt from the floor by the couch and slipping it on as I hurry back to her room where my boxers and pants are... somewhere. I run my hands through my hair as I search, finally finding them half under the foot of the bed on the side opposite me. I step into my underwear, then hop on one foot as I tug my pants on. The sink runs as Lor brushes her teeth in the bathroom.

I slip my phone in my pocket and search for my jacket next, nearly bumping into her in the hallway when she comes out the door.

"Ah, hey," I say, breathless. "Can I borrow some mouth wash?"

"Sure." Lor waves me into the bathroom and I take a gulp, swishing as I head back into the kitchen. I spit in the sink, then request a travel mug.

Lor pauses and eyes me, suspicious.

"I've got some things to do, so I'll just head out with you," I say.

Perhaps a misdirect, but it's not a lie. I do have things to do. Namely, following Lor, making sure Lor's safe, and in general, obsessing over Lor. I should probably call my therapist, too.

We're on the road in no time, and I take a wrong turn to throw her off, grinning with mischief and devious intent. I saw her grab her backpack before she left, and I have a hunch she's headed back to the same creepy warehouse I've followed her to before.

The urge to follow, to protect, to *know her*, has taken priority, and I'm not fighting it anymore. I know I should let her share her secrets in her own time, and while I'm happy to let her share whatever she wants with me, I'm also happy to find them out on my own. Especially now that I know the truth of her family.

Star-chasers.

Demons might have magic, but Lor is *magical*.

I up my speed, weaving between traffic as I race against the clock to beat her there. I'm not going to lose her this time.

HAND OVER HAND, I steadily climb the fire escape on the back side of the building Lor went into. I'm careful to step softly so my boots don't thump on the metal ladder, and soon enough voices drift through the glass above me. I slow down and peek into the bottom corner of the window to see Lor in the middle of a concrete room facing three men. One looks to be the leader, standing between the other two and reaching to take the cloth bag from Lor, then passing it to one of the others, who snaps his fingers. A man in a lab coat sprints up to them and takes the bag, then disappears out of my line of sight.

I look back at the three men facing Lor, but can't make much out. Their backs are to me, so I can't see them clearly. I lean forward, straining to make out the words, when the leader raises his voice.

"You know this isn't acceptable, Alorra," he booms, and I frown at the condescending tone he uses, especially with her full name. "Do you need a reminder of what happens when people fail me?"

Lor shakes her head, her mouth pinched shut and eyes trained on the floor between them. The man waves a hand imperiously, and a few moments later more bodies appear. Two massive men, muscles bulging, are hauling a third between them. He's limp, feet dragging on the floor and head lolling to the side. The leader gestures at them, then clasps his hands behind his back and faces Lor again.

The goons drop the beaten man, the thump of his head hitting concrete reaches me all the way up here in my hiding spot. I wince, then freeze when my boot squeaks on the metal. I duck out of sight, holding my breath.

Voices continue to rumble inside, and there doesn't seem to be any alarm or shouting, so I peek back up to see the two muscular goons have disappeared. Only the beaten—possibly dead—man and the first three remain.

Lor has her face turned away from the grisly scene.

I don't blame her. Nausea rises, making my mouth water and my gut heave, but I'm determined to sit through this with her. She may not know it yet, but she's not alone anymore.

I steady my breathing and strain my ears again, picking up the boss' voice one more.

"Continue underperforming, and that—" he pauses, angling his head at the maybe-dead man, "will soon be your fate."

My blood rushes to my ears and flames leap to life on my fingers. White noise and my pounding pulse are all I can hear. My demon is thundering in my chest, my entire body vibrating with rage that he would dare to threaten *my* Lor. My Starfire.

Flames lick at my sleeves and I look down to see my hands fully engulfed. My lip pulls up in a sneer and I push the flames away from my clothing, uncaring that my cuffs are already singed. I turn back to the window and am briefly surprised when I see my reflection.

There are flames in my eyes. My pupils are blown out, fully dilated and glowing with only a thin ring of iris around them. I close my eyes and suck in a breath.

I haven't lost control like this since I was a kid first coming into my powers, and even then it never made my eyes glow.

I open them again, and peer into the warehouse to see the leader turning around. Finally. I burn his image into my brain; I'll be seeing him again soon.

The other two could be statues for how still they've been this whole time, and that doesn't change now. Lor waits for my new enemy to leave, then turns on her heel and strides out. A flare of pride shoots through me at her composure, but it's quickly followed by worry, then rage. Has she been living like this her whole life?

I back down the fire escape, hands trembling and knees nearly knocking together until I drop to the ground and let out a shaky breath. My heart is racing, and fire still licks between my fingers, coating my palms. I won't be able to touch anything flammable until I get it under control.

My mind flashes back to elementary school, when my powers first started emerging.

I was at a friend's birthday party, in the backyard. They had an awesome play set with swings, a slide, a climbing wall and a rope ladder. We were playing pirates, waiting for the other kids to arrive. My friend was at the top, standing above the slide with an arm outstretched, pretending to hold a sword. We had just stolen all the treasure from the evil king and were making our great escape. I was climbing up the rope ladder, laughing and yelling about how fearsome we were.

I didn't notice at first, still climbing, but then the rope started smoking. I smelled it first, then looked down to see blackened marks on the last few rungs I'd just climbed. I pulled my hand back, but it looked normal, so I kept going. I ignored the tingling warning that was zinging up the back of my neck. I ignored the smoking handprints. I even ignored it when my hand burned straight through one of the rungs; I was close enough to the wooden platform that I just hopped right up.

My friend shouted with triumph as he turned to me, his face pure joy, and I pushed back the apprehension lining my gut to join him. I fisted my hands and threw them in the air, yelling and hollering and forcing laughter.

But then he leapt toward me, pulling me into a jumping hug. My hand grazed his arm, and his joyful shouts morphed into a scream of pain. He shoved me away from him and I fell back, catching myself on my hands as my butt hit the wood while he stumbled to the slide. He gave me a horrified look of betrayal as he slid down, his mom already running outside toward us.

I was frozen with shock, having no idea what happened.

And then there was more than just smoke.

The wood of the play structure caught fire beneath my hands. It was old and dry, so it went up in flames quickly. I don't remember much of what happened in those moments, only that the fire burned my clothing away, burned the entire play structure to the ground, but no part of my body was injured. Not even my hair.

The fire department arrived before the fire could spread, and it was quickly doused. The party was cancelled, my friend was taken to the hospital with second degree burns, and I learned what my demon affinity was.

Fire.

I shake the memory away and will my inner demon to settle, but the memory on top of what I just saw Lor going through has me too worked up. The flames rise again, and I shake my hands in a desperate attempt to put them out. I know it won't work, but I'm stuck here until the flames recede. I spin around, searching for a puddle, a random bucket of water, even the sky to see if it might start raining. There's nothing, and the flames grow alongside my panic.

I thought I was better than this. I thought I had control over the flames, but with every moment it gets worse.

I run down the alley, needing to get away from that warehouse, but also somewhere I can't hurt anyone. I turn a corner and find a different alley lined with brick buildings, and there's a metal dumpster on one side. My heart is pounding, the blood rushing in my ears again as I start running toward it.

I fling my hands out as soon as I get close, and flames spiral away, shooting through the air into the dumpster. I bend forward, my arms thrust in front of me as I drop my head and pant. The flames are still pouring out of me, heating the air and sizzling over the metal. The stench of burning garbage rises, my chest heaves for breath, and my gut clenches with nausea. My thoughts spin and spin, so fast I can't sort one from the next, and still, the fire rages.

My arms burn with the effort of holding them up and my hands shake, my eyes glassy with tears as I clench my jaw. The air shimmers with heat, and a sob lodges in my throat.

This isn't me.

This isn't who I want to be.

Then another voice pops into my head. It sounds like my therapist, but then it sounds like me, or some strange combination of the two. It's saying I can do this, that I'm more than the urges, more than the flame. I've controlled them before and I can control them again. Find my center, find my peace, stay grounded.

I stomp my feet and focus on the ground beneath my boots instead of the burn rushing from my fingertips. It's solid, hard, with a stone beneath the ball of one foot.

I tense my legs, then unlock them and shift my attention to my lungs.

I focus on taking deep breaths, slowing my breathing until I feel more steady. It takes ages, but it's helping.

I picture Lor. The newness of her smile, the affection she's learning to accept from me and Kahlo, the bracelet around my wrist tying me to her.

I raise my head, seeing the flames sputtering rather than streaming from me. Another breath, then I straighten my spine and seek out my center. The peace and safety I feel when sitting on Lor's couch. I close my eyes and pull the flames back. They shorten and flicker until I'm holding two small balls of fire in my palms.

I close my hands, gently fisting them and dousing the fire.

My head tips back as I suck in a breath of cool air. Then I walk on shaky legs to the dumpster and peek inside. Everything in it is burned, only glowing embers remain. I reach a hand out, mentally connecting with the lingering flame, and douse that too.

The fire didn't spread; it stayed contained to the dumpster. There's not even a smudge on the brick wall above it, so what felt like ages to me must have been only a few minutes at most.

I'm lucky no one saw that. An out of control demon gets a one-way ticket to the supernatural prison, and I don't think I'd survive there. I flex and relax my hands, ensuring there's not even a tiny spark of flame before I make my way back to the block where I parked my bike.

As I'm weaving between traffic, my mind shifts between two topics: the threats against Lor, and my deepening feelings for her. It's obvious they're stronger than I anticipated; I wouldn't lose control like that otherwise.

The question is, what am I going to do about it?

18

STAR-SONG

April 20, 1992: My mind plays tricks. The darkness is darker, deeper, heavier. Even when I follow the pull of the stars, even when I find the ancestors' remains, what am I to do with a box of dirt? A bag of ashes? Screams in the flames, a blinding light. No more. Please, no more.

LOR

"You might think I need you, but I don't. I'd rather eliminate an asset entirely than maintain an underperforming one."

The words ring in my ears as I watch him stride away. He had leaned toward me after his thugs dropped the poor bloodied man on the ground, lowering his voice for my ears alone as he made his threat clear. His bodyguards haven't moved a muscle since entering, and they stare at me as I back away a few steps, then turn and attempt to keep my head high as I leave on shaky legs. I hope my nerves aren't noticeable; weakness is a danger in this world.

I don't let my defeat show until I'm back at my bike,

blocks away. I don't know how to move forward. I'm not too worried about myself; despite his threat, as long as I'm bringing in stardust, I don't think he'll kill me.

What I'm truly worried about is Ro. He's been getting closer, wiggling his way through the cracks in my walls, and now he knows more than he should. If he realizes what's going on, who I'm working for and what is required of me, I fear what his demon side will do. He seems good-natured and cheerful, easy going with a quick smile, but he's still a demon.

Not to mention what would happen to him if the big boss man found out I have a weakness. My mind starts offering flashes of worst case scenarios: Ro being threatened, harmed, his face taking the place of the bloodied one from the warehouse, him being used against me to force me to comply. Even worse, they might find a way to use him too, somehow harnessing his demon abilities for evil.

That would break him.

And I can't allow that.

Which means I can't have him. It's the only path forward that keeps him safe.

I unlock my apartment on autopilot as my brain conjures more and more images. Ro with bloody stumps instead of colorful fingernails. Ro being forced to beat someone, or being beaten for my failures. Ro being held hostage in a dank cell as I try desperately to find more stardust.

Ro losing his spark, the life draining from his eyes.

I pull out my grandmother's diary, the only thing I have left from my family, and clutch it to my chest. It's cool in my hands, the leather soft under my fingertips. I don't even have anything of my mom's, but this at least makes me feel slightly less alone sometimes. My mind shifts from Ro to my mother, and I wonder what country she's in. Is she happy? Is she still jumping from boyfriend to boyfriend, city to city? Is she safe?

My fingers start to drum the cover of the journal, and my

knee bounces as my thoughts spin. I try to avoid it, but one thought punches through the others anyway.

Has she lost her mind yet?

I jump up from the bed and pace down the hall, around the coffee table and couch, through the kitchen, and back to my room before spinning on my heel and doing it again. How much of her sanity is left? Can she still take care of herself, keep herself safe, feed herself? Does she remember she has a daughter?

Is she even still alive?

I thrust my fingers into my hair and grip my scalp, shaking my head to try to dislodge the thoughts, but they stick in my brain like taffy. Stretching and pulling, one thought leading to the next, but refusing to let go. My mood is plummeting, getting darker, the thoughts filling me with despair. I feel helpless, hopeless, like there's no way out of the horrible situation that is my life.

I grab my keys and sprint to the door. Only bad choices will come if I stay here alone, so I fling myself back onto my bike in search of the open road.

The dark sky welcomes me, and I blink in surprise. I didn't realize the whole day had passed already, but evening brings a sense of relief. I'm always more calm when I can see the stars, and tonight is no different. I catch a glimpse of another bike turning a corner behind me as I pull out onto the highway. I spare a moment to wonder if it's Ro, and if so, what to do about it, but I don't have the capacity tonight.

When tingles light up my spine a few minutes later, I know I was right, that it is him, but I pretend he's not there. I drive to one of the only spots that brings me peace these days. A remote area along the beach of Lake Michigan where my feet sink in the soft sand. It's a place of solitude where I can listen to the waves crash, and bathe in the light of the stars.

Their song resonates in my chest and I close my eyes, absorbing it.

It feels like loss.

My eyes prickle with tears, but I don't let them fall. I shift on the sand, pulling my knees up to my chest and wrapping my arms around them as I tip my head back. I stare up at the night sky, letting each star wink at me as their song echoes in my heart.

I'm not surprised when soft footsteps approach and Ro sits next to me. He leaves a few inches of room between us, not saying anything, and I appreciate being given space right now. His silent support is more than enough.

From my periphery, I see him stretch out his legs and lean back on his arms, hands planted in the sand behind him so he can tip his head back and look at the stars with me. I shift my attention back to the sky, focusing on my breathing. The silence is calm between us, but not peaceful.

I don't know if I'll ever feel peaceful again.

"I moved a lot as a kid," I say, my voice surprising me as it cuts through the night.

Ro glances at me, hazel eyes soft and wide, but then slowly returns his focus to the stars. I can tell he's listening though, ready to hang on every word. My lips pinch and my eyes burn. I hadn't intended to speak, but thoughts tumble from my mouth anyway in the face of his quiet support.

"My mom... She was a star-chaser, too. She couldn't ever stay in one place for long. A year at the most. It made it hard to make friends. I didn't even graduate high school. Got my GED on the road instead, while my mom moved us from state to state. At least she stayed in the country, I guess that's something."

I swallow hard, my brows drawing down at the memory of trying to survive with a chaotic, barely-present parent while also dealing with my own emerging star-chaser urges surrounds me. Ro shifts, moving a couple inches closer.

"I haven't seen her in years," I whisper. "I have no idea where she is, what country she might be in. I hear from her sometimes, every few months maybe, and she's always somewhere new."

Ro sits up and crosses his legs, angling his body slightly toward mine, but his gaze turns to the crashing waves down the beach. I'm glad he's not looking at me. I don't think I could continue with his eyes on me this time.

"I think she resented me when I was little. She never seemed to want me around, and it always felt like I was holding her back. Like she'd be able to be so much more—do better—without me," I say, my voice catching with the admission.

Ro lets out a low noise in his throat, and he reaches for me, then tenses and pulls back. I shove my hand into the sand between us, the dry grains sticking to my sweaty palm and digging under my fingernails. My fist clenches around a handful and I pick it up, letting it slowly trickle out between my fingers and back to the ground before doing it again. It takes me a few moments to gather the courage to continue.

"I get it now," I say, glancing at Ro. "The urge to follow the stars, to keep moving. It's intense, demanding. Impossible to ignore."

I shrug and open my hand, letting the sand drop between us. Ro snags my palm, gently brushing the sand away before enfolding it in both his hands and bringing my knuckles to his lips. He kisses them softly, then turns my hand over and feathers his lips over the inside of my wrist, eyes intent on mine. I meet his gaze, letting him see all my sadness, all my fear. The hopelessness that consumes me.

I know I shouldn't. I know I should put up my walls, push

him away, protect him from the consequences of being part of my life.

But his pull is nearly as strong as the stars.

"You still deserved better," Ro says. His voice is tentative, like he's unsure how I'll react.

I look back down at our clasped hands, shifting toward him. "Maybe," I whisper.

I can feel the heat from his body inches from mine, and I shiver on the cold sand. I yearn to lean into that heat, to take comfort from him. To not be alone.

Ro makes the decision for me, closing the space between us to pull me into a hug. I melt into his arms, and he tugs me onto his lap. I curl into him, burying my face in his neck as he tucks my legs up, looping his arms around me and holding me snug against his body.

His warmth seeps into me, loosening my muscles and slowing my breathing. We sit there for long minutes, with Ro trailing his fingers up and down the outside of my thigh and nuzzling his nose into my hair.

It softens the grief inside me, dulling the song of my kin in the sky. He places a soft kiss on my forehead, and it sends a sharp pang through my heart.

I ignore it all, closing my eyes as I let myself accept the comfort he offers under the light of the stars.

When my legs prickle with discomfort from being folded up for too long, I shift and stretch, settling on the sand between his legs instead. I lean back against his chest, and one of his arms winds around me. My head tips back to rest against his shoulder as we both look up at the clear night sky.

"I can feel them," I say softly.

Ro twists to look down at me, then follows my gaze back up to the stars. "What do you mean?"

"The stars. They sing to me. I can feel it," I say, taking his hand in mine and moving it to the center of my chest, between the hollow of my throat and the top of my breasts.

"Here," I say. "It's like... a resonance. Within me, but coming from above."

Ro presses his palm into my chest, his entire body stilling behind me.

"I can't feel it," he says, dejection lining his tone.

The corners of my lips tip up in a sad smile. "No," I murmur, "I can't imagine you'd be able to."

Ro grumbles an incoherent noise, and my lips tilt further. I turn my face to press my nose into his neck again, taking a long inhale of his bonfire scent. He sees my smile and squeezes me once before letting go. I'm glad he doesn't make a big deal of it. Of me opening up, or the unbelievable things I've shared.

"How about a distraction?" he says.

My face drops and I eye him warily. "What kind of distraction?"

His grin turns wicked, flushing my skin until it's hot.

"The fun kind, of course."

Ro urges me up, standing and pulling me with him. Then he starts stripping off his clothes. He reaches one hand back to grab the collar of his shirt and pull it over his head, biceps flexing, and then the shirt drops to the sand. His piercings blink in the faint glimmer of night, catching my attention. My mouth waters when his hands drop to his pants, unbuttoning them and shoving them down as he kicks his boots off.

Before I know it, he's butt naked, standing proud in front of me with his hands on his hips and cock jutting out like it's reaching for me. He bounces his eyebrows, then turns toward the water. My gaze drops to his ass, firm round muscles rippling as he strides away.

"I dare you to skinny dip with me, Starfire," he says, throwing the words at me over his shoulder as he walks away.

My jaw clenches. Does he know I hate turning down a

dare? I can't let a challenge go without meeting it. I reluctantly agree—in my own head, of course—that it does sound like a great way to get my mind off everything that's been plaguing me.

I roll my eyes with a sigh, then strip out of my clothes, dropping them on the sand next to Ro's as I stomp after him.

Is he still keeping score between us? Because if so, I'm pretty sure I'm losing.

Badly.

19

A DISTRACTION OF
THE NAKED VARIETY

Ro

I can practically feel her stomping behind me toward the water and I grin. She can pretend she's grumpy about it, but I know perfectly well that Lor doesn't do anything she doesn't want to do.

My demon urges have taken a sharp turn in the last few hours, shifting from general chaos and destruction to a singular focus of protecting Lor. From others, from herself, from anything that might hurt her body, mind, or soul.

It's killing me that I can't help with her star-chaser gift, but I'm trying to meet her where she's at and give her what she needs. Starting with letting her talk, giving her space, and then offering a distraction when I sensed she needed an escape.

I glance over my shoulder to see her scowling at the water ahead, and bite my lip to hold in a laugh. She's so fucking cute it kills me.

"Race you in," I say, letting a taunting tone underline my words as I raise my eyebrows at her again.

Lor turns that sweet little scowl on me, but her lips twitch, and I know she's trying not to grin. I let mine grow to make up for it. I can smile for the both of us until she's ready to let hers shine.

Her gaze flicks down to my straining cock before jumping back to the water, but mine doesn't stray from her face. This moment is for her, not for me to ogle, although it's mighty hard to resist. She's stunning, her silky bare skin like a siren song drawing me in.

I keep my eyes fixed on hers, though. She heaves a dramatic sigh and I chuckle, then she nods once.

"Fine," she says, taking a step closer to me. "Count us down, then."

Lor braces herself in a lunge position, and my heart jumps in my chest. She's about to be so mad. It's gonna be great.

"Ten... nine—"

"What the hell," Lor interrupts.

Her back leg steps forward as she straightens and turns, hands on her hips while she glares at me. "Who the fuck counts down from ten?"

"You didn't specify. What's wrong with ten?" I widen my eyes and blink, giving her my most innocent puppy-dog look.

"Oh my god," she says, rolling her eyes again with a huff and getting back into position. "Whatever, just go."

"Go!" I yell, my feet pounding the wet sand as I race into the water with a rambunctious cheer.

I dive under as soon as I hit waist-deep, then surface and turn, slicking my hair back and the water out of my eyes. Lor's scowl has turned magnificent where she stands on the beach still, glaring daggers at me.

"I win!" I holler.

Her chest starts to shake and she purses her lips, then twists them to the side as her eyes crease at the corners. I break out into a little happy dance, shimmying my chest at her as I twist and turn, swaying my hips through the water in an incredibly over-the-top celebration.

Finally, she gives in. She lets out the most glorious rolling laughter, and wades into the water toward me. I whoop with victory, her grin lighting me up inside.

"You cheated," she says with a crooked smile on her face.

"Did I?"

I reach forward to scoop her into my arms, one behind her back and the other under her knees. Before she can get her hands around my neck, I turn and toss her further into the water. Lor lets out a laughing shriek as she goes under, but then she disappears and doesn't come back up.

My smile falters and my heart pounds in my chest as rush toward where she went in. I didn't throw her far, I'm not a bodybuilder or anything, so she should be... right here... Where is she? Flames jump to my fingers and distort my vision, creating rippling reflections across the surface as I attempt to search the water for her. I plunge my hands below the water, which would normally put the flames out, but I guess my demon is so panicked that the flames keep coming. Fire flickers below the rippling water as I spread my arms out and spin around, searching.

"Lor?" I call, my voice frantic. "Lor!"

I yelp and leap straight up when something bites my ass cheek under the water. Then Lor pops up behind me. She's cackling before her mouth has even breached the surface, throwing her head back as she laughs. Water streams from her silver hair, and her wet skin shimmers in the light of the moon.

My breath hitches in my throat. She's so gorgeous it's dangerous, and when she laughs... There's no better sound in the world. I think I might die without it.

Her laughter trails off as she meets my heated stare.

"Ro?" she says, her voice a soft rasp.

"Lor," I reply just as quiet, drawing out the end of her name.

Her nipples harden, and she shivers. I'm not sure if it's

from cold or want, but I sweep her up against my chest either way. Her legs circle my waist, and her arms loop around my neck, one hand trailing into my hair as she draws me closer. I palm her ass, then slide one hand up her back to press her into me. Her nipples scrape across my chest, and she shudders at the contact. Her eyes dip down to my lips as she licks hers, then parts them.

Our mouths are a scant few inches apart, but it feels like miles as I wait for her to close the distance. I won't push her. Not tonight, anyway.

Lor releases a shaky breath, and then her eyes gently close as she leans forward and presses her lips to mine in a sweet, soft kiss. My arms tighten around her, and she arches into me, my warmth seeping into her chilled skin. I squeeze her ass, and she tightens her legs, her kiss turning harder, more demanding. She licks the seam of my mouth, then twirls her tongue around my lip ring. I can't hold in the groan of desire, and she smiles against my lips in response.

Then her tongue is plunging into my mouth, hot and wet and demanding all of my attention. I'm dizzy with desire for her. Physically, yes, but emotionally too. No one has ever affected me this way, and I don't care that I'm gone for her already. I just hope I'm good enough, that I can be what she needs.

I break our kiss to lick the fresh water off her jaw. Lor tilts her head, giving me more access, and I grin, knowing I'm about to push her buttons again.

"That's my good girl," I murmur into her neck.

As expected, she stiffens in my arms, but I also feel her nipples get impossibly harder as her thighs clench around me. I smirk and continue moving my lips in a lazy path to that soft spot beneath her ear.

"I'm not..." Lor rasps, panting. "Don't... call me that."

I simply 'hmm' into her skin as I kiss, suck, and lick my

way down the column of her throat to the hollow between her collarbones. I lick up the droplets of water pooled there, her skin cool against my tongue. She's already relaxed against me again, settling all her weight into my palm cupped under her ass, buoyed by the waist-deep water.

"Alright," I say, bending lower as I lean slightly away from her. "My naughty girl, then."

Before she can deny it this time, I suck her nipple into my mouth and pinch it between my teeth, then tug gently. She gasps and arches into me, shoving her tit further into my mouth when I release her nipple. I groan at the feeling of her soft breasts against my mouth as I switch to the other one, giving it the same attention.

"Ro," Lor chokes out.

"What do you need, Starfire?" I say between sucking marks into the pale skin above her breast.

"You... Your..."

I pull back, palming her breast and arching a brow.

"My?" I tease.

She attempts a scowl, but it's not even half as fearsome as she normally manages. Lor reaches around her legs to fist my cock beneath her, and I jump, not expecting it, but then she doesn't move. She holds it, squeezing, and glares straight into my eyes.

I grin, loving her ferocity. "Yes, Starfire? You want to come?"

"You know I do."

"All you have to do is ask," I say, pressing a sweet kiss to her sharp cheekbone.

Now her scowl turns properly fierce. She grips my dick tighter, but when I moan and thrust into her, she seems to realize her threat is having the opposite effect she wants it to. She shifts her grip to my balls instead, but that won't get her what she wants either. There's nothing she can do that will come close to my cock cage, so she can go ahead and do her worst.

I dip my head to lave my tongue over her stiff nipples again, switching between them and nipping every so often until she's writhing against me. Lor grinds her hips into me, pressing her hot pussy into my pelvis. She's so slippery with desire I can feel it, even though our waists are still submerged in the water.

She's panting, breasts heaving and eyes half-lidded when I pull back.

"Ask, Lor," I murmur into her neck, then take her earlobe between my teeth.

Her needy whimper almost makes me give in, but then she caves.

"Please, Ro," she pants. "Make me come."

I figure that's close enough; we can work more on her begging later. "As you wish," I whisper into her ear.

I adjust my grip, shifting her so I can fit one hand down between us. As much as I'd like to fuck her, that's pretty much asking for a UTI for each of us, so I'll stick to fingers this time. I don't expect or want anything other than to make her feel good, anyway.

My palm settles over her pussy, hot against my skin as I press the heel of my hand into her clit. Her forehead drops to my shoulder, and I shudder at the idea of her wanting to watch as I pleasure her. I drag my fingers over her slit, then slip one inside to stroke up into her.

"More," she says, and I grin.

"Greedy girl," I murmur, but I don't know if she hears me this time.

I plunge my middle and ring fingers inside her, curling them toward me as I press my outer two into her folds. Lor's breathing is shallow, sending goosebumps across my chest with every quick exhale. The heel of my hand is still pressed up hard against her clit, and she starts rocking her hips. I swipe my fingers side to side, then curl and uncurl them, pressing harder and softer until I find what she likes.

"There," she gasps. "Right there. Don't stop."

She throws her head back, body shuddering as I hit that spot over and over. My eyes trail down her pearly skin, taking in every freckle and baby hair and drop of water covering her. Lor arches her back, and I have an out-of-body moment where I'm looking down at us together and marveling at how incredible it is that I have this woman in my arms. That she would trust me enough to share her story, to give her this pleasure, to be so vulnerable with me... A demon.

I jolt back into my own skin when her fingers curl into my biceps and her body tenses.

"Pinch your nipples," I say, my voice hoarse. "Play with your tits."

Lor's hands fly to her breasts. She squeezes and kneads them, then twists her nipples. Her body goes rigid, tendons standing out on her neck as her pussy starts to tighten around my fingers. My eyes are glued to her face as her mouth drops open, and she lets out a desperate, breathless moan.

"Look at me," I demand.

Her eyes flutter open to meet mine just as her pussy clenches around my fingers. Her eyes flare, and her entire body pulses with her orgasm. I gentle my strokes when her inner walls relax, and she trembles, dropping her head back to my shoulder. I pull my hand from between her legs and bring my fingers straight to my mouth, licking them clean with a groan.

Lor's breathy laugh catches me off guard, but I squeeze her tighter to me, relishing the closeness of this moment. Air saws in and out of her lungs as she struggles to catch her breath, and her body sags against me.

Precious, vulnerable, strong.

I'm in awe of her.

She kisses my neck, and my heart leaps at being gifted such a sweet gesture. I know how much that means coming from my prickly star-chaser. I hold her close as I start wading through the water to get us back on dry land. When we reach the packed sand, I gently lower her to her feet, thrilled when she runs her palm down my arm to settle her hand in mine.

I never want to let it go. My demon is all but purring in my chest.

Then I realize the folly of my plan: we have no towels. I grab my t-shirt and shake it out, then turn and start drying Lor with it.

"I have no say in this, do I?" she says, a small smile pulling up one side of her mouth.

"Nope," I reply, continuing to soak as much water from her skin as I can. "That's probably the best you're gonna get."

As I straighten, Lor squeezes my shoulder where her hand was resting for balance. "Thanks, Ro."

WE'RE FLYING DOWN the highway with me alternating between riding next to Lor and dropping back behind her as we return to Chicago. My body thrums with the memory of her in my arms, her slick skin against mine, the vision of her pleasure at my hands. I absently rub at my chest while my eyes remain locked on her. I'm admiring the strong lines of her body, her straight back and the angles of her arms and legs as I contemplate my next moves.

Things with Lor are looking up, much more than I could have anticipated. Of course, I always hoped she'd share more of herself with me, but I never expected her to be carrying so much generational trauma. Perhaps I should give her my therapist's information?

I shake my head, that's probably pushing it. She'd ask if

she wanted it, and it's not my place, but I can't help wanting the best for her.

And that brings up the topic of whatever mob boss she's involved with. I have no doubt she's working for him against her will, otherwise he wouldn't threaten her so blatantly—and she wouldn't be absolutely miserable day in and day out.

Now my body thrums for a different reason.

Vengeance lights up my veins, and I take a deep, slow breath to avoid lighting myself on fire while on my bike. But then I realize the flames aren't hounding me like usual. It feels like they're banked, but ready and waiting.

Like they know their time is coming.

20

SCRATCHING VULNERABILITY
WITH HUMOR

*September 7, 1993: The emptiness gapes. A
hurt too deep to heal. Return to the stars.
Dirt on my brow, ashes beneath my nails,
stardust in the wrinkles of my skin. No
rest for the weary. No peace for the
wretched...*

LOR

I leave for the club the next evening right when it opens.
It's been another long day of pointless research trying to find
impact sites that I haven't already scoured. It feels hopeless,
and after the big boss man upped his threat level, the pressure
is oppressive.

At least I get to see Ro today.

Or... maybe I shouldn't. He's relentlessly smiled his way
under my skin, and started to convince me that maybe I can
have *some* good things, even if they're only temporary. But
everyone leaves in the end, so is it worth it to put him in
danger for my own short-term desires?

My head splinters with indecision, my steps faltering as I

turn the corner toward Tempo. Before I can make up my mind, my feet do it for me while my hand pulls open the door.

Ro is bent over the bar, resting his elbows on it while his eyes stare off into space. I pause on the threshold, tilting my head to observe him. He looks more distant than usual, less joyful. My brows pinch with concern as I take in his strange mood.

I slide onto a stool and rest my cheek on my fist, fine with waiting until he comes back to himself. It gives me a few moments to take him in. The lines between his eyebrows and around the corners of his lips. The darker clothing than he usually goes for: navy pants with a tight, blood red t-shirt. Silver rings cover his fingers as usual, but he wears no other jewelry on his wrists or around his neck.

Perhaps most strange of all—his stillness. It's bizarre, and none of my business, but I assume something must have him twisted up inside to be so out of it. I've never seen that on him before, but of course, we all have our demons.

I internally snort; some of us more literally than others.

Finally, Ro's unfocused gaze turns my way. His eyes take me in, blink once, and then he jumps, a tiny ball of flame rising from his hand and fizzling out in the air.

"Lor!"

"Hey," I say, my lips quirking up on one side. Has he always been this cute?

"Hi," he says, flustered.

A grin finally stretches across his handsome face, and it settles a piece of me that I didn't realize until now needed settling.

"Gay purple drink?" he asks, raising his eyebrows with exaggerated hopefulness.

I roll my eyes, but nod. "Sure."

He springs into action, no hint of the vacant, disconcerted mood I sensed when I first sat down.

"So, what brings you in today, my lovely little Starfire?"

I shrug, glancing around at the empty bar and club. I suppose that's to be expected, as it's fairly early on a weekday. My fears are still hounding me, intruding thoughts reminding me how dangerous it is to be seen with him, that I'm going to get him hurt or worse. I take a gulp of the shimmering drink and immediately regret it; whatever is in this is more suited to sipping than chugging.

"Can I get a shot?" I ask.

Ro eyes me, then nods once. He reaches beneath the bar and fills a shot glass without breaking eye contact. Why is that so hot?

I look down at the tiny glass, willing my heart to steady, then throw it back. Ro's eyes are still on me. I can feel them, but I'm avoiding meeting his gaze. I guess I've got some demons of my own I'm battling with.

"What's going on, Lor?"

I shake my head as my throat closes. I'm unable to get a single word out as my emotions surge and—to my horror— my eyes prickle as my sight turns blurry.

"Sweetheart," Ro murmurs, quickly rounding the bar to my side. He takes my hand and pulls me from the stool, gesturing at someone with his other arm. I fix my gaze on my feet as I let him lead me to a back room.

As soon as the door shuts, he envelopes me in his arms. I try to turn away, but he easily tucks my head under his chin and sways us side to side. My body slowly relaxes into his as his steady pulse thumps beside my ear.

I don't know the last time I was held and comforted like this, if I ever was. Did my mom ever care enough to? Did she even notice when I needed it?

"You can tell me anything," Ro says, his voice soft as he lays his cheek on the top of my head.

It's hard to swallow, hard to breathe, but I force myself to do both. I have no idea where it comes from, but at some point, part of me must have decided to trust this demon.

"I'm afraid," I whisper.

Ro tenses for half a second, then his muscles relax against me again.

"Afraid of what?" His voice is careful, perfectly neutral.

"Being a star-chaser... It means I'm going to lose my mind. I don't know when. I don't know how fast. But it's the one thing I know to be true. All star-chasers go mad, or well, I don't think that's the right way to say it—going mad—whatever you want to call it."

I chance a glance up at him, seeing his brows furrowed in confusion. Like he was expecting something else. I look away to give myself the courage to continue.

"My life is dangerous, but even if it wasn't, it still wouldn't be fair to make you part of it. You'd have to deal with my madness, and there'd be nothing you could do about it. It wouldn't be fair to you, Ro. It would be awful for us both."

My voice trails off into a dejected whisper, but he replies immediately. "That's not true at all."

I stiffen. How could he say it's not true? It's the only thing I have no doubt of. One of two truths I've been told my entire life. The only thing I've fully accepted—all star-chasers go mad.

"You might lose your mind, go insane, whatever. I don't know what the right thing to call it is either. But you don't get to tell me what's fair. You don't get to decide for me what I want, or what's best for me."

I jerk back to stare at him as my thoughts spin. His face is open, raw with determination and so much passion it almost makes me take a step away.

"You think I can't handle what you might someday be like?" He scoffs, a wry tilt to his lips. "Lor, have you met me?

I'm the literal definition of crazy. Wild. Weird. Wacky. Out of control demon, right here."

He points his thumb at his chest with the last sentence and I blink, trying to catch up.

"If anything," he continues, "that makes us a *better* match."

He finally pauses—boy has some lungs on him—and gives my head a chance to process everything he just said.

"A... What?"

I'm still processing, obviously.

Ro nods decisively, tugging me back to his chest, and bracketing a hand on the back of my head to cradle it under his chin again.

"Yep, the more I think about it, the more I know I'm right." His voice is arrogant, and far more assured than he has any right to be.

I scoff into his shirt, and his chest hitches with a suppressed chuckle. I hate to admit his strategy is working.

"After all, I'll need a partner who can match my level of crazy," he says.

That gets a short laugh out of me, and I turn my face up to his. "Your level of crazy, huh? What, like stalking me?"

Ro turns sheepish, his eyes darting to the side before meeting mine again.

"Yes, well, that... among other things."

He shifts me into his side, still hugging me with one arm while rummaging around in his pocket with the other. When he finds what he's looking for, he holds his hand up between us with something dangling from his fingers. It takes a moment for the sight to register.

"Is that my bracelet?"

I reach out, but before my fingers make contact, he jerks his arm away with a literal, godsdamned *hiss*.

I gape at him, my mouth falling open as I stare in shock.

Ro cringes and pulls away, cradling the bracelet protectively to his chest with an apologetic look in his eyes.

"Shit, sorry." He fights with his instincts as his fingers clench, and he forces himself to move his hand toward me, as though to give the bracelet back.

With gentle fingers, I take the silver strand from his hand.

"No," I whisper, clasping the bracelet around his wrist instead of my own. "It's okay. You can keep it."

Ro freezes, his eyes leaping to mine as I gaze up at him. I see myself in his eyes. My heart is thundering in my chest as I wonder what this means, what's happening, if I'm already losing my mind.

I clear my throat, a scratchy jolt of sound jarring us both back into the present.

"Is this what you meant by 'among other things' then?" I ask.

"Yeah, so uh, I kinda have some other issues besides just ... stalking you."

He stumbles over the word stalking, and it shouldn't be nearly as cute as it is. He runs a hand through his already messy hair, avoiding eye contact with the admission.

My emotions are going haywire, and I feel like I could sleep for a week from this conversation alone. At the same time, I'm lighter, more energized with every moment. I want to soak up each of his words and lock them in a box to keep them safe with me forever.

"I have some klepto tendencies, and... Um... Pyromania is a thing I struggle with too."

Ro shrugs like it doesn't matter, but I know him too well for that now. Tension lines his eyes, and his fingers are fidgeting with the bracelet.

"I've already got issues, so I know what it's like. You don't have to try to protect me from you, Lor."

His eyes meet mine, dark with emotion, and I suck in a

breath. Then his skin starts to flicker like it's lit from below, prompting me to look down. There's a flame cradled in his palm.

My eyes widen and I take a step back.

"It won't hurt you," he whispers. "I would never let that happen."

"I..." My fingers itch to reach for it, an urge I've never experienced before. Surely this must be the star-chaser curse eroding my mind already. "Can I touch it?"

Ro nods and his gaze lightens, a tenuous smile touching his lips. I dip my fingers into the flame and feel only a slight warmth, like sun rays through a window.

"Fire is the hardest," he murmurs. "My demon always wants me to set things on fire, but I can control what I allow it to harm. Most of the time, anyway."

He closes his fist, dousing the flame, and his expression shutters. I don't know what to make of it, other than the fact no one has treated me the way he does. Like I'm special, like I'm trustworthy, like I matter and deserve... goodness.

It's baffling and confusing, and the only way I know how to repay it is by sharing more of myself in return.

"Maybe..." I whisper, unsure what I'm trying to put into words. "Maybe."

Ro nods, perhaps understanding better than I do.

He steps back, then walks over to some stacked boxes a few feet away. I look around, realizing we must be in a storage room. It's lined with metal shelving units, boxes and supplies stacked on the shelves and along the back wall. He sits on a box and pats the one next to him until I sink down on it. Then he dances a small flame across his knuckles and between his fingers.

"What's it like?" Ro asks, eyes on his flame. "Your call to the stars?"

"It's a curse," I reply without hesitation, my voice bitter.

Ro frowns, and the flame stills on the back of his hand before he rolls it into his palm. Then his eyes meet mine as he tilts his head in question.

"This undeniable compulsion. I have no control, no power. It's something beyond my physical body. I don't know. It's hard to describe. Like my soul itself needs to be close to the stars, but I can't manage that, so the best I can do is find the ones that fall. Rescue the stardust from the earth and treasure it, at least until..." My voice trails off, and I hope he didn't catch the grief that started to seep into my tone.

When I glance at him from the corner of my eye, he looks thoughtful.

"That sounds remarkably similar to my demon urges."

"Really?"

"Yeah," he says. "My therapist is treating it similar to OCD, since I have obsessive thoughts and compulsive behaviors, even though it's not the same. But it feels deeper than that. Like you said, something in my soul. A need that isn't being met."

He shakes his head with a self-deprecating smile before continuing.

"Although, it's been better since I started following you. *Stalking* you, I mean," he chuckles. "I was trying to be politically correct."

I roll my lips between my teeth and bite down on them. "I don't think that's a thing," I say dryly.

Ro huffs a soft laugh. "Even using the word 'stalking' settles my demon side, which is frustrating. I don't want to be a demon. I don't like how it feels like I have no control over myself."

I contemplate that, empathizing with him far more than I expected to.

"Yeah," I say, my voice soft. "Yeah, I get that."

Ro's flame blinks out, and he moves his hand closer to me,

right next to my leg, then flips it up. I eye it for a long moment, glance at him, then turn my eyes back to the far wall as I place my palm in his. He twines our fingers together, palm to palm, sending a tingling warmth up my arm. Then he looks straight at me and grins. I can see it from the corner of my eye.

"Stop it or I'll take it back," I say.

"Too late, you already gave it to me," he says, tightening his grip. "This is my hand now."

My lips twitch, but I'm saved from admitting anything when there's a shout from the hallway.

"Ro! Customers!"

"Ah, that's Finn. Gotta get back out there."

Ro sweeps his thumb across the back of my hand, then squeezes it once. I reluctantly let go, and he slaps his palms against the boxes as he stands. Then he spins around with the most manic grin I've seen yet.

My eyes widen as my heart skips a beat. My defenses are ready to shoot up again.

"Ro..." I say, wary. "What's that grin for?"

He saunters backward to the door as he replies.

"Just imagining what it'll be like when we're both happily mad together in our old age."

21

———

A DEMON UNLEASHED

Ro

It's official. I figured things were going this direction, but it's undeniable now. I've found my calling: to protect Lor. Protect her from those who would use and abuse her, but also protect her from herself. From her own self-deprecating thoughts, her inclination to not take care of herself, her disregard of her own physical and emotional safety.

It puts a bounce in my step as I head back out to the bar. I want to protect her future and allow her to grow. I want to nurture her joy so she can be the best version of herself, and live a long, happy life. I also want to protect her from the madness she's so fearful of, although I'm not sure if that one's possible. The mental health stuff doesn't bother me one way or another, but I don't like how she treats herself with regards to it. So at the very least, I'll protect her from being mean to herself about it.

For all I care, we can go mad together.

That actually sounds kind of fun. My inner demon picks its head up with interest, reigniting the wild grin on my face.

I wasn't lying before. I do think we're a good match.

"What the fuck, man," Finn says. "I don't mind covering for you for a minute, but you can't just disappear like that."

"Sorry," I say, slapping him on the back. "Something came up."

"If it was your dick I'm gonna be pissed."

I let out a guffaw and throw him a wink. "No, it wasn't, and stop asking after my dick. I'm taken."

"Why do I put up with you?" he grumbles.

"Because I'll share my tips as a thank you?"

He flicks his eyes to the ceiling with a reluctant grin and steps out from behind the bar, heading to the side stage where his DJ booth is set up.

"Thanks for covering!"

He raises his hand in an almost-wave, then lowers all but his middle finger as he glances over his shoulder. I throw up a hand-heart, and he rolls his eyes so hard this time I worry they might not recover.

I shrug, then step up to the first of a few customers waiting at the bar. It doesn't take too long to fill their drinks, but I'm starting to wonder if Lor is ever going to emerge, or if I should go check on her. Just as I'm getting antsy, she drifts out from the back room and eases her way to the far corner of the bar, sliding onto a stool.

I drop off a glass of water, but when I ask if she wants anything else, she simply shakes her head with a tiny, polite smile. I've never known Lor to be polite, and it would worry me if I wasn't aware of the emotional rollercoaster we just went on together.

I keep an eye on her over the next couple of hours, refilling her water as needed. She seems to be in her own head, and I assume she's thinking things over. I don't blame her for needing some time to process through it all; I know I'll be doing the same as soon as I get a chance.

I am glad she stayed, though.

Eventually Lor raises her glass to catch my attention. I dart over and angle my head to hear her over the music.

"I'm gonna head home," she murmurs.

I nod. "You okay?"

"Yeah," Lor says. She reaches out to rest her hand on mine, sending a frisson of warmth through my body. "I'm okay."

My heart feels tender, and I slowly lean across the bar, stopping a mere inch from her lips to give her time to pull away if she wants to. She doesn't, so I press a soft kiss to the corner of her mouth, then whisper in her ear before I pull away.

"Sleep well, Starfire."

I spend the rest of my shift trying not to contemplate murder as images of those goons and their boss rattle through my brain. I settle on fire as an acceptable alternative, and devise a strategy for scoping out the area tonight and tomorrow, then setting my plan into motion.

As soon as my shift ends, I clean up faster than I ever have, and nearly sprint outside to my bike.

THREE DAYS later and I'm dead on my feet. Apart from working, my nights have been spent spying on criminals, and my days spent spying on Lor. I'm honored she's trusted me with so much of her truth, even if she hasn't yet told me about her criminal employers. It doesn't bother me that her work is illegal. It bothers me that it puts her in danger.

It just so happens that I have the power to eliminate that danger.

I'm satisfied with my plan and ready to put it into action, but part of me worries what will happen if they don't heed my message. I guess in that case, I'll have to reconsider the murder idea.

I'd do it for her.

With that decided, I fall into bed for a few hours. I won't be able to pull this off if I can't keep my eyes open, and since this is the one night I have off this week, it's now or never.

When I wake, my heart is already pumping. I pull on all black: leather pants, t-shirt, loose hoodie, combat boots, riding gloves, and tuck a ski mask into my pocket. I grab a can of lighter fluid, just in case, and head out the door.

When I get to the warehouse, it's mostly deserted, as it has been every other night. I pull on my ski mask and double check the perimeter, then launch myself up the same fire escape I previously used to spy on Lor. I found a loose window a floor further up when I was here a couple nights ago, and I use it now to carefully lower myself inside.

I start on the opposite side of the building, lighting small flames on boxes, desks, in a waste basket, and under a flight of stairs.

I've been practicing with my flames as well; how to light and control multiple at once, even if they're not in sight. It's not easy—in fact, it's really fucking challenging—and my forehead beads with sweat at the effort it takes to split my mind between so many different fires. I picture each of them, willing them to hold, to stay small, not to sputter out and not to flare, not yet.

Then I wait until the goon on watch steps outside for their hourly walk around the building to go to the middle of the empty warehouse floor. I use the lighter fluid to write a massive message, then I sprint back up the stairs to my loose window. I swipe the back of my wrist over my eyes, flicking away the sweat that has dripped from under my mask as I flatten my back against the wall. Then I peek outside and wait, wait, wait.

As soon as the goon rounds the corner out of view, it's time.

I drop the lighter fluid beneath the window, hop out onto the rickety metal ladder and grip it tight, then close my eyes. I find the flames and will them to grow. To catch, to flare, to rouse, but to leave a circle around my message clear. In my mind's eye, they rear up, engulfing the desk, the boxes, the stairs. When I'm sure they've all caught and aren't at risk of going out, I let go of them one by one, releasing my control for them to blaze on their own.

Then I turn my sights to my message. My lungs rattle when I suck in a deep breath, the air shaky in my chest as I push my power to its limit. I only need one more flame, just one more to catch, and I'm done.

The door opens, and it's now or never.

I whip one glove off and reach through the window, closing my eyes to focus on my inner fire. I let it build within me, feeding it with thoughts of Lor: the threats to her life, her sadness and despair, all her hurt and everything that's been stolen from her. I feed it all to the inner flame until it's roiling within me.

Then I open my eyes, and will it to pour out.

Fire flies from my fingers straight down into the warehouse. It catches on the first letter, then whooshes through the rest and the lighter-fluid roars to life.

LEAVE HER ALONE OR YOURE NEXT

I also added shooting stars on either side, just to make it extra clear.

Flames shoot into the air, and my arm falls to the window sill as my shoulders droop. I heave a sigh of relief; there is no more fire within me. I'm drained, a hollow, empty spot where my flames usually roll. I've never used it all up before, but I can tell I have nothing left to give tonight.

Then a shout rends the air, and I glance back inside to see

the goon staring up at me. His eyes dart from the fire to me, then back to the flames before he turns to run.

"Shit," I say, my hand slipping on the metal ladder as I pull away from the window.

I fumble to pull my riding glove back on, then make my way unsteadily to the ground. I don't know if he's planning on coming for me himself or calling for backup, but I'm in no state to take anyone on right now. I turn and stumble-run down the alley.

I parked close in case I needed a quick getaway, and I've never been so relieved to see my bike before. I throw myself onto it, clumsy, but managing to get my feet in the right places as I push the throttle and tear out of there.

I don't look back as I weave my way through the back streets, sticking to alleys when I can, and avoiding stoplights for fear of cameras. I take off my mask and gloves as soon as I'm a couple miles away, then I continue to drive in circles and twist my way through random neighborhoods until my entire body is too heavy to keep going for much longer.

When I finally pull up to my place, I barely make it to my bedroom before yanking off my clothes, and collapsing on the bed.

FEROCIOUS POUNDING on my door jolts me awake. My head is pounding too, and I groan at the splitting headache. Did I drink too much last night? I never drink enough to be hungover this bad, but clearly I was not making good choices.

I holler that I'll be right there in an attempt to get whoever is outside to stop beating my door, and then immediately regret shouting as it exacerbates my headache, shooting streaks of lightning across my vision. I roll off the bed, one hand pressed to my eyes and the other reaching into my closet as I attempt to orient myself.

Pants, I need pants. And a shirt.

When I'm adequately clothed, I stumble to the door and pull it open, then stare in shock at the two officers glaring at me.

"Uhh," I say, rubbing my eyes again. What the hell is going on? "Can I help you?"

"Foras Cromwell?" one of them says.

"Yes?"

"You're under arrest."

LOR

My mind has been spinning for days, but this afternoon it finally seems to have settled. Kahlo is on the counter next to me as I fix my coffee, and they head-butt my hand for pets. It's something new we've been trying, and I quirk a smile at the temperamental feline.

Ro hasn't been quite as up-in-my-space the last few days, which has allowed me the time I didn't know I needed to reflect on everything. Of course, he hasn't been absent, but I think we've both been processing.

Or at least, that's what I've been doing.

Then when I woke up this morning, things finally clicked in my brain. It's been weeks, and Ro hasn't wavered even once. I've shared more with him than I have with anyone else, and despite knowing I'll end up losing my mind, he hasn't balked.

In fact, it didn't seem to bother him at all. I don't know how that's possible, but at this point, I don't bother trying to understand the infuriatingly chipper demon. He somehow takes everything in stride and makes good out of the bad.

So if he knows pretty much all of my bad, and still hasn't gone anywhere… I need to tell him the rest.

The decision rests across my shoulders like a comforting blanket, his previous actions giving me the strength I need to share this one final piece with him. The danger I'm in, and the danger it would put him in, if we were to move forward with a relationship.

He's an adult, perfectly capable of making his own decision if given all the information.

My heart shudders with anxiety at the idea of him leaving, but then it pangs with fear at the thought of him staying, too. Fear and longing, they both swell side by side as I think about what it would mean for him to choose me.

What if he doesn't leave?

I truly don't know what that would be like. I've never experienced it before, but I desperately want to. My heart feels like it's crying out for him, and I absently stroke down Kahlo's back and twirl their tale around my finger as the emotions surge and sweep through me. A relentless tide that stalls the breath in my lungs as I contemplate it.

I'm startled back into my body when my phone rings with an unknown number. I normally don't answer unknown numbers, but something has me picking it up.

"Hello?" I say.

The call connects, and I hear Ro's strained voice on the other end. "So, uh, hey."

"Ro? What's going on?"

"Don't freak out, but I got arrested—"

"What!"

"Lor, listen, I need you to contact an attorney for me. The ones they provide, well, they're no good for…" His voice is hesitant, and he lowers it so I have to turn the volume all the way up to hear the rest. "Someone like me."

A supernatural, he means, and a demon at that. Shit shit shit.

"Okay, right." I'm already opening my laptop. "Are they charging you? What do they have you on? Wait, don't say anything that could get you in trouble. Just tell me..." I pause to think for a moment.

"Remember when we talked the other night?" he says.

"Yeah," I say, relieved to have confirmation. "Yeah, okay, I got it. I'll do some quick research, can you call back in a few minutes, or do we need to stay on the line?"

There's some muffled talking on the other end.

"He says I can call back, but..."

"You'd rather stay on if you can."

I'm only half paying attention to him as I scroll, searching for an attorney who can actually help. I've got nothing against the court appointed public defenders. It's a thankless and much-needed job, but their work is hard enough for regular folks. Defending a demon is going to be near impossible, so we need someone who has done it before. My eyes skip over listings until finally I land on one that looks promising.

"Got it, you ready to write down this number?"

I slump in my seat after hanging up with Ro, exhausted by this day already. I've managed to convince myself that it was probably a small charge; he got caught stealing something most likely. He said he would sign a release for the attorney to contact me, so I turn my phone volume up and check it constantly, even though I know they likely won't call today.

Naturally, I turn to the internet, as one does when they're trying not to panic while knowing the internet inherently makes everything worse. I search for other cases involving demon defendants, going down a rabbit hole of information that becomes less and less comprehensible with my limited understanding of legalities. I do my best to parse through the dense information, but it only serves to confuse and worry me more, so I turn to my own research instead.

I pull up all the usual websites: American Meteor Society, NASA, the Global Meteor Network, a couple different meteor maps run by independent research companies, and a handful of user-based forums. There's nothing new, as I feared, so I expand my search across the entire midwest and southern Canada, hoping against hope for anything I might have previously missed.

All the while, I ignore the little voice in my head taunting me about how I had just convinced myself Ro wasn't going to leave me, only for him to get arrested.

22

TO LIE OR NOT TO LIE

November ~~13~~ 16, 1994: Send them back. Never fall. Take them in. I Need. Where is their home? Try to find, but. They must be free, just like me. But do we have a home? What is such a thing... as free? Earth and sky. Back to ash...

LOR

A few hours later, I'm idly scrolling across another meteor map when the TV I have on in the background catches my attention. There's breaking news of a fire. Arson, they're saying.

I stand from the table and snag the remote off the couch. It's a story on a massive warehouse fire that just so happens to coincide with the building I normally drop off the stardust at. The blood drains from my face, and I drop onto the couch.

Kahlo mrows a scolding at me for bouncing the cushions, but I don't acknowledge it. I can't tear my eyes from the TV and the roaring flames. They show a clip of the blaze with firefighters spraying down neighboring buildings to contain it, then reveal an after-shot of the charred remains. There's hardly anything left; even the metal supports are twisted and warped.

Ro did this.

This is why he's in jail.

My mind blanks, and I click the TV off. The silence is monumental, both inside and outside my head. I don't know what to think. Was anyone hurt? He must have followed me one time when I thought I lost him, but why did he burn it down? Was it an impulse, something he couldn't control? That doesn't feel right, he wouldn't have let it get that out of hand.

Which means it was on purpose.

My heart starts thumping in my chest, pounding so hard I'm half-convinced something is wrong. The muscles in my legs tremble before I tense them to stop it, and it feels like I'm not getting enough air into my lungs. I need to get out of here, to get away from all this.

I jump off the couch, startling Kahlo enough for them to hiss and dash away, but I'm already by the front door. I snag my keys, and am on my bike before I know it. My hair flies behind me, a tangled mess, but I don't care enough right now to worry about it.

That's future Lor's problem. Current Lor has enough problems she's already running from.

And now I'm talking to myself in the third person. That can't be good.

I try to empty my brain, try not to think about fire, or jail, or the club, or anything to do with Ro. It's impossible though, when I don't feel his eyes on me. I've become so used to the sensation, that to go without it feels bizarre. It's an uncomfortable feeling, like when you think you forgot something, but can't remember what it is.

I clench my jaw and twist the throttle harder, desperately hoping to leave my fears and worries behind, but the further and faster I go, the more wrong it feels.

When the sun dips from under the heavy clouds and nearly blinds me, it shocks me out of my stupor enough for me to realize what I'm doing. I have no idea where I am, no destination in mind, and the ride has not cleared my head like it normally does.

Because he's not here following you.

As soon as the thought crosses my mind, horror slides down my throat to settle heavy in my stomach. I *left him.* He didn't leave me, not intentionally. If he really did set that fire, I have no doubt it was to protect me. Somehow, he found out what was going on, and this was his response.

"God-fucking-damnit!"

I continue to curse up a storm, throwing a leg out as I whip the bike around in a 180. It leaves skid marks along the road, and my front tire leaves the pavement for a moment when I gun it back the direction I came.

I don't have time to be out here. Ro needs me, and I was ready to abandon him.

My heart feels like it's lodged in my throat, and anger at myself pulses scorching heat through my veins. I'm sweaty when I get back, bursting through the door and earning myself another hiss from a different room. I toss my helmet and gloves on the couch as I sprint to the kitchen, then scramble back to my laptop and pull open the tab with the attorney's information. My fingers shake as I type the numbers into my phone.

"Shirlene and Associates, how can we help you?"

"Hi, yes." I pause, panting between words as I try to catch my breath.

"I gave my... boyfriend," another pause as I stumble over

what to call Ro, "your information. He was arrested earlier for arson but hedidn'tdoiticanproveit."

"Ma'am, I need you to slow down. Please provide your name, and the name of the person you referred to us, and I'll check if we have any releases on file."

I suck in a breath, willing my hands to stop shaking.

"Right, my name is Alorra Seren, and I referred Foras Cromwell, he goes by Ro. He would have called this morning."

"Thank you, one moment while I check please."

An eternity of pacing around my coffee table and kitchen passes before she returns to the phone.

"I'm sorry, ma'am, I don't have anything on file for you."

"That's okay, can someone just take my statement? You don't even have to confirm you're working with him, just... I need to tell someone he wasn't there, he didn't do it."

There's a pause on the other end of the line, then muffled talking like she covered the phone with her hand.

"I'm going to transfer you, please hold."

I heave a breath of relief, and then I'm talking to someone I assume is on his legal team. I have no idea how expensive they are, but I'll gladly help foot the bill. He did this for me, after all.

"Ms. Seren, you said you referred Mr. Cromwell to us and that you have information about his case?"

"Yes! He was with me, he couldn't have set that fire."

Another pause, this one heavier, then the woman on the other end clears her throat.

"Alright, please start from the beginning."

My mind is already moving onto the next piece of my plan when I hang up with the attorney, the pieces falling into place right as I need them. I drop some food into the bowl for Kahlo, refill their water, and then head back out the door.

I practically sprint to Tempo, then twist my way through dancing bodies until I get to the DJ's turntable. Finn glances at then away from me, then does a double take. He holds up one finger for me to wait, and I bounce on my toes, twisting my fingers together until he puts on a playlist and steps away.

"Hey," he says, placing one hand on my arm, and turning me toward a quieter area so we can talk.

I want to slap his hand away for how casual and unconcerned he's being, but I'll give him a pass for now. He doesn't know what I do.

"What's up? I don't think Ro came in tonight, although he's supposed to," he says, brows furrowed.

"Yeah, that's what I need your help with. He's in trouble, and, um..." I trail off, darting my eyes around as though one of the big boss man's goons will be eavesdropping on us. "Well, I don't really have anyone to ask, and I figured you must know a lot of people from working here, right?"

He nods slowly, looking more confused than concerned as he waits for me to continue.

"Okay, yeah. So. I think I need a hacker."

Ro

I'm notified that my attorney is here, and escorted to a private room even though I just saw her a couple hours ago. I'm pretty sure that's not normal, but I don't have anything else to do.

She pins me with a calculating look as I lower myself into the hard metal seat opposite hers, and I'm half convinced she's a supernatural of some sort that can read minds.

"Um," I say, glancing around. "What's up?"

"You tell me," she says, voice steely.

The woman is honestly terrifying. Her brown hair is slicked back in a neat bun, and she wears thick red cat-eye glasses. A navy power-suit and heels show off an intimidating form, and there's a tattoo peeking out at her wrist. I have no idea what to make of her, or how to handle myself in her presence, other than to gulp and hope for the best.

"I... tell you?" I practically squeak the words and my face burns. I wish I had something to fidget with, but I don't dare call on my flames, and they took all my rings and bracelets. I clear my throat, then straighten. Lor said she was good, and I trust Lor, so I need to trust this woman too.

"Do you know a Ms. Alorra Seren?"

"Lor? Yeah, did she contact you?"

"And what is your relationship to Ms. Seren?"

My mind whirls as I try to figure out where this is going. I should probably be honest, right?

"She's, well, it's a bit complicated—"

The woman interrupts the start of my nervous ramble with a huff. She takes a folder out of her briefcase, flips it open, and slides it across the desk to me.

"Ms. Seren called my office, insisting to talk to your legal team. She stated she had evidence that will exonerate you. She *claims* you were with her all night, and therefore could not possibly have started the warehouse fire."

She pauses to tap a blood red, coffin-manicured fingernail on the papers in front of me. My own nails are abysmal, chipped flecks of purple remaining on only a few. I blink the printed words into focus as the message trickles into my brain.

Lor said I was with her? I wasn't, and I'm pretty sure my scary attorney knows it. But Lor's statement is right here. I look up at her, half expecting this to be some sort of joke or trick.

"She said she'd be willing to testify for you. I have no doubt we'll have to take her up on it if this is to be our plan of defense. Luckily for you, no one was injured, so the worst we're dealing with is property damage. I'll give you a minute to read this over."

Her words are crisp, and she continues to stare, dissecting the innermost parts of me like she can see all my secrets. I blink back down at the papers in front of me, taking in Lor's words.

She's *lying* for me. My heart thumps as my eyes flit back and forth over the first page, then the next. None of this is true, and I don't know if it will work, but would it give me a chance? Thank goodness I didn't share much of anything with my attorney earlier. Most of what we did was sign paperwork, and she instructed me in no uncertain terms not to speak to anyone but her.

"Now," the attorney says, leaning back in her chair and crossing one leg over the other. Her suit pant pulls up enough for me to hope she never comes near me with those pointy as fuck, sky-high heels. "Let's try this for the second time today. Would you care to share your side of the story with me?"

I'M BACK in my holding cell, pacing the small space as my mind turns in circles. Half of me thinks I did the right thing, and half of me wishes I had done the opposite. I only ever wanted to protect Lor, but I don't know if that's what I'm doing anymore.

Flames tingle beneath my skin, and my fingers itch to snatch something.

"No more fires. No more stealing. No killing," I mutter the words under my breath, hopefully too soft for anyone or anything to pick up.

The mantra repeats in my head, and I time the words with my steps, but it's not helping as it used to. I need Lor. I think I protected her, and I hope it'll stick, but then another thought pops into my head.

My parents will be so disappointed.

I drop onto the bench bolted to the wall as the energy leaves my limbs. They wanted better for me than this, and Lor won't be happy I protected her at the sacrifice of myself. This is so much more complicated than it was supposed to be.

I hunch over, hiding one hand behind the other as I let a spark of flame out. I twist it between my fingers, the tiny concession easing my demon urges enough to keep the rest in check.

It's a long night, and the following days don't get much better.

Between arraignment and my court date for trial, I'm held in custody. Apparently, they've deemed me too great a risk to public safety to be released pretrial, so I'm stuck in the county jail for the next two weeks. My attorney contacts me whenever she needs additional information or to clarify something, but otherwise I assume she's coordinating with Lor, since I signed a release for them to speak.

I spend every day debating with myself. Lying to a courtroom is definitely not the definition of "good person" behavior, and all I've wanted my entire life is to be good. But if I don't, and Lor has already put in her statement as evidence, would that get *her* in trouble for lying and trying to cover for me? Could she then be charged as a co-conspirator or something?

For once my demon likes the idea of lying, mostly because it means protecting Lor, but also because if it works, it means I get to be with her again. I don't know what to do. I wish someone would come tell me so I didn't have to make this decision myself.

The worst part of this entire situation isn't the food, or the cold cell, or the lack of freedom. It's that I haven't been able to talk to Lor.

My demon is losing it. I'm not able to sleep, I can hardly keep food down, and my mind is filled with thoughts of her. The only thing that helps is the visit from my therapist, but even she can't save my mind this time. All I can do is remind myself to stick to the plan, and that it's all worth it for my Starfire.

23

WHY CAN'T ATTORNEYS
JUST TALK NORMAL?

*~~Febru~~ April, 1995: It comes... I go. To be free,
regrow. Renée, my sweet Renée. I'm sorry.*

Lor

I sleep terribly the first night Ro is in jail, and I'm up with the sun the next morning. A first for me. I have no idea if his attorney bought my story, but I'm moving forward with my plan either way. If there's anything I can do to diminish his sentence or help prove him innocent, I'll do it.

Finn calls that afternoon telling me to come down to the club, that he found someone who can help, so that's where I'm headed after getting lost for hours on the internet again. I managed to at least wash my face and brush my hair before I left, but I can't say the rest of me is well taken care of.

"Lor, hey," Finn says, waving me to the back room when I walk in. He motions to a slight figure leaning against the far wall. "This is XingXing, they/them. I'll just let you two work things out back here, yeah?"

"Sure, thanks Finn. I know this puts you in a tough spot, but I appreciate your help."

He nods, a conflicted look of worry and relief lining his face as he backs out and closes the door behind him. I wonder for the millionth time if I'm doing the right thing as I take in their casual t-shirt, chin length black hair, and the graceful way they slide into a chair.

"So, what can I help you with?" XingXing asks. They clasp their hands in front of them and cross their legs, the picture of nonchalance.

I eye them warily, questioning if I can really trust this person. I've been weighing the risks all morning, going back and forth in my head. The risks of trusting them... And the risks if I don't.

I'm willing to sacrifice my secret if I need to, it's worth it to save Ro from what would surely be a lifetime sentence in the supernatural prison. Supernaturals aren't given a second chance, and they're not given lenient sentences either.

I pinch my lips, hating the deal I'm about to offer, but deep down I've already decided. When it comes down to it, there's no other option.

"I need you to help me clear someone's name. I gave myself as an alibi, but..."

"Let me guess," their mouth quirks up in a wry grin. "They did something bad and you need the footage scrubbed?"

"Yes." I sigh, slumping with relief that they said it and not me.

"Alright," XingXing says, pulling out a laptop and plugging a black box into it. "I need the details. Where, when, who, anything else relevant, so I know where to start looking."

They type and click as I talk, dark brown eyes flicking across the screen as they do... whatever it is hackers do. When they run out of questions and I run out of information, they settle back in their seat and cross their arms.

"I'll need payment."

"Right." I bite my lip. I knew this moment was coming. I can do this. "How much will it be?"

The number they give makes my eyes pop. I take a deep breath, then do the one thing I swore I'd never again do.

"Do you accept payment other than cash? Like, what if I had something valuable to trade?"

The hacker tilts their head, hair swaying with the movement, but their eyes don't leave mine. "Depends what it is."

I suck in a shaky breath, steeling myself, then blurt it out.

"I can pay with stardust."

XingXing freezes. They don't even blink as they stare at me, then their eyes flit between mine. It's only now I consider that they may not know the value of what I'm offering. I tense, kicking myself internally for being so stupid as I hope I didn't just ruin everything. If they think I'm crazy, or don't believe me, or... My lip hurts from how much I've been chewing on it, and my leg starts to bounce under the table as I wait for their answer.

"How?"

I gulp, and my eyes dart around the stacked liquor boxes in the back room of the club. Does that mean they *do* know about stardust? And that they believe I can get some? Their stoic expression gives nothing away, but I've already started down this path, so I might as well see where it goes. I don't have many choices other than to trust them.

For Ro.

I lean forward and lower my voice. "I'm a star-chaser," I whisper.

XingXing must know we're real, because they don't look surprised. It's only slightly reassuring.

"Prove it."

"I—what?"

"If you're as you say, and you can pay with stardust, I want proof that I'm not being scammed."

Now, it's my turn to stare. How am I supposed to prove that?

"Um, I could..." I shake my head and my entire body slumps. "I don't know how to prove it," I whisper, defeated.

Their eyes narrow, but XingXing doesn't look put off as they continue to eye me for long moments. I take one breath, two, feeling like an ant under a microscope when they finally speak again.

"Tell me what it feels like."

How would that... Wait, are they also a star-chaser? Or do they know someone like me? My heart rate kicks up a notch.

"It's, well, do you mean like, when I get the urge to follow the stars? Or just like... being a star-chaser in general? Because that doesn't feel too much different from what regular people feel, I don't think at least—"

"Star-chasing," they interrupt. "What does following your ancestral gift feel like?"

My *ancestral gift?* I nearly scoff, but manage to hold it in. I've never heard it referred to in such generous terms before.

"Uh, it feels like this urge that I can't deny. A pull like something is hooked into me, into who I am inside, dragging me toward the fallen star. If I ignore it... well. I can't ignore it, not really. The pull just gets worse and worse, and I can't help but follow it no matter how much I try not to. But once I give in, then I guess it doesn't feel too bad. It's just a sense of urgency, like I'm needed somewhere really important and I'm almost late so I have to rush, but no matter how fast I go, there's no getting there on time. And then when I do find it... I normally ignore how that feels, to be honest."

XingXing nods slowly, a thoughtful look on their face.

"Why wouldn't you want to?"

I blink at them. "What?"

"You said you try not to follow it sometimes. Why?"

"Because... because it's a curse. Because I hate being unable to control it. Because it has killed everyone in my family."

They make a noncommittal humming noise, their eyes squinting as they take me in, but then jerk their chin once.

"Alright, agreed. One scavenging of stardust—no matter how much or how little, I want it in its entirety—in exchange for my help in clearing and covering all of *these* feeds."

They turn their computer around and show me a number of video stills of Ro on his bike in various parts of town the night of the fire. Then they click to another screen with more video stills, and then a third with another click.

"Shit, what was he doing?" I mutter under my breath.

"Trying to lose any tail that might have been on him, I assume," XingXing replies, spinning the laptop back around. "Lucky for your friend, there was no one tracking him. He got in and out clean, apart from these videos."

"And you can take care of all that? Make it look like he was with me all night?"

"Yeah, I can. It'll be done tonight. I'll contact you to collect the payment."

Before I can reply, they snap the laptop shut, slide it into their bag, and are striding out the door.

I hope I didn't just make the biggest mistake of my life.

Two Weeks Later

I'm a jittery ball of nerves, an anxious wreck, and I need to get it together if I'm going to do any good for Ro today. It's his court date, and his attorney seems optimistic.

She's been drilling me all week on questions and counter questions. I think there are proper terms she used, but I can't remember them. All I know is I'm going to testify as a witness that Ro was with me all night, and I'll be questioned by both his legal team as well as the prosecution.

She says I'm ready, I just hope I can keep my story straight, and that Ro doesn't say anything to dispute it. I'm also feeling slightly nauseous at the thought of facing the big boss man, or whoever they send in his place. He hasn't contacted me at all over the last two weeks, but I have caught glimpses of his goons hanging around. I suspect he's waiting to see how this trial turns out before delivering whatever horrendous punishment he's cooked up for me.

I won't let my mind go there. I need to be focused on Ro right now. I have to trust that he'll still want me after this; that despite his efforts at being a good person, he won't hold it against me that I'm lying for him, essentially forcing him to as well.

Lying in court, no less.

I cringe. It's really not a good look. Best case scenario, it appeals to his demon side, and he appreciates my efforts to protect him in return. Worst case... nope, not going there either.

When I step into the courtroom, the chilly air sends goosebumps up my arms. My fingers reveal a slight tremble, and I clench my hands behind my back in an attempt to look strong, confident, anything other than what I'm feeling right now, which is like I'm about to puke.

The buzzing of the air conditioner is loud in my ears, or perhaps that's just my nerves drowning out the murmurs of the prosecution as their cold eyes track me. Ro's attorney nods, her fierce glasses and mile-long heels giving me a confidence boost. Just having her on our side feels like a win, and I hope it translates to one at the end of the day, too.

When they march Ro into the courtroom, my breath hitches in my chest. He looks haggard, like he hasn't seen the sun in years and isn't eating enough. No makeup, no silver jewelry, no colorful clothing. Then his eyes meet mine, and a part of me relaxes while another part low in my stomach tightens. His hazel eyes sparkle despite the tense situation, and he grins my favorite lopsided grin.

My heart pinches in my chest when I realize how much I've missed him.

I try to smile back, but it feels wobbly, so I stop. He doesn't seem phased as he's escorted to his seat, and plops down next to his attorney. This is the closest we've been in weeks, and I'm dying to race up the aisle and touch him, kiss him, pull him into my arms. Maybe also slap him for doing something so reckless and stupid.

The next few hours last an eternity. My throat is parched, but I only take sips of water as I fear I won't be able to keep anything more down. Ro periodically turns around in his seat to wink, grin, or waggle his eyebrows at me. I can't return his playful gestures. I don't know how he's handling this trial with a smile.

When I'm called to the stand as a witness for the defense, I steel my spine and clench my fists, determined to do the best I can to get Ro out of here. I'm sworn in, although I really don't understand what swearing on something I don't believe in is supposed to do, and then I sit down and face a plethora of terrifying faces. Even Ro's attorney is intimidating, despite knowing she's fighting for us.

She stands and walks around the desk, then leans back against it. I think she's going for nonchalant, but the woman is a powerhouse, and nonchalant isn't in her repertoire. I start to relax, though, when she goes through each question we've already practiced multiple times. I give the same answers, and she nods each time. I take that as approval, giving me another little confidence boost.

The prosecution's cross-examination isn't nearly as bad as

I was expecting. Sure, the attorney is a big bully-looking man, but I've dealt with plenty of those in my life. The big boss isn't here. There's another man sitting at the desk that I don't recognize, but I don't get a chance to wonder about it. His attorney dives in, throwing question after question at me, all the while our attorney continually interrupts to object.

I hear calls of, "leading the witness" and "speculative" and "irrelevant" among others, but much of it I can't keep up with. I answer as best I can, relying on our practice sessions to get through them all. My brain is spinning, my breath starting to speed up as anxiety takes root, and I wonder what will happen if I get up and leave.

Before I have to find out, the judge calls for a recess.

My eyes dart to Ro, but he's already being dragged out of his chair and escorted to the back of the room where he came in from. His eyes are locked on me, concern edging out the smile he's held on to until now.

"Lor."

I see more than hear him call my name, but his attorney steps between us, and we're cut off.

"Take a breath," she says, her voice no-nonsense. "You're doing well."

Surprisingly, her unconcerned attitude actually helps. I'm able to draw in a slower breath now that everyone's eyes aren't on me while attorneys talk over one another in a verbal battle I don't understand.

"Here," she says, handing me a bottle of water. "Drink."

I take a few sips, and my eyes wander around the room.

"Don't look at them, look at me," she says.

It pulls my attention away from the media lining the seats, and back to her with her badass suit and stabby cat-eye glasses.

The free time passes before I'm ready, and I'm called back up to the stand.

"You've stated the defendant was with you all night," the prosecuting attorney says. "In what ways could he have snuck out—"

"Objection," our fierce attorney calls out, her voice steely. "Again, leading the witness."

"Sustained," the judge says.

The other attorney dips his head to the judge, then turns dead eyes back on me. My thoughts are already spinning again.

"Is there any chance the defendant could have left your presence during the night without you knowing?"

"No," I say.

Keep it short and sweet, don't elaborate if you don't have to. That's what Ro's attorney keeps telling me.

"And how would you ensure that?"

"I'm a light sleeper," I say, starting to get nervous again.

"How do you know?"

"Objection, speculative."

"Overruled," the judge says. "Continue."

Sweat gathers in my armpits while goosebumps from the cold air shiver up my arms.

"How do you know you're a light sleeper?"

I glance at Ro, then his attorney, whose eyes are narrowed. I don't know what that means.

"Uh, well, I have a cat," I glance at Ro again, who is now grinning in triumph, then continue. "And my cat is an indoor-outdoor cat, so, um, I have to be able to let them in or out when they want. Mostly they're wanting to come in during the night, and they'll tap on the window or meow, but it's pretty quiet, so I sleep lightly, and any little noise wakes me up."

The prosecutor's lips pinch, which I assume to mean that was a good answer.

"No further questions, your honor," he says.

"Defense?" the judge asks.

Ro's attorney stands again, nods her head to the judge, then faces me once more. She told me she'd ask more questions if she felt anything needed clarifying after the prosecution's cross-examination, and I assume that's what this is.

"Ms. Seren," she says. "Can you please clarify? You said any little sound would wake you up, correct?"

"That's correct," I say.

"So, we can assume that if Mr. Cromwell got up to use the bathroom or get a snack in the middle of the night, you would hear that?"

"Objection, leading the witness," prosecution says.

"Overruled."

She tips her head to me that it's my turn to answer now, and I nod.

"Yeah, actually, that has happened before," I say.

Meanwhile, I'm kicking myself internally. We literally practiced this exact scenario and it flew right out of my brain. Why did I think the cat was a good example? This is much better evidence.

"Please explain," Ro's attorney says, her stance relaxing slightly now that we're on the same page again.

"Yeah, he's spent the night before and had to get up to use the bathroom. I always wake up as soon as he gets out of bed. If somehow *that* didn't wake me up, my door creaks, so I'm sure that would have woken me up too."

She nods at me with a tiny twitch of her lips before turning to the judge.

"No further questions."

I'm escorted back to my seat and I slump into it, tuning out the rest of the proceedings. Our attorney submits video evidence that Ro's motorcycle was outside my apartment the entire night. She vehemently opposes their "evidence" from a witness who says they saw Ro shooting fire from his fingers into the warehouse, claiming it's circumstantial based on the fact they previously described the arsonist to be wearing a black mask, and therefore unidentifiable.

I'm starting to think we're actually going to win this.

24

DOWN BAD FOR HER

Ro

She's amazing. Absolutely incredible.

I can't help smiling the whole time, even though I probably shouldn't. It makes me look like I don't take the charges seriously, or so my attorney says, but come on. How am I supposed to *not* smile when Lor is only feet away from me?

And the way she owns every single answer, and has evidence to back herself up while on the stand is so impressive. I mean, I know my attorney helped prepare her just the same as she helped me, but still. I'm thrilled to see Lor in person after two weeks of no contact, and I don't care one bit that she's lying to help me. In fact, my inner demon is delighted at her manipulation of the system.

I have no idea where the "evidence" of my bike outside her apartment all night came from, because it sure as hell wasn't there even once that night. I keep that to myself though, obviously. I'll ask her later, when I'm out of here.

After hours that pass in minutes, thanks to my gorgeous distraction, I'm declared not guilty, and taken to retrieve my belongings before I'm released back into the general public.

The fresh air has never felt so crisp, and the sun never felt so welcoming. Perhaps it's a bit of a dramatic thought, but I indulge myself in it regardless, as I close my eyes and tip my head back.

I can't believe I got away with that.

After everyone has dispersed and I've thanked my badass attorney, my eyes land on Lor. My smile hasn't dropped since we came back from the recess, yet somehow it gets even bigger now. My nails have almost no paint left on them, and I wasn't afforded any makeup during my brief stint in jail, so I feel a touch out of place as I ruffle a hand through my hair. She doesn't seem to care though, as I jog over and sweep her into a hug.

Lor lets out an "oomph" at the contact, and her muscles are tense for a long moment before she relaxes into my hold.

"What were you thinking?" she hisses in my ear.

I set her down and immediately palm the back of her head to pull her into a kiss. The surprised noise she makes as she melts beneath my lips is music to my ears. I figure it's probably not the place for a make-out session, so I pull back much sooner than I want to.

"I missed you," I say, swiping a strand of silver hair out of her face.

I cup her jaw between my palms and let my eyes feast on her. She's so fucking gorgeous it makes my heart hurt.

Lor's lips twitch into a small smile, and then she steps out of my hold.

"Come on," she says. "Since your bike isn't here, you can ride bitch on mine."

I cackle with delight, and she spins away, but not before I see the answering grin stretch across her face.

I swing on behind her and she revs the engine, handing me my helmet.

"How'd you get this?" I ask.

"You're not the only one with some tricks up your sleeve."

Honestly, could I be any more in love?

I band my arms tight around her, pleased when she doesn't protest my viselike grip. She's literally perfect. Smart, fierce, strong and resilient, loyal. I've always heard perfect isn't possible, but obviously whoever said that hasn't met Lor.

The wind whips around us as she tears out of the parking lot, and I let out an exhilarated, laughing whoop as I throw an arm out in celebration. I set a warehouse on fire, threatened Lor's ugly, blackmailing boss, and got away with all of it. I just hope it made a difference.

Lor twists around at a red light and pushes her visor up.

"I know you haven't been home in weeks, but," she grimaces. "I have to..."

She gestures toward her chest and her nose wrinkles, then she looks to the horizon. Ah, her star-chaser magic.

"You feel it?" I ask, pressing my palm to her sternum.

Lor nods, and the light turns green, but she doesn't go yet.

"Let's go then," I say, jerking my chin forward.

"You don't want me to drop you off?"

I scoff. "Do you know me? I'm not leaving your side if I don't have to."

Lor rolls her eyes and flips her visor back down. Soon enough, we're shooting down a country road to the middle of nowhere, and then she's off the bike, stalking through a section of forest until she finds what she's looking for. Her hair shimmers in the dappled light beneath the trees, and the peaceful sounds of the forest surround us as I stumble over roots in her wake.

Then she's collecting more stardust. My heart trips, and I wonder if I didn't succeed in protecting her.

"Lor?"

"Yeah," she says absently.

"Did it work?"

Lor pauses sifting through the dirt and leaves to look up at me, her brows scrunched. "Did what work?"

"My fire. Are you still working for that man?" I don't know why I'm so nervous, but it kind of feels like I've done something wrong and am about to get in trouble for it.

Lor stands and walks over to me, dusting her hands off on her pants.

"Ro," she says, her words slow and deliberate. "Thank you for protecting me, but if you ever pull something like that again, I'm going to chop. Off. Your hands."

My eyes go wide as she speaks, then I sag with relief at her last words.

"Why the hell do you look relieved?" she exclaims.

"I thought you were going to say my dick!"

Lor snorts a laugh as she turns away. "Nah, I enjoy that too much to chop it off."

A manic grin spreads over my face as I skip after her. "Oh yeah? You like my cock, do you?"

"Are you fishing for compliments, Ro?"

"From you? Always."

Lor stops and turns to me again. "Yes, you've got a great cock, and you know how to use it. I certainly like that. But what I like more is *you*, Ro."

She places her hand on my chest, and it feels like she's the one with fire. My smile drops as I take note of her serious tone.

"When I got that phone call..." she trails off, then swallows hard. "I've lost everyone in my life that I've ever cared for, Ro. Everyone."

Her eyes bore into mine, like she's trying to will my understanding. My stomach plummets when I realize what she's saying. She thought she lost me too.

I drop to my knees and scoop her toward me, banding my arms around her thighs. Lor's body is rigid with tension, and I press my forehead to her bare stomach.

"I'm so sorry, Lor. I wasn't thinking about getting caught. I just needed you to be safe, and when I saw him threatening you... I'm sorry."

"I know, I understand," she says. Her fingers thread through my hair, then she sinks to her knees in front of me. Her dark grey eyes meet mine, and I hate how heavy they are.

"I would never abandon you. Never, Lor."

I take in her wary posture, the way she seems to be fighting against her own instincts. Her hard swallow and jerky nod. The glassy sheen to her eyes.

"Starfire," I whisper, cupping her cheek. "I would sell myself to hell to keep you safe. I'd burn down the world for you."

"Please don't," she whispers, her words choked. "Just stay with me. That's all I want."

I press a soft kiss to her forehead, then pull back with a tender smile. "Don't you know? I'm yours. I'm hopelessly in love with you, Lor."

Her glassy eyes round and she starts to pull back, but I scoop her up and cross my legs, then plop her into my lap.

"And neither of us is going anywhere. I don't expect you to say it back, not ever if you don't want to. But Lor..." I trail off, waiting for her to gather the courage to meet my eyes again.

When she does, I grin extra wide, showing way too many teeth, and her eyes turn the slightest bit wary.

"I'm so fucking obsessed with you, you couldn't get rid of me if you tried."

I smirk, then bite my lip ring. Her eyes fall to it, then fly back up to mine and... *there's* the heat I've been waiting for. I lean forward, brush my lips along her cheekbone, and then whisper in her ear. "Stalker, remember?"

I pull back and wink, and finally the tension drains from her slender body. She huffs out a husky laugh, and my cock hardens beneath her ass at the sound. Lor glares at me, then rolls her eyes, all while trying to hold back my favorite smile.

That's okay, I remind myself. It's a work in progress, and soon enough she won't have to be afraid of smiling anymore. I'll be here every second to prove it to her.

WE GO BACK to my place instead of Lor's this time, since I haven't been home in ages. I'm a bit surprised to realize it's the first time I've had her over. She takes in my colorful, eclectic aesthetic with wide eyes.

"Wow," she says, turning in a circle. "This is... a lot."

I glance at the multi-colored frames decorating the wall she's starting at.

"Are you surprised?"

Her eyes meet mine and her lips twitch up with a small chuckle. "No, I guess not."

"Make yourself at home, I'm gonna go—" I wave a hand up and down my body, then glare at my horrendous nails. "Fix all this."

Lor's tentative smile cracks into a real grin, and it sends warmth cascading down my limbs. I grab the first set of fresh clothes I see—a cropped t-shirt with a massive pink daisy on the front and a pair of ombré purple/pink sweatpants—before slipping into the bathroom. I rush through my shower, even though I haven't had this luxury in weeks, then swipe on some eyeliner before grabbing my eco-friendly nail polish remover and an old washcloth. The whole time I'm in here, my skin itches to get back to Lor, so as soon as I step out and see her sitting on my mustard velvet couch, I stride over and plop down beside her.

Then I loop my arms around her waist and haul her into my lap.

She lets out a surprised squeak, and I chuckle as I nuzzle my nose into the back of her neck.

"Needy," she grumbles.

"Mhm."

Then I angle her body so I can reach around it, grab the nail polish remover, and get to work on my nails. Lor huffs and attempts to wiggle out of my hold, but I don't have to fight very hard to keep her there.

I don't think she really wants to get away, she just wants to know she's wanted.

I'll happily provide that reassurance for her every day of our lives. I press a smile into her neck and inhale her lightly floral scent. She shivers as my lips kiss up to her earlobe, and I suck it into my mouth, then nip the shell of her ear.

"Ro," she says, voice breathy.

"Lor," I reply, my own voice gravelly with need.

I suck the tender skin of her neck into my mouth as she twists in my hold to straddle my hips. I drop the washcloth to the ground, and clamp my palms to the bare skin of her waist instead. She presses down and rocks into me, forcing my already hard cock to pulse in my pants. I groan, unable to resist anything about her. It's truly a marvel that we're here, together, after everything we've both been through.

Momentous. That's how this feels, like my heart might explode at any second, and I'll happily let it if Lor's the one causing my destruction.

Then her fingers are tugging at my shirt, and I gladly let her strip it off me. I nudge her jaw to the side, and she angles her head to give me more room. I want to devour her, and the sensation of having Lor back in my arms, her weight settling me into the couch, her heat pressing into my crotch—it's world-ending. I could never live without this, and suddenly I'm desperate to be inside her.

I lurch to my feet, ignoring Lor's surprised gasp as I wrap

her legs around me and stride to my bedroom. I turn and sink onto my bed, then my lips meet Lor's in a fiery kiss. I feel like I'm glowing, and I have to be careful to keep my flames contained inside me.

I slip my fingers beneath Lor's black lace crop top, and she quickly shimmies out of it, probably so I don't burn it off. I grin when I find that she's not wearing a bra beneath.

"Naughty girl," I say, dipping down to suck a pointed nipple into my mouth.

Lor arches into me, and her fingers tangle in my still-damp hair. My hands on her hips urge her to rise so I can tug her pants off. They're so tight that her black panties come off with them. Another delightful development.

Then she's tugging at my sweats, tossing them to the floor and pulling my cock out. She drops to her knees and immediately sucks it into her mouth.

"Shit," I gasp as my hips punch forward and I hit the back of her throat.

Lor flicks her eyes up, a heated glare burning into me.

"Sorry," I groan. "You're so goddamn sexy."

Her glare lightens with mirth. Then she flattens her tongue, licking up the bottom of my shaft as she pulls back while sucking hard. It feels like she's sucking my soul out through my cock and I'm *absolutely* going to come in two seconds flat if she doesn't stop.

"Jesus."

I fist a hand in her hair and yank her off. She lets go with a pop, then licks her lips. My cock throbs, straining for her, and I can feel her breath on it as she exhales.

"What's wrong, demon?" she says. "Can't handle me?"

"Oh, I can handle you just fine," I say.

She smirks like she doesn't believe me, but I continue before she can reply.

"It's your fucking mouth that's the problem. If you keep

that up, you're going to suck me dry far too soon for what I have planned."

I thumb her lower lip and her smirk drops, her eyelids growing heavy as she stares up at me. Her chest rises as her breathing grows more shallow, and it's my turn to offer a wicked grin.

"Yeah, I've had too much down time lately," I murmur, slowly leaning toward her.

She inches back, sensing the predator peeking out at her.

"Too much time to think... To imagine what I'd do if I got my hands on you again."

I snap my hands out and wrap them around her waist, then yank her back up into my lap. I groan at how hot and wet she is when she rocks her hips against me. There's no way I'm lasting like this either, so I twist our bodies and toss her on the bed. She bounces once, eyes wide, then tries to scoot back away from me.

A laugh punches out of me, perhaps a touch maniacal, but we're both going mad, so what does it matter?

I crawl over her, grasping her wrists and dragging her hands above her head. I shackle her wrists in one hand, then lightly trail the fingers of my other down her arm, across her shoulder and collarbone, then circle her delicate neck with my fingers.

My palm rests over her throat, so I can feel it when she swallows. One side of my mouth tilts up as I take in my prize. Her breath hitches, and I pause a moment to admire her beneath me. Her pearly skin, the shimmery silver hair splayed out beneath her, her rosy nipples straining up toward me. She's my fantasy come to life.

"More incredible than I ever could have imagined, my Starfire," I murmur.

Lor's cheeks flush a delicious pink, and my eyes wander

back up to meet hers. I press her palms into my headboard and squeeze her wrists once.

"Hands here, gorgeous," I say.

She nods, and I tighten my grip on her neck before letting go of both. Her hands don't move an inch.

I nip along her jaw to her ear, then lick around the shell of it.

"That's my good girl," I say, wondering how she'll react this time.

She tries to stifle her moan, but I hear it, and it sends my cock bobbing again as it strains for her. I lean back on my heels, careful to keep most of my weight off her, and take a moment to admire the goddess splayed out before me. My eyes trail every inch of her until she starts to squirm.

Then I unfurl one hand, palm up in front of me, and call on my power. My eyes are fixed on Lor's face as I watch for her reaction.

A ball of fire flickers to life in my palm, and Lor's eyes widen.

"Eyes up here," I murmur.

Her gaze meets mine, and I search it for a long moment. I see no fear there, only heat and desire. My lips slowly curve into a satisfied smile. I don't know what else I was expecting; as I've already previously established, Lor is perfect.

Of course she wouldn't be afraid of my flames.

25

BRINGING THE HEAT (LITERALLY)

LOR

Ro tips his hand, slowly turning it over as his fingers move in a rolling wave with the flame dancing between them. Then he lowers it to my body.

I suck in a sharp breath, my heart pounding with anticipation and the thrill of danger. I trust Ro not to hurt me, but that doesn't mean I know what to expect from the chaotic demon.

He drops the glowing flame to my navel, just under my belly button, and it spreads a delicious warmth across my skin. It's like nothing I've felt before. Similar to a blast of heat from sitting too close to a fire, but not quite as intense. More like the deceptively inviting warmth of the sun on your skin when you know you're getting a sunburn, but it feels so good you endure it anyway.

Ro eyes me carefully, his gaze burning into my skin in a different way as he slowly rolls the ball of fire over my skin. He sends it circling beneath the curve of one breast, tongues of glowing red and orange licking up towards my nipple, then curling around the other. I shiver, the heat from the blaze leaving an icy path behind when my hot skin meets the cool air. Goosebumps break out along my arms and legs, and my brain empties of all thoughts.

I'm a creature of sensation, fire and ice, tingling shivers. I gasp when he tweaks my nipple with his fingers, then sucks the other into his mouth. He trails his hand down my ribs, tendrils of fire dripping from each finger. The contrasting sensations are so foreign my body doesn't know how to react.

My heart pounds and my breaths turn even more shallow as my gaze follows the flickering lines. The fire coalesces and settles on my hip bone, shimmering and dancing, seeming slightly more *alive* than a normal flame would be.

My breath stalls in anticipation, but nothing happens for long moments. I flick my eyes up to Ro's to see him drinking me in, his gaze avid and intense as it caresses up my body, my face, then finally meets my eyes.

His smile is comforting and thrilling at the same time. Somehow a juxtaposition of danger and solace, but I guess that's what we are to each other.

Ro pointedly darts his eyes down, then to my eyes again, telling me with a look to watch. I turn my focus back to his fire, and his hand squeezes my opposite hip before he removes all physical touch. The only stimulation comes from his flickering flame, the heat intense with all other sense of touch removed.

As I watch, Ro flares it lightly over my hip bone, then lets it melt down the crease between my hip and my leg. My breath stutters in my lungs and I bite my lip with anticipation, but then it contracts, skipping over my most sensitive area, only to flare up the opposite crease and around to the outside of my hip. Air leaves me in a whoosh of disappointment, and I sense Ro's smirk from the corner of my eye.

I stay focused on his flame though; I have a feeling if I get distracted for even a moment, he'll take advantage, and I'm not sure if I'll survive it.

Ro's hands move to my knees and he applies gentle pressure, dragging them further apart as his glowing flame ripples into multiple spirals that swirl random patterns along my hip and outer thigh. He pulls my knees up and plants my feet outside his bent legs, giving him an alarmingly vulnerable view.

His fingers raise more goosebumps as he lightly trails them up my inner thighs, then grips right below where my thighs meet my hips. He trickles fire along the same path, the heat blinking in and out, sparking along my sensitive skin and flickering from one leg to the other until it gets to the juncture where his hand clenches me tight.

My pussy is weeping, my mind spinning out of control as my body strains to keep up with the foreign sensations. I've never been so wet and ready in my entire life, and I hold my breath for so long I start to see black spots. He's going to kill me if he goes any slower, but finally, after ages of staring, he makes another move.

Ro again condenses the spreading embers down to a single, flickering flame that shines with a burnished golden radiance. He's gentle as he sweeps it across my puffy outer lips, the scorch making me clench up with a surprised gasp.

Ro's forearms strain as he prevents my thighs from snapping closed, and my eyes dart up to his. Then he does it again, the glowing ember licking over me. I'm sucking in quick, desperate breaths, and confusion flares in my hazy mind when I notice he's talking.

"That's it, my needy girl," he murmurs, "I love to hear you beg."

My brows are already tight with want, but they furrow further with his words. Then I realize I've been pleading with him. Hoarse whispers and cries leave my lips without my permission.

"Please, Ro," I say, "More, I need you, don't stop. Please."

I don't have it in me to be embarrassed. I might care later, but he owns me in this moment, and as long as he keeps going, I'm happy to babble whatever nonsense he wants.

"The prettiest words from the prettiest lips," he croons.

My eyes are locked onto his mouth, his lip ring glinting—taunting me—when he strikes.

His thumbs had moved while I was distracted, pulling me open and exposing my sensitive nerves. He sends tendrils of sparking heat from my outer lips straight up my slit to circle my clit, and I scream out a hoarse cry at the intense sensation. I throw my head back, arching my neck and body as everything tightens. I don't even get a chance to catch my breath when his wet tongue follows the same path.

I can't breathe.

I can't think.

Fire rolling over my clit, then his tongue soothing the burn. Heat again, over and over until I'm a shaking, gasping mess of garbled pleas.

Ro spears two heated fingers into me, curling them toward that sensitive spot, and my orgasm crashes over me. Flame under his tongue nearly burns my throbbing clit as my pussy clenches, his tongue laving me, licking and sucking as his fingers press exactly where I need them. Lights flash behind my eyelids, my lungs burn for air, and my entire body convulses as the orgasm pounds through me.

It's brutal, the most intense climax I've ever experienced, and when I finally crumple back onto his bed, I wonder if I'm dead. I don't know how anyone could have survived that.

I heave in great pulls of air, my breasts shaking with desperate attempts to catch my breath. My throat is dry, raspy from whatever noises he was drawing out of me, and my limbs feel boneless. I don't know if I'll ever be able to move again.

Soft lips trail gentle kisses across my hipbones, then up my sternum between my breasts. I shiver as his breath puffs over my sweat-slicked skin. The last traces of fire caress my body in gentle waves as his hands soothe me.

"Ro," I murmur, my voice hoarse.

He glances up at me, dark-rimmed gaze gleaming with wicked satisfaction. "Yes, Starfire?"

"Am I dead?"

His eyes flash with amusement, and an embarrassed flush sweeps across my skin. Of course I'm not dead, although he may have literally blown my mind if that nonsense is any indi-cation. I huff and throw an arm over my face.

"I'd never forgive myself if I killed you, even if it was from pleasure," Ro says.

His hard body brackets mine as his gentle fingers circle my wrist and pull my arm away. His eyes flick between mine, then one side of his lips lift in a mischievous smirk. "What a way to go though, huh?"

I roll my eyes, but can't contain the loopy smile. I feel incorporeal, disembodied, like he's somehow changed me on such a fundamental level that I'll never recover. My eyes lift to meet his again as he traces his fingers along my jaw, down my neck, over the shell of my ear. It's like he's memorizing every last curve and detail.

I blink in astonishment at the reverence on his face, then my lids fall closed in bliss when he scratches his nails along my scalp, threading his fingers through my hair.

"Shit, that feels good," I murmur.

He does it again, causing tingles to race from my scalp down my neck and along my spine, and I arch into him. Ro lets out a low hum of approval, tightening his grip on my hair and tilting my head back, exposing my neck. Then he hovers over me, letting the anticipation build. I don't know how I can possibly want more after he just destroyed me so thoroughly, but I can't deny the throbbing warmth radiating between my legs.

"Ro," I whisper.

He's blasted through all of my defenses, and I know the desperation is clear on my face. I can feel it, and there's nothing I can do to hide. His eyes glimmer, the dark eyeliner making the ring around his iris stark and striking in the low light. His piercings glint as his expression darkens, his own want rising to meet mine.

"Starfire." His voice is an octave lower than usual, sending lines of fire through my blood straight to my oversensitive clit.

I clench my thighs together with a strained whimper, begging him with my eyes. To take me, to fuck me, to care for me, to not hurt me, to keep me safe.

Asking for an impossibility that he may have already granted me.

Ro dips his head down and licks a line up my bared throat, the warmth of his tongue nearly scalding. I want him closer, need him inside me, and my fingers scrabble for purchase along his lean back. His muscles flex under my palms as he adjusts our bodies, settling himself between my legs.

"Are you ready, love?" he asks, slipping his fingers between us.

Love.

That word again, but it feels different now. It doesn't feel sarcastic or manipulative. It feels *relevant.* Significant. Meaningful.

My eyes turn glassy as I blink back my cresting emotions and swallow the defensive urge to push him away. I circle my hands around his biceps. Press my fingertips into his skin while he waits, patiently paused above me. I think he knows I need a moment to collect myself, and the fact he's so in tune with me gives my protective instincts another flare of defiance.

I don't want to be seen.

But... It's not so bad when it's Ro.

I open eyes that I had clenched shut, looking up through my lashes to meet Ro's steady gaze. He tilts his head and offers me a soft smile that quickly takes on an impish slant. It's a safe way out of the emotional mess I've landed in and I take it, meeting his smirk with a glare.

His eyes light up as his grin grows. "There she is," he murmurs.

He dips down to nudge his nose against mine, then nips my bottom lip. My lips part, and Ro groans into my mouth.

"I want you, Lor," he says.

"Yes," I reply with a frantic nod, giving him all the permission he needs.

He pushes inside me, a decadent stretch as my pussy sucks him in. I angle my hips and pull one leg up, stretching it above us and allowing Ro to push even deeper. He growls out a string of profanity and leans into my leg, adjusting it on his shoulder so my foot is behind his head. Then he grips my opposite knee, bending and pushing it wide to give himself room to pound into me.

I gasp and arch off the bed, the angle hitting something deep inside, triggering a cascade of trembles to wrack my body. I don't understand how we fit together so well, how after only knowing each other a short time, we can have what feels like an instinctual connection.

I also don't have the capacity to think about that right now, as Ro obliterates me for the second time tonight. He's a different person in this space; no longer the ridiculous demon whose eyes sparkle with mischief. It's like something has been unleashed inside him, something allowing him to dominate and control every facet of me. My body, my mind, my pleasure are all his to command.

I've never opened myself so fully to someone before, and yet it feels right with Ro. Like this is exactly the moment I'm meant to be in.

Ro's thrusts are relentless as he drives me higher and higher, tightening every muscle in my body as he forces me to the edge. I'm so close, it won't take much to push me over.

"Open your eyes," Ro growls, not softening his punishing rhythm for a moment. "Look at me, Starfire."

I force my heavy eyelids open, and take in his form above me. His rumpled hair hangs down, falling over one eye as his shoulders bunch, and breath heaves in and out of him. I gasp, my eyes flaring wide when they meet his.

His eyes are wild, lit from within by his demon fire so they're glowing a rich golden bronze. The knowledge that I could have such an impact on him, combined with the gorgeous image of his luminous eyes, is the last nudge I needed.

I careen straight into euphoria, my raw throat letting loose a harsh cry as Ro's hips punch into me. He answers with a low groan of his own, his eyes not letting go of mine, and I see every moment of his pleasure as he flies off the cliff with me. The gold in his eyes pulses in time with the warmth I can feel flooding me, and it sends aftershocks scattering through my trembling muscles.

I collapse beneath him, blinking heavy eyes as I will them to stay open, to hold onto his fiery gaze, but I quickly lose the battle as exhaustion pulls me under.

GOOSEBUMPS FLARE up and down my ribs as light touches tickle my skin, and I shiver.

"Are you awake, Starfire?" Ro's soft voice rouses me from whatever passed out state I was in, and I grimace, curling into myself.

"Nuh-uh," he says, tugging me back into him. "None of that closing off nonsense. I've seen every part of you, Lor, inside and out. I want it all."

My cheeks heat at the brazen statement, and I lick my dry lips, but allow him to pull me flush against his body again. Then I realize... I want to be there. My instinctive reaction to pull away and wall myself off isn't who I want to be with Ro.

I nuzzle my face into his neck and sling my arm over his waist, pulling myself tight against him as his chest rumbles with approval under my ear.

"That's better," he murmurs, dropping a kiss on the top of my head.

It's another struggle to let myself enjoy the small gesture. I don't know what to do in this situation; none of my previous hookups involved waking up to cuddles.

"Soooo..." Ro says, dragging out the word, and I tense at the seriousness of his tone. "You claimed your cat in court."

It takes me a moment to sort through the jumble of words that just came out of his mouth, but he's not done yet.

"And you know it's illegal to lie to a judge."

My eyes narrow as my body turns rigid in his arms. I'm still lying next to him, molded into his side, so all I can see is the bare expanse of his chest and shoulder. I hope he can feel the glare I'm attempting to burn into his skin.

"That means," the demon continues, his tone blithe as though he has no care for his impending demise. "Kahlo really is yours now. No takesies-backsies."

My lip pulls up in a snarl as I realize he's right, and that I'm happy about it. I think I really like that goddamn cat.

"Fuck you," I mutter, pressing my bared teeth into his neck.

Ro tips his head back and laughs, his entire chest bouncing beneath me so I have to pick my head up for fear of brain damage. A smile tugs at my lips as he pulls my entire body onto his, so I'm lying flat on top of him. I cross my arms over his chest and rest my chin on my forearms as he stares down at me, a grin stretching across his face.

I twist my lips sideways, and he wrinkles his nose. It's such a surprisingly cute look that it forces a laugh to break past my defiant lips.

"There it is," Ro says, his eyes glimmering with joy. "I love your laugh, and your smile."

I bite my lip and attempt another glare, but I know it doesn't work. Somehow this demon makes me *happy*. An entirely foreign sensation for me, but one I'm trying to embrace for the first time in my life.

"I love your glares too," he says with that stupidly endearing grin still plastered across his face.

26

INTRUSIVE THOUGHTS
FOR THE WIN

Ro

We're up and moving before too long—once Lor finally realizes it's the next day and we have a lot to talk about. Personally, I'm not in any hurry for her to put clothes on, but she seems to think it's important, so I go along with her ridiculous notions.

For now.

There is one specific thought that won't stop circling my brain, though. One worry that won't let go. Ever since she dragged me out to the forest yesterday as soon as I was released and collected more stardust.

"What will you do with the stardust if you're not going to sell it?" I ask, curiosity and wariness warring in my brain.

Lor freezes with one leg halfway into her pants, and my guard instantly goes up. She glances at me, then finishes dressing. Her movements are unhurried, intentional in their slowness.

She's hiding something.

Alarm shoots through me and I sit up, swinging my legs over the side of the bed. "You're not going back to him, right?"

Her head whips toward me, a look of outrage twisting her features.

"Never," she says, vehement.

I blink as my brain tries to figure out what's going on.

"Okay, then what? Is there someone else you're going to sell to?"

I secretly hope not, but if that's her plan I'll support her and do my best to keep her safe.

Lor grimaces, then her shoulders slump with a sigh as she turns to face me fully. "I traded it."

My brows shoot up, but she averts her eyes from mine.

"I went to Finn, I didn't know who else to ask, and he set me up with a hacker..." she trails off, giving me a look of expectation.

A hacker.

She traded stardust to a hacker in exchange for... me. Shock has me jolting my head back from her, but the rest of my body is reacting the opposite in a confusing turn of events. My feet step forward as my arms reach out, wanting to scoop her up and twirl her around.

She's frozen in front of me, eyes wary as her gaze flits across my face. But really, why shouldn't I scoop her up? She broke the law for me, *again*.

I grin, delighted to witness my angry little star-chaser turning into a law-breaking goddess. With that, I stride forward and follow that intrusive thought. The one that says she's mine, she belongs to me, she should be in my arms at all times.

I sweep her off her feet with a playful growl and throw her over my shoulder.

"Ro!" she shrieks, her voice a mix of bewildered shock and amusement.

Naturally, I slap her ass, then swing her back down into

my arms as she lets out another amused huff, which she tries to turn into an angry scoff. Unsuccessfully.

"You're becoming a right little devil, aren't you? My cute little criminal," I say, so pleased I can't possibly contain it. "I *told* you we were perfect for each other."

Lor flicks her gorgeous grey eyes up in a tiny eye roll as one side of her mouth twitches into a crooked smile.

"Admit that I'm right," I say, narrowing my eyes on her.

When she sticks her nose in the air and pinches her lips firmly shut, I adjust my hold on her, then tense my fingers along her ribs.

Her eyes widen.

I cock one eyebrow, tickle threat activated.

Her body tenses as her lips part, ready to protest, but it's too late. I tighten my hold, and my fingertips dance along her sides as she shrieks with tortured giggles. She swats at me, her hands flying as she twists in a heroic attempt to get away—unsuccessful again—unfortunately for her. I love her laughter, and I love that she doesn't tell me to stop. She wants my hands on her just as much as I do.

I pause my tickling, and she pants to catch her breath while I eye her expectantly. She scrunches her face up, and I tighten my fingers against her ribs again, ready for round two if she doesn't concede. We stare at each other, and I'm about to tackle her back into the bed when she gives in.

"Fine!" she says. "Stop! Stop, you're right."

"About what?" I demand. I'm not falling for any tricks. I want her to admit what I've known all along.

She sucks in a breath as her eyes grow serious, and I loosen my demanding hold, my touch turning worshipful instead of teasing. Lor pushes into me, molding her body to mine as she tips her head back. My breath catches at her willing vulnerability when she places one hand on my bare chest, right over my racing heart.

"We're perfect for each other," she whispers.

Her eyes are intent on mine, a flicker of uncertainty in their depths. I hold her gaze, keeping it strong and steady as I nod once, then crash my lips to hers, sealing the words between us. I yank our bodies together as our lips blaze with heat, keeping her tight against me for a long moment before pulling back and letting her see that I'm right there with her, only I don't have any doubts.

"Damn right we are," I say.

Her insecurity dissipates in the light of my confidence in us, and a small smile touches her lips. I grin in return and spin her around, snagging my pants off the floor.

Then I march us out to the kitchen for some much needed sustenance.

"YOU CAME THROUGH," the hacker says a few days later, surprise lighting their voice as they peer into the cloth sack Lor sets on the table in front of them. "Successful on all accounts, it would seem."

Their warm brown eyes flick to me as they cinch the sack closed, and then they focus on Lor again. They tilt their head, eyeing her up and down where she stands across the table from them.

"You're different than I thought," they say.

Lor glares at them, her entire body tense and ready to lash out, but they don't seem perturbed by her outward hostility. If anything, they relax even more as they rise with languid grace and step back from the table.

"I'll take care of them," they say with a solemn nod.

It takes me a moment to work out what they're saying as they lift the sack, give Lor a respectful nod, then turn and stride out the back door of Tempo.

Lor stares after the hacker, the door closing behind them and bringing what feels like a finalizing silence down between us.

"Well, that was..." I say, unsure what to make of it. "Something?"

Confusion flickers in Lor's eyes as she flexes her hands in what I'm assuming is an attempt to let them leave with the stardust. Or perhaps to let them leave with her secret.

I can't believe she did that for me. My heart leaps in my chest when I think about the risks she took, and I vow to never again put her in that position.

She sucks in a breath, holds it for long moments, then exhales in a gust as her shoulders slump and she turns to me.

"Yeah," she says. "That was weird."

Finn pokes his head in the door to the back room before I have a chance to ask if she's okay.

"Hey, you guys good? I gotta open soon."

Obviously, I've been replaced after not showing up for weeks, but I don't mind. Working this job isn't conducive to the future I have planned for us, anyway.

"Yeah, we're good."

A few minutes later, I'm munching on fries and my eyes are fixated on Lor's lips. They're forming a perfect O around a paper straw as she sips on a fountain drink, and I can't help but remember when her lips sucked on my dick like that.

Lor snaps her fingers in front of my face and I startle. She glares at me and points at her eyes, but then hollows her cheeks as she drinks.

Torturous little star-chaser.

"Lor," I growl in warning. "Keep it up and see what happens."

One side of her mouth tilts up, but she releases the straw and I blink, finally able to inhale. The breath in my lungs freezes though, when she slowly licks her tongue across her top lip. I clench my jaw and my gaze darts to hers. I wouldn't be surprised if my eyes were glowing again; I want her desperately.

Confidence suits her.

She full on smirks this time, and my belly swoops out from under me. She's so stunning it hurts; the best kind of painful.

I snatch her drink and suck it down to the dregs just to avoid any further torture at her hands—or lips. Whatever.

Lor laughs and I grin, then we get down to business.

We decide to move clear across the country, getting nearly as far from the midwest as we can. Truthfully, I'm willing to go anywhere, but Lor's star-chaser gifts are what dictate our next moves. She feels a strong inclination to go west, wanting to try an area with less frequent impact sites. I'm more than happy to get as far away as possible from Chicago's underground. Neither of us have heard or seen anything to indicate her former blackmailer is planning any sort of retaliation, but that doesn't mean he isn't. I suspect he's biding his time, letting things settle down before making a move.

All the more reason to disappear.

So we spend the next couple weeks packing up Lor's meager belongings and selling most of my eclectic collection, then set off for Oregon with Kahlo in a brand new cat backpack.

It's a blissful few days of riding through fields and then mountains with only what we can carry on our bikes. We often drive late into the night, which suits me just fine as it gives one of my surprises time to heal. Lor has a sense of freedom about her, a loosening of her limbs and softening of her face that allow her to truly shine. She's been hiding, protecting herself, and I never want her to feel like she has to live that way again.

We periodically veer off-track when Lor has a pull to follow the stars, and her bags are quickly filling with extra sacks of stardust. I don't know what she's going to do with all of it, but she seems content to have it with her for now. I offer to carry some to help distribute the added weight, but she gives me her previously packed bags instead. If she keeps it up, soon all she'll have is stardust, and I'll be in charge of the rest of her belongings.

I wonder if that means I get to decide what she wears?

A devious smirk crosses my face as we pull into a motel parking lot on the outskirts of a small town in northeastern Oregon, only a few hours from our destination. Kahlo yells their displeasure at being confined for so long, and I cringe. Poor cat did not sign up for this, although they've been doing surprisingly well.

"Just one more day," I say, reaching a hand into the backpack to rub their soft cheek.

I'm itching to tell Lor about the surprise I've been working on. Ever since she expressed a desire to go west, I've been hunting for the perfect place for us, but I want to see her face when she realizes for the first time what it means.

So I bite my cheek as I stride into the dingy lobby, and drop some cash for a room. It's not the best, or cleanest, but they allow pets, so it'll do for our last night on the road. I let Kahlo out, and set down a tin of wet food as Lor situates her many bags.

I don't know if she intends for her impromptu strip show as she drops her clothes on the way to the bathroom to be an invitation, but I'm certainly taking it that way. Little does she know, I'll be holding the rest of her clothes hostage.

"You ready to be done moving?" I ask Lor as I follow her

lead, leaving a trail of clothing on the floor, and then dropping my rings next to the sink with a series of plinks.

She shrugs in answer to my question as she sticks her hand around the curtain to test the water.

"I don't know if I'll ever be done moving," Lor says. Her eyes hold a depth of sadness I wasn't prepared for. It guts me, but I refuse to let her history dictate her future. I'll hold onto hope for both of us.

"Then we'll move," I say. "Whenever you want, wherever you want."

I step into the shower, not caring how hot or cold it is, and tug her in with me. She hisses at the chill, sending me a scathing glare while melting into the heat I push through my skin.

I swing one arm around her waist and palm her ass, then twine my other hand into her hair as she arches into me. I don't care that we should probably be wearing flip flops, or that the towels will undoubtedly be scratchy.

Having Lor in my arms, languid and trusting, is all I want or need.

Then she freezes, and her eyes latch onto the new tattoo above my heart. The one I got right before we left, that I haven't let her see yet. It's still healing, but doesn't look too bad.

Lor's eyes flick up to mine for a split-second before returning to my chest. She reaches up with one finger, but doesn't touch, tracing the air a scant inch above my skin as she follows the thin lines of the tattoo. It's all black and grey with intricate line work, and her lips part as she takes it in.

A shooting star with a fiery tail, exploding right over my heart.

"Ro," she whispers, still staring at it. "Is this..."

I tilt her chin up, and she tears her eyes away from the tattoo to meet mine.

"Yes, Starfire," I say, dipping down to brush my lips against hers. "It's for you. My star-chaser. My heart. My everything."

Her beautiful grey eyes turn glassy as they dart between mine, and her lower lip starts to tremble before she sucks it into her mouth and bites down on it. I smile, a gentle, understanding one, knowing this is a lot for her. I can't hold the words back any longer, though.

"I love you so much, Lor," I murmur.

I know she's not ready to say it back, even though I also know she feels the same. So I thread my fingers through her hair, and tip her head back into the water now that it's warmed up. Her silver locks darken, a metallic sheen bending the light as water sluices down her hair and along the gentle curves of her body.

She closes her eyes, and I take in the strength and beauty of the creature before me. It'll take time for her to stop avoiding her pain, but for now I'm happy to give her a distraction. I unwrap the stick-thin bar of soap and lather my hands, then I caress them over Lor's soft skin. Over the swallow tattoos behind her ear and down her neck, her strong arms, the curve of her waist and hips.

It feels like worship as I lower to my knees to wash her legs and feet.

When I glance up, Lor is staring down at me. Emotions flicker through her eyes, one after the other. It's like a slideshow of confusion and lust, doubt and hope. My lips tip up in a tender smile, and my eyes catch on a stream of bubbles as they flow down her body.

27

HANDS ON THE HEADBOARD

LOR

I think Ro is the one turning me insane, not the star-chasing. My thoughts swirl as his hands flex and glide across my skin. Every time I open my eyes, they go straight to his new tattoo.

The one he got for me.

I don't know how to feel about it. The anxious part of me is stuck on our future, wondering how we're going to possibly make it work, while every other molecule of my being is yearning to be here with Ro. Of course, that also sends my anxiety spinning, because what does it mean that he's here with me?

He said he loves me, but my mom was supposed to love me and she didn't stay. Could he be telling the truth? Can I trust him not to hurt me, not to leave me? Can I trust myself to...

My eyes flick back to the tattoo, and I quickly clench them closed. My avoidance is legendary by now, and to prove my own point, I force all my thoughts and worries aside to focus on the man in front of me.

I trace his other tattoos with a heated gaze—the old, safe ones—as he leans back and takes my foot in one hand. He props it on his shoulder, spreading me open as his eyes devour me, and a clenching ache moves through my core. I suck in a breath when he swipes his hands up my leg to the crease where it meets my hip, then he stops and looks up at me.

Those gorgeous hazel eyes are my undoing. His lips twitch as his eyes spark, then he drops his hands back to my ankle where he massages slow circles into my skin.

A demon, no doubt.

I groan at his teasing, and his lips slant further, enough that he can't hide the smirk this time. I narrow my eyes when I realize if it was up to him, he'd likely drag this out all night. I lick my lips and tilt my head as I survey our positions and the demon before me.

Then I tense the muscles in my leg, the one he has propped up, using it to my advantage to shove him back against the shower wall. He lets out a surprised yelp as his eyes dart up to mine.

It's my turn to smirk as I pin him to the wall, and his hand tightens its grip on my calf. I lick my lips as my heart rate speeds up, the playful glint in his eye spurring me on. I leave my foot where it is against his shoulder as I angle my body closer. His eyes flit between my face and my pussy, and I slide a gentle hand into his hair, pressing my fingers into his scalp. Ro closes his eyes and lets his head fall back into my palm.

Silly demon.

I clench my hand into a fist, gripping a handful of his hair tight enough to sting, and his startled eyes fly open to meet mine. One side of my mouth tilts up, and his eyes somehow widen even more.

"Lick me," I say, my voice coming out low and husky with desire.

Ro's eyes flash as his gaze darts back down between my

legs. He attempts to jerk forward, but he's stopped by my fist still tight in his hair. He shoots a glare up at me and I eye him, holding him away from me for another moment.

"Give me what I want," I say, narrowing my eyes. "No more teasing. No more playing. No edging."

To my surprise, Ro's face splits into a delighted grin.

"I'm not sure if I like that mantra more or less than my old one."

Before I can question what he means, he rips his hair from my grip, loops his arms around to grab my ass, and shoves his face straight between my legs. His tongue is hotter than normal when he swipes it up to circle my clit, and I gasp at the sensation.

I can feel him grinning against me as he licks and sucks, circles and nips. True to my instruction, he doesn't tease, or play, or edge me even once. It's overwhelming how good it feels.

His every touch is a demand, and my body has no choice but to obey. I'm coming hard before I know it, an inferno lighting me up inside and scorching every nerve as it crashes over me. Too much, too fast, and then it's over.

I pant above him, not sated in the least, and Ro licks his lips as he leans back.

"Not quite what you were looking for?" he says with a cheeky grin.

I press my foot hard into his shoulder, ensuring he gets the message to stay, then I drop it so both feet are on the shower floor as I step back to rinse and attempt to catch my breath.

Ro doesn't heed my nonverbal warning, of course.

He bites that infernal lip ring of his, then slowly raises his body as he steps forward, looming over me. This diabolical man can't let me have one win, can he? I tip my head back to glare at him, pinching my lips to prevent my smile from answering his.

Much as I pretend to loathe it, I love our games. He brings out a playful side of me I didn't know I had.

I eye him warily as my brain jumps from one thing to the next, trying to figure out what he's going to do. Before I land on any likely scenarios, Ro scoops me under the ass, latches his mouth onto my nipple with a hard suck, and steps out of the shower.

Without turning it off or even touching a towel, he strides into the bedroom and tosses me onto the bed. I'm still bouncing when his hands are on my hips, pushing me around so I'm flat on my back with my head hanging off the edge of the bed facing him.

Upside down.

I open my mouth to—I don't know—ask what he's doing, protest soaking the blankets, try to inhale after the air was knocked out of me? Whatever it was going to be is interrupted by Ro shoving his cock between my lips.

I suck in a quick breath through my nose, and then he's pumping into me, smooth and hot along my tongue. I suppress a groan at the feeling, the taste of him, the demand in every stroke between my lips.

Ro's fingers twist my nipple, and his other hand settles along my jaw and throat, feeling himself as he fills me. I moan at the overwhelming sensations, the rough treatment turning me on more than I would have thought possible.

My pussy clenches on nothing, a most unwelcome sensation, so I reach down between my legs to bury my own fingers in it. Ro snags my wrist, then both of my hands are shackled in one of his.

To my horror, I whimper.

Ro grins and tightens his grip on my wrists, then slowly pushes his cock further, nudging it into my throat. The lack of oxygen and upside down position are making my head tingle, but all I can focus on is my throbbing clit and the emptiness I need filled. I can't move to fix it, and more fiery incredulity sweeps through my veins.

I try to protest, but Ro is still filling my mouth, so all that comes out is a rumble in my throat that he seems to enjoy, if his answering groan is any indication. My face flames with indignation. I'm incensed, and so turned on I'm pretty sure I'm dripping down my ass.

"You're perfect, Starfire," Ro grunts as he pumps into my mouth. "So pretty and weeping for me, desperate to be filled."

His dirty words are scorching, and I try to squirm out of his grasp as I clench my legs together and twist my hips, desperate for any sort of friction.

"So needy," he says, then moans when I try to speak around his cock again.

I'm afraid I might resort to begging if he were able to understand me.

"Yeah, keep telling me how much you like it. That's my good girl, taking me deep in your throat." His hand squeezes my neck, and I practically convulse as I try to hold back a gag while my body breaks out in delicious shivers.

"Fuck, Lor." Ro's voice is decadent, sweeping under the rush of blood in my ears to send more flaming need through my body.

"Gonna come all over you, mark you as mine."

I'm only half listening at this point, as I've managed to find a position that I can clench and rock against my own legs to get the tiniest spark of stimulation. It's not enough to come, but with Ro's hands on me, restraining me and controlling my breath and tweaking my nipples, it's almost enough to get close.

I suck in a startled gasp when he pulls out of my mouth, a rush of cum landing on my lips before he releases my throat to stroke his cock. He groans deep in his chest, and I can feel his eyes on me as he shoots ropes of hot liquid across my body. He covers my breasts and belly as I heave for breath, coughing as air scalds my sore throat.

"Gorgeous," Ro says, panting. "And all fucking mine."

He reaches down, and I think he's going to clean me off, but instead he rubs his cum into my skin. He swirls it around my breasts, then swipes some onto his fingers and shoves them in my mouth. I groan at the salty taste, and my back arches, his possessiveness inflaming my need.

"If I let go, will you be a good girl and ride my face?" Ro says.

My instinct is to snarl in reply.

The thought of being a *good girl*—of doing what he says —prickles along my skin, but the need thrumming through my body wins out. I glare at him as he pulls me up, my body somehow both tense and lax at the same time. He maneuvers me on top of him so I'm straddling his lap as he leans against the headboard. Then he grins and pinches my nipple before sliding down the bed until my pussy hovers over his face.

"Hands on the headboard," he says, nipping at my sensitive inner thighs.

My legs tremble, and I obey without thought, leaning forward to grip the top of the headboard as he pulls me down to sit on him. Ro sticks out his tongue, swipes it up my center, then sucks my clit into his mouth. I can barely focus as I look down at him through dazed eyes, his dark-rimmed gaze intent on my face while the lust swirling through me mixes with too many emotions.

"Take your pleasure, Starfire," he growls into my skin.

And finally, I have all-encompassing, searing relief.

WE HEAD out the next morning after the best sleep of my life. I've been looking over my shoulder the entire trip, disbelief painting the landscape around me every time I fail to find one of my former evil boss' goons following us.

It makes anger boil in my chest, the fact he's put so little work into holding onto me after the years of threats and emotional torture. I don't know if or when I'll be able to fully relax and trust that we've gotten away, but at least I have hope sparking in my chest again. A demon bringing hope... Who would have thought?

I glance over to see Kahlo being wrangled into the cat-backpack Ro bought for them, then slung onto his back. They hiss at everyone we pass. I roll my eyes at the creature, then startle when I realize I'm already smiling at the devilish duo riding next to me. I blink and turn my attention back to the mountains and massive trees as we make our way toward Portland.

Ro weaves through the city and I follow, unsure where he's going. He finally pulls over next to a park along the river in what looks like a nice downtown area. I follow his lead and kill the engine, then pull off my helmet.

"What are we doing?" I ask.

"I heard they have great donuts here," he says. "Figured we could stop for brunch on our way through town. Check it out a bit before we get to our final stop."

He grins and I look around, then my stomach rumbles.

"Fine," I say, realizing donuts actually sound pretty incredible right now. "I wish you'd tell me where we're going, though."

I'm pouting, and I hate it.

Ro swings his arm around my neck and tugs me into his side. He nuzzles his nose into my hair, then kisses my temple before sliding his arm down to clasp his hand around mine. He's really very sweet and affectionate, and I have no idea how to return any of it.

My face flushes and I look down, a small smile playing on

my lips. Ro doesn't comment on my reaction, instead angling his back toward me.

"How's Kahlo doing?"

I glance at our cat and they stare up at me with big, curious green eyes.

"Seems fine," I say with a shrug.

Ro snorts. "Very convincing, I'm so relieved."

He shrugs off the bag and holds it in front of him so he can see Kahlo, then he starts cooing to them. "Hey little bug, how you doing in there?"

The cat freaking meows back at him and raises a paw, pushing it against the clear bubble of the backpack. Ro places two fingers on the other side of the material like they're trying to touch through it, and the damn cat's entire being somehow relaxes.

My heart melts and I start to smile, then screw my face into a scowl. I cannot handle this, and I refuse to admit why. Never will I think of a cat or a demon as cute.

That is *not* happening.

"I know, you want out. You're gonna have to wait just a little longer though, okay? I promise it'll be worth it. You'll see. Maybe you can even have a little sneaky taste of donut," Ro whispers the last sentence and I close my eyes, taking a deep breath to ground myself.

Can I really survive living with those two?

Yes.

My heart beats the word. Yes, yes, yes.

I start walking, no idea where I'm going, but I can't stand still anymore. I've only ever experienced—and expected—bad things for myself. I don't know how to handle so much good in my life. It feels unsafe, even though logically I know that's not true.

Ro carefully swings the bag back over his shoulders, then catches me in a few quick strides. He slips his hand around mine again and gives it a squeeze, shooting me a knowing smile. My heart eases, and my lungs loosen.

Then he tugs me around a corner and into a donut shop.

After I've eaten my fill of sugary sweets, and Ro has finished letting Kahlo lick the remnants of glazed bacon bits off his fingers, we're walking back to our bikes. Ro is bouncing with excitement, and Kahlo is protesting loudly enough that I can hear his furious mrows.

"Okay," I say, snagging one strap of the backpack so Ro is forced to stop. "Let me take that, you're going to kill them before we even arrive."

Ro grins and bounces in place as he hands over the cat with far too much giddy excitement at my care for Kahlo's safety.

"It's not a big deal," I grumble, carefully threading my arms through the loops.

We walk past an ethical blood bank I hadn't noticed before, and I do a double take when I realize it's for people to sell their blood so vampires have a reliable source of sustenance. I blink, stumbling a step as Ro tugs me along behind him.

Then we're back on our bikes. I drive extra carefully with Kahlo on my back as I follow Ro's lead again. He zooms through the city, continuing west as we hit more forest and winding roads. Then he's slowing, pulling onto a narrow dirt drive in the middle of nowhere.

I look around, curious and feeling lighter than I have in years. The trees are wide and tall, with light dappling through the canopy, and there are dense ferns covering the forest floor along both sides of the trail. It opens into a clearing with a small cottage set in the middle of it.

My mouth falls open, and I follow Ro on autopilot as he parks and shuts off his bike, then swings off it. My movements mirror his, my brain stunned into silence at the image before me.

The house is a rich brown color that matches the trunks of the trees. A few stairs lead up to a wide porch with double doors and windows on either side, dark green shutters framing them.

"Ro?" I say, my voice cracking as I turn to look at him with wide eyes.

His eager expression softens into a look that makes my bruised heart thump with yearning.

"This is ours, Starfire," he says. His voice is soft, almost tentative.

I search his face, not sure what I'm looking for, and then turn back to the quaint cottage before me. It's like something straight out of a fairytale, although perhaps in need of a bit of work.

I blink—hard—but it's still there when my eyes open again. So I reach over and pinch my own arm.

"Ouch." I grimace, then break into a wide grin as I turn back to Ro.

"It's ours?" I say. Did this absolute maniac seriously buy us a house? "How?"

Ro nods and bites his lip, then raises one eyebrow. "Yeah, you know how my parents are. They helped me out. They just want us to be happy." He shrugs, like parents caring and wanting the best for their child isn't incomprehensible. "Want to check it out?"

The inside is gorgeous. With an A-frame roof, the front door opens up to an airy living space. Two stories of windows look out over the small, overgrown meadow. A tall stone fireplace takes up one wall, and there's a massive, colorful painting hanging on the other. I look at Ro in question.

"Frida Kahlo," he says.

My heart skips a beat, and Kahlo meows from my back. I

twist around and bend down, unzipping the bag to let them explore our new home.

It's nearly off the grid, with only electricity and running water, spotty cell service, no internet or cable. Practically nothing to connect us to the rest of society.

I love it.

There are skylights in multiple rooms, and the bedroom has an entire wall of windows. I'll be able to see the night sky from any angle, and nearly any room. My eyes burn as I blink back tears.

"It's perfect," I say, turning to Ro as he envelopes me in his arms.

28

STAR-CHASERS
ALWAYS LOSE THEIR...

October, 2025: We've been here for nearly three months now, living in the middle of the woods in a cottage where I can always see the stars. And I think... I wonder if I might be okay.

LOR

I'm curled up in an oversized, blue velvet armchair, staring out the window at the rain. Ro convinced me to give therapy a try, and now we both attend weekly. I haven't decided how I feel about it yet though, and dredged up emotions swirl through me as I try to relax after my last session.

There's a dried yellow flower, a sparkly stone, and a metal jigger from Tempo sitting on the windowsill. Trinkets that Ro has collected from our time together. We've done a lot of work getting this house fixed up, and now it's the first place that has ever felt like a home to me.

Fat raindrops hit the sprawling fern leaves beneath the trees, and occasionally one will roll down the window in front of me. It's peaceful, something I never thought I'd experience.

The chair is a second-hand piece Ro ordered last week, and it's become a constant battle between myself and Kahlo over who gets to use it. Today, Kahlo is happily curled up on the back of the couch behind Ro. He got a bartending job in the city as he explores if and what else he might want to do, but it's his day off, and we were planning to go star-chasing. Then the rain hit and we decided to wait it out instead.

A decision I never thought I'd be able to make.

The urge to follow the stars hasn't been weighing on me like it used to. For one thing, I feel the pull much less often here, so my idea of moving somewhere the stars fall less frequently seems to have worked.

But I think it has to do with Ro, too. Even when I do feel the pull, it's not as urgent. Ro has shared some of his therapist's techniques and coping skills with me, which help, but he's also made me question everything I thought I knew.

He thinks I can embrace being a star-chaser, like he's embracing being a demon. A few months ago I would have denied it was possible, but now... I'm not so sure. I wonder if the star-chaser madness was due to always being alone. Or maybe because we never knew what to do with the stardust when we found it.

It's not like being a star-chaser comes with an instruction manual.

Ro encourages me to meditate, to let my instincts guide me. I hated it at first, but now I think there might be some magic in it. After every star fall, when we get back home with the stardust—my ancestors' remains—I let the universe tell me what to do. Most often, I'm inclined to mix the stardust into the earth in a special garden we have along the edge of the tree line. Sometimes I follow the urge to sprinkle it through the trees deep in the forest, or into a river that runs about a mile back.

Everywhere the stardust touches, after being reverently

spread or mixed into the earth, beautiful plants grow. Flowers that glow in the dark, thick moss that covers the ground in a protective layer, trees that grow far faster than normal and have strange, hollow centers like they're meant to house tiny creatures.

I don't know what to make of it, but it feels right like nothing else ever has. It helps me feel settled, a sense of comfort, like I'm giving myself and my people a protected home where we can always see the sky. A home where we can be together in the only way possible.

Inevitably, my thoughts turn to my mom, and my heart skips a beat when I wonder where she is. Kahlo, perhaps sensing the distressing turn of my thoughts, rises in a languid stretch, then pads over and jumps into my lap. They give me a threatening side eye before kneading my legs and settling into a fluffy cat loaf. I crook a small smile; we're learning to show our appreciation for each other in more healthy ways now.

I haven't heard from my mom in many months, longer than normal. I have no way of reaching out to her, as her old phone number is disconnected. I hope she's okay, and I wish she'd call so I could tell her what I learned. I don't know if she'd listen, and I don't know if I'm ready to talk to her yet, but I want her to be okay. I haven't forgiven her for abandoning me, but I think I might be able to, in time.

I don't know if my anxiety will ever fully go away, but I already feel less inclined to madness with Ro by my side—or, more accurately, stalking me.

Because yeah, that hasn't stopped.

Although it tends to be more of a planned stalking these days, rather than whatever unhinged nonsense he was doing back in Chicago. I truly don't know what I'd do without him. If I'm honest with myself, I know he saved my life.

He's like a bridge holding all the different parts of me together, turning something I despised and resented about myself into something I look forward to. He's somehow able to twist the most mundane or uncontrollable moments into joyful memories, and it makes my heart skip a beat for a different reason when I think about our plans to go star-chasing after the rain lets up.

I look down at Kahlo when they start purring, a tiny motor rumbling on top of my legs. Then I glance at Ro, with his bright green nails and glinting piercings. His easy grin and demonic urges. He's a contradiction I can't get enough of.

When he first showed me this place, and I expressed my worry about not being able to stay in one spot forever, he made it easy.

"We can always go, and we can always come back." He said it so simply, so matter of fact, that I had no choice but to accept it as truth. Those words have become my lifeline, my mantra. A consistent reminder of his love, and devotion, and acceptance.

"You want to head out after we eat? Looks like the rain is done for now," Ro says, his eager voice interrupting my reflections.

I glance outside to see sunlight streaming through the trees.

"Yeah," I say, turning to narrow my eyes at Ro's wicked grin. My lips twitch up in an answering smile of my own. "Let's go."

Ro

My stomach flips as my heart races with excitement. I've been planning this outing for weeks, figuring out how I can make it work with the knowledge that I can't plan where the stars will fall. It needs to be flexible, but still cover all the bases for safety, and I think I've got it.

Lor throws a suspicious look my way as I dump extra food into Kahlo's bowl, then drop a kiss on their head.

"No parties!" I say, then amend my statement. "Actually, you can party, just don't wreck the house."

"We're not going to be gone that long," Lor says, eyeing me.

I hum a noncommittal noise as I grab her hand and our go-bags, then skip out the door to our bikes. We take off down the gravel driveway, winding our way through trees and mountains as Lor follows the pull in her blood, and I follow her. My mind wanders as my body sways on autopilot with the movements of my bike, but I can't contain the grin stretching across my face.

I never expected to create a life like this, one I'd be happy with. Where I like who I am, and have learned to work with my demon urges instead of suppressing them. They're mostly satisfied by our "stalking" games, plus setting controlled fires when we go camping or stardust hunting.

Lor loves curling up against my warm flames; she claims they feel different than a regular fire. It's helped me realize I can do good with my urges, that my demonic side doesn't define who I am as a person, and I don't have to change who I am to be good. That I can embrace all parts of me equally.

My parents are just pleased I've found someone and am happy. I realize now how they were modeling for me all along that being demons isn't bad, but none of us knew how to handle my inclinations for fire and stealing. They also ask far too many questions about my sex life, and love to give unsolicited advice.

I no longer wish I was a sex demon like them, though, because if that was the case, I wouldn't have ended up here with Lor. I tighten my hold on the handlebars as excitement floods my veins.

Finally, she pulls off the road into a forest of towering

trees. I swear, every time we drive somewhere new, the trees are bigger than the last place. I take in the surroundings, my brain whirring as Lor pulls over and kills the engine, then saunters off into the trees. Her tight black pants look painted on, the curve of her ass making my mouth water in the dappled sunlight as I follow her further into the forest.

I force myself to look away so I can keep track of where we are this time; I don't want to get lost later. After what has to be at least a mile of weaving through trees, Lor finally comes to a halt alongside a rushing river. The impact site is obvious. A decent sized crater disrupts the surrounding greenery like an open wound.

Lor is already pulling out a cloth sack and spade. There's nothing I can do to help with this part of it, so instead I start plotting.

Trying to look casual, I stick my hands in my pockets and slowly walk around. I check the nearby areas to see if there are any distinguishable landmarks, widening the perimeter of my circle as I go. There's a grouping of boulders near a small ravine that looks treacherous and I grimace, making a mental note to make sure we don't go that way.

I try the opposite direction, walking along the river as it curves away from Lor's fallen star. I push through the thick foliage, then stumble when I nearly face-plant into a serene pond. The river takes another turn here, but it's created a small, secluded oxbow lake alongside it. My eyes widen as I take in the picturesque setting. There's even an open grassy area along one side that's been dried by the sun already.

It's perfect.

I'm giddy with anticipation as I swing my backpack off and unload my supplies. I stamp down some of the overgrown grass, then spread out a blanket and weigh it down with a couple rocks and my pack. I flop down, and am instantly surrounded by grass with a clear view of the clouds above, tree branches fringing the edges of the sky. I nod with satisfaction and jump back up, snagging the last thing I need from my bag.

I scope out the rest of the areas surrounding Lor's crash site just to be sure it's safe, and then make my way back to her. The cloth sack filled with the newly collected stardust is set to the side of the turned up earth, and she's walking around with her hands on her hips, a look of fierce concentration on her face.

29

A SURPRISE ENCOUNTER

Ro

"Got it all?" I ask.

Lor barely glances at me as she nods absently, her gaze tracking across the dirt one last time. I snag her bag of stardust and loop it over my shoulder, then grin as I let the wicked glint of my demon enter my eye. Lor's gaze widens as she takes a step back, but I dart forward and snatch her wrist. I spin her around, folding her arms across her chest and banding one of mine around her to hold her in place.

"Not so fast, Starfire," I murmur.

She shivers against me and my entire body heats.

I light a small fireball and hold it out in front of her, then slowly bring it closer to her body. Lor presses her back into my chest; we both know I would never hurt her, but it's human instinct to recoil from danger.

I dance the flame across my fingers, then turn my palm up and let it rest in the center of my hand. Her breathing starts to slow again as she settles, and I grin with wicked satisfaction.

I snap my hand closed, fisting the fire to put it out and Lor jumps in my hold at the sudden movement and her heartrate spikes again, higher than it was before. I can feel it in her wrist where I'm gripping her against me, and see it in the pulse thrumming in her neck. I tighten my grip on her as I lean down again.

I want to consume her, but first I want to catch her.

"Run, little starchaser," I growl into her ear.

As soon as my hold loosens, Lor darts out of it. I cackle with glee as Lor sprints away, her hair flowing behind her. I enjoy a good chase, but that's not the purpose of today, even though Lor might think it is as I take off after her.

I laugh as I catch glimpses of her silver hair flashing between the trees. Thanks to my earlier casing, I know the paths she's likely to take, and I catch up to her within minutes.

Lor is breathing hard and her pupils are dilated, but she grins when she catches sight of me dashing through the trees to her left. She ducks to the right, towards the river, and I whoop with wild abandon. I'm right behind her, within lunging distance, when she looks over her shoulder and stumbles. It's exactly what I was waiting for, and I pounce.

I twist to take the fall with Lor landing on top of me, then we roll through the ferns and undergrowth until I have her pinned to the spongy moss beneath me. I flip her onto her stomach as she lets out a breathless laugh.

"Ro," she says, panting. "What—"

I unfold the black bag I've been hiding, and whip it over her head.

She shrieks, her hands flying up to grapple with the edge of the bag, but I snatch her wrists and tug them behind her back. Lor's chest heaves and I lean forward, hovering over her.

I savor this moment, more satisfied and excited than I've ever been as my demon side thrills in the capture. Leaning down, I lick a long, slow stripe along the side of her neck where the skin peeks out beneath the bag.

Lor shivers, and I groan at the feel of her tight body

against mine. My blood heats as it thrums through me, and a heady euphoria sweeps my inhibitions away.

"You wanna play?" I whisper against her skin, sending goosebumps scattering down her neck as I stroke my free hand down her arm in a deceptively gentle caress.

Lor swallows hard as her breathing picks up.

"Yes," she says, voice ragged. "I want to play."

Admittedly, the chuckle I let out is more demonic than usual, so I can't blame her for struggling a bit in response. My hand is loose around hers though, and she hasn't used her safe word or movement, so I'm not worried.

She agreed to this, after all, she just didn't know when it was going to happen.

I release my grip on her to Velcro the bag around her neck, ensuring it's loose enough that she could get out if she wanted, but not so slack that it'll fall off.

My grin is wicked as I let my inner demon take control. I pull us both to standing, then I spin her to face me and toss her over my shoulder. Her startled screech of protest is music to my ears as I stand, hook her stardust bag around my elbow, and start walking into the woods with my trophy. My arm tightens over her thighs as I hold her to me.

"Ro!" Lor yells, her voice covered by the bag and muffled against my back.

"What's that?" I say. "Can't quite hear you!"

Her cute fists pound against my lower back, and I cackle in response. Then I turn my head to the side and bite her sexy ass. It would be more satisfying if she wasn't wearing pants. I pause, considering.

"Can I take your pants off first?"

"Oh my god! No!"

Ah well, it was worth a shot. I pick up my pace again, carefully stalking my way through the thick foliage along the river.

LOR

Why did I agree to this? Being carried over someone's shoulder is not as fun or sexy as it sounded. I should have known this game was coming, though. Ro's been acting cagey all morning, not nearly as overbearingly cheerful as he usually is.

Him avoiding me should have been my first clue he had something like this planned. We didn't even finish the conversation when we first tried to talk about it a couple months ago. We both got so turned on that we ended up fucking on the rug right where we had been standing.

We agreed to a 'no touching' rule for the duration of the conversation the second time we approached it. But going through with it in real life is a whole different experience. My breath is hot inside the bag, and I can only catch faint glimmers of light through the dark fabric.

My face heats when I imagine what we look like in the fading light of the evening. Me slung over his shoulder with my arms dangling, a bag over my head, and him probably stomping proudly through the trees like he won some sort of olympic medal.

I scoff and roll my eyes, even though he can't see it.

"Got something to say, Starfire?" Ro jostles my legs, then palms my ass, squeezing one cheek and then the other.

"No," I huff, then wheeze when he stops suddenly, putting unexpected pressure on my stomach. His hand tightens on my thighs as his back muscles flex against me.

There's a strange sounding growl, but before I can even register the sound, Ro speaks.

"Oh, hello. I didn't see you, we're just... Uh..."

Is someone else here? Mortified, I yank the bag halfway off

my head and brace an arm against his lower back, propping myself up so I can peer around him.

"Ro? What's going on?"

He shifts to the side slightly, probably trying to hide me, but the angle lets me peek underneath his arm. There's a man staring at us, a look of anger slowly turning to confusion as his eyes widen. He could be any sort of person or paranormal, and the fact he's out here in the middle of the woods... My throat goes dry as possible scenarious, each one worse than the last, flit through my mind. I raise my hand to give Ro our safe-word-signal when...

Some sort of gazelle bounds up next to the mystery man.

I blink, then squint at it. I'm pretty sure that animal isn't native to the pacific northwest.

Then the gazelle shifts into a human. A very naked woman, to be precise. My eyes widen in surprise, but the man quickly shoves her behind him with another growl. Is he some sort of shifter too? All he's done is growl at us so far, so it seems like a good guess.

The woman pokes her head around the man's arm as she glances around, taking in the situation. Her dainty fingers press tiny dents into his forearm as she tugs at him.

"Ash?" she says.

She looks up at the man who still has his eyes narrowed at Ro and me, and the moment feels surreal. I guess we do look suspicious. To be fair, he does too, though.

Is this real life? Me, being pretend kidnapped with a black bag barely hanging onto my hair as my demon lights a flame in his hand behind him, clearly preparing for the worst. Her, naked in the middle of the woods with a big, angry creature of some sort protecting her.

I laugh, a single, loud guffaw, and everyone jumps. I glance at the naked woman, the first to recover, and she breaks into a mischievous smile. Her hands creep around the man's sides to curl up over his shoulders as she rests her cheek against his biceps. Her blonde wavy hair floats alongside them in the stray breeze.

"Uh, Lor?" Ro whispers.

"Aww," naked girl stage whispers, intentionally loud enough for us to hear. "Are you making new friends, Ash?"

The angry man looks stricken, like he just learned he was fatally poisoned or something. He glowers at her, a gruff "no" punching out of his chest.

That makes me snort-laugh again, but this time it doesn't stop. I feel like I'm outside my body. Disconnected from reality. I mean seriously, what the actual fuck is happening?

I drop my hands and my face hits Ro's back as I lose control, laughing hysterically. Is *this* what finally does me in? Playing Ro's demon games in the middle of the woods and apparently *not being the only ones doing it?*

Un-*fucking*-believable.

"Hey," naked-girl says. "I'm Raya, and this is Asher."

I can hear Ro's answering grin as he douses the hidden flame and replies. "Nice to meet you! I'm Ro, and this is Lor."

He pats my ass in what would be a fond gesture in any other context, but here it comes off as possessive with a side of demeaning.

And now, I'm the one growling.

I can't believe that sound comes out of me, but who does he think he is? I thrash in his hold, but he tightens his grip with a low chuckle. I flatten my hands on his back and throw a glare up at him as I twist around to look at naked-girl, whatever her name was.

"I guess our game is intruding on your game, huh?" she says, a wide smile stretching across her face.

A surprised huff leaves my mouth as my face swivels between her and Ro. This woman is like a spirit twin to him, isn't she? I grimace. Too much sunshine in one spot.

Unimpressed, I meet her partner's eyes, taking in his lack of amusement in the situation as well.

"Yes," I grumble. "You are."

Then my arms give up for a final time, and I flop limply into Ro's back.

"Sorry about that!" she chirps. "We'll just go a couple miles over that way, right Ash?"

"Perfect, we're heading this direction," Ro replies. I assume he points or gestures.

"Awesome, we'll stay out of your hair. And hey, cute setup over there!"

"Thanks for understanding," Ro says, far too chipper in this situation. "Have fun, new friends!"

"You too!" Raya says, then she's back in her gazelle form and leaping away into the trees. A blur follows moments later, one I just barely catch out of the corner of my eye before the bag shifts and covers my eyes again. I blink. That was... a vampire?

Ooookay, then. I heave a sigh, accepting that I have no idea what is happening anymore.

"Well, they seemed nice!" Ro says, then continues on his way to whatever unknown destination he has in mind.

30

WHO IS TEASING WHO?

Ro

I try to hurry the rest of the way, grimacing when I imagine how uncomfortable it must be for Lor to stay in this position for so long. She hasn't complained, though, so she must be doing okay. Those two—the shifter and the vampire —seemed like loads of fun. I wish I had gotten one of their numbers... I wonder what game they were playing?

My mind returns to the firm ass next to my face, and I trace my fingers up and down Lor's calf, carefully stepping over roots and around low-hanging branches. Soon enough, I break through the undergrowth, and cross the small meadow. Long shadows stretch as the sky darkens, and the evening birds call back and forth beyond us in the trees. The river burbles faintly in the distance, while fireflies blink over the swaying grasses.

I sling Lor down from my shoulder, then settle her on her back in the middle of the blanket.

She's pouting, I can tell. I grin and bite my lip, fiddling with my lip ring as my eyes devour her. She's so fucking pretty, with her bared stomach and long legs, breasts heaving and hair sparkling across the blanket, a silvery halo in the setting sun. I'm going to show her how good life can be, convince her every single day that she deserves good things. Prove to her that she's strong, and resilient, and worthy.

Someday, she'll believe those things about herself, just like I do. I mean, she has to put up with a demon day in and day out, so how could she not be incredible?

"Ro?" Lor's voice startles me back to the present moment.

"I'm here," I say.

I kick my boots off, then tug hers off, too. My demon side preens, pleased beyond measure that I've successfully kidnapped my soulmate—who trusts and plays with me—and will be claiming her under the stars. I slip my hands up her legs, over the tight fabric of her pants to the waistband. Lor sucks in a breath as my fingers skim her navel, raising goose-bumps in their wake.

I lean in to press light kisses to her bare stomach as I unbutton her pants, then strip them down her legs. She took her riding jacket off earlier and left it with her bike, so she's laid before me in a black lace crop top and black string bikini panties. Her skin glows in the evening light, a stark contrast to the dark clothing.

"So pretty," I murmur, gliding my hand along Lor's collar-bone. "All mine."

She tries to steady her breathing, but I know her senses are heightened from the bag covering her eyes. I follow the path of my fingers with my tongue and teeth, nipping and licking as I pull down one strap of her top and expose her breast to the cooling air. Her nipple tightens, and I suck it into my mouth, bathing it in heat as I'm rewarded with Lor's hiss of pleasure.

Her hands tangle in my hair and I close my eyes, reveling in her touch, her presence, her willingness to give me this. I flick my lip ring against her nipple, and her fingers clench, pulling my hair and stinging my scalp. I grin into her breast as I tug the other strap down, restricting her arms.

Lor grumbles under her breath, but it's just for show. She's so cute.

I drag my teeth around the curve of her breast, then lick along the side before circling her nipple. She arches into me, begging without words, and I have no reason not to give her what we both want. I suck that nipple too, rolling my tongue around it before tightening my teeth and tugging.

Her whimpers and moans are better than the most decadent food. I kind of want to record them, set it as my ringtone, play it in the background while I cook or read or...

Lor's hips jut up into mine as she tugs on my hair, pulling me—again—back to earth with her. I debate what to do with her top, then decide to figure it out later when she presses her hot pussy into my groin. I slip my fingers under the silky fabric and yank it down her legs, then I quickly shed my own clothes and pile them up on the blanket next to us. Lor bends her knees and opens her legs, baring herself to me.

I groan, and dive down. She knows I can't resist feasting on her, and I don't even try. I hook my arms under her thighs, throwing her legs over my shoulders as I palm her ass and squeeze, spreading her open and lifting her up to my face. I flatten my tongue and lick from asshole to clit in one long swipe.

Her head shoots off the blanket as she chokes on an inhale, then she slams it back down with a drawn out groan. I smile against her slick folds, then work my way back down while she gasps for breath. I circle my tongue around her puckered hole, licking and sucking as she writhes in my hold. I slip one hand up to toy with her clit as I eat her out, happily driving her wild while she can't even see anything.

I could be anyone. I'm not; I'm hers, and she knows it, but

still. The thought is there, and I'm sure it's entered her mind, too.

Lor's back hole clenches and relaxes as I tease it with my tongue, then press the tip inside.

"Ro," she gasps, pressing further into me.

I suck and lick, not letting up as my fingers circle her clit. She's pulsing beneath me, her breath hard and choppy, loud inhales that break the music of nature around us. She's close, and I want her to come before I fuck her.

I shove my tongue in her asshole and pinch her clit, rolling it between my fingers. She comes with a shuddering gasp, her entire body clenching as her pussy throbs, wetness leaking from it to meet my circling tongue. I lick it up and gentle my touch until she collapses, panting beneath me.

Then I drop a kiss on her clit, grab her hips, and twist, flipping her onto her stomach. She goes easily, my satiated star-chaser, but I'm not nearly done with her yet. I pull her hips up, but she keeps her shoulders and head down on the blanket. I guess she's more worn out than I thought, but no matter. I don't mind working hard for our pleasure.

I settle behind her on my knees, nudging hers wider as I roll on a condom, then slide the head of my cock up and down her pussy.

"Ro," she says, an underlying note has me focusing in on her. I tear my eyes from her perfect ass to see her fingers fumbling with the bag covering her head.

I drop my dick and lean forward, batting her hands out of the way so I can rip the Velcro apart. I sneak a hand under her cheek to lift her head as I tug the bag off, and her dazed eyes flutter open to meet mine. I stroke my fingers through her silky hair, inspecting her face and neck to be sure the cloth didn't chafe or irritate her skin. A crooked smile spreads across her face as I look her over.

Not finding anything to be concerned about, I crush my

lips to hers. Lor's tongue battles mine, and I grin into the kiss. She hasn't lost her spark yet, my Starfire, and hopefully she never will. Gently, I set her head back down, and pull away to kneel behind her again.

She sighs, then wiggles her goddamn ass like I'm taking too long.

I swing my palm back and smack it, a crack ringing through the air at the sharp contact. Lor jolts with a surprised squeak.

"Act like a brat, get treated like a brat," I say, then spank the other cheek for good measure.

Red handprints bloom on her pale skin, and I lean down to do what I wanted to earlier. I bite right on top of one red mark, hard enough to leave tiny dents in her skin when I pull back.

"Mmm." A pleased sound rumbles up from my chest at seeing my mark on her ass.

Then she snorts a laugh, ruining my satisfying moment of possession. I narrow my eyes, certain she can feel my disapproving glare when she smirks into the blanket. She's not even looking at me.

I slam my cock into her pussy, effectively wiping both the smile off her face and all coherent thoughts out of my head. She's hot and tight, slick and perfect.

Made for me.

LOR

"Fuuuuuck, Lor," Ro grinds the words out between his teeth as his hips pull back. A slow drag, forcing me to feel every inch of him as my pussy tries to suck his cock back in.

"Shit, you feel good." His hands clench on my hips, holding me in place. I don't think I could move if I wanted to.

He thrusts back in, overwhelming hardness filling me until I can't breathe. Then he starts up a relentless rhythm, in and out, over and over, punching into the perfect spot deep inside that not even his fingers can reach.

I try, but there's no holding in my moans of pleasure. He may not have been born a sex demon, but I wouldn't think he was lying if he told me he was one. The man knows exactly what to do to drive me wild.

Ro lets go of my hips with one hand, skimming it up my back and then clenching it in my hair. He yanks my head back, baring my neck to him. He folds his body over mine, hips circling and rocking with his cock buried deep inside. His presence is overwhelming, pushing every other thought out of my head until I'm consumed with him.

Then his lips meet my neck right above my pulse point and he sucks hard, leaving a hickey and marking me as his. It feels so good, his possessive streak, his hard cock filling me up, his lips and hands all over my body.

"Are you going to come for me, Starfire? Clamp down on my cock with that perfect pussy and claim me as yours? Let me feel it, show me how good you feel with my cock filling you up."

My pleasure builds, a relentless heat firing along every nerve and pooling in my core. Each word from his mouth, every rock and stroke he makes, fuels it until I'm ready to explode.

"Yes, there Ro, don't stop." I chant his name, a hazy impression of demands leaving my lips as the world disappears around me, and every sense is focused on the blinding pleasure he's stoking. "More, more, I'm—"

It crashes over me, a pulsing wave of euphoria that rips a drawn-out moan from my lips as the most spectacular feeling overwhelms me. Ro's cock hardens and thickens as he roars his own release, pumping deep inside me. It sends me spinning even higher. Wave after wave, the orgasm flows through my body, my nerves sizzling and muscles clenching until it releases me, and I fall back into reality. My body melts into the blanket, languid with satisfaction.

Ro strokes a hand across my face, brushing the sweaty strands of hair from my forehead.

"You good, Starfire?"

"I'm good, Ro," I murmur, fluttering my eyes open.

He's hovering over me, glowing golden eyes staring into mine with the most reverent expression of devotion I've ever seen. He's so open with his feelings, so vulnerable and soft. I try to meet him there, forcing myself to leave my walls down so he can see me too.

He smiles, a tender thing, then leans down to press an equally gentle kiss to my forehead. Ro pulls out and takes care of himself, then flops down next to me and pulls me into his side, rearranging my body until we're situated how he wants.

I'm on my side, one leg thrown over his hip and my head pillowed on his shoulder with his arm around my back, holding me to him. He wiggles a little, getting comfortable, then lets out a long, slow sigh.

I quirk an amused smile as I glance up at him. His eyes are on the sky above, but his lips hold the traces of his perpetual joy.

Sensing my gaze, he glances down at me, then tightens his hold.

"I love you, Lor," he says.

I stare at him. He knows those words are dangerous. He knows I've never known how to love, or how to accept love. But he's also insisted that I'm learning. I cling to that hope, his belief that I can do this. That *we* can do this, together.

My throat is dry, but I lick my lips, refusing to look away from his knowing gaze.

"I love you too, Ro."

He grins, satisfaction sparking in his eyes as he squeezes me, then jerks his chin up. My eyes follow his gaze to the sky where the stars are out in full force.

My heart yearns for them, but it yearns for Ro now, too.

His hand is warm on my waist, his body steady and solid under mine. I ground myself to him, then find that hum in my veins. The song of the stars that resonates through my blood into my very soul.

It sounds different than it used to. Less demanding, less sorrowful, more welcoming.

I sigh as I sink into it, allowing the stars to pull me into their embrace as the twinkling lights fill my vision, knowing I have Ro here with me—a rock tethering me to earth.

It's a new feeling, this version of star-chasing. I don't think anyone in my family has felt this way before, but I'm doing my best to record it in case there are other star-chasers out there who are lost, like I was. I'm learning that my mom and grandmother weren't right, maybe not even about that one thing that I was convinced was truth.

Maybe not all star-chasers go mad. Maybe it is possible to trust, to find happiness and hope.

To enjoy our life here on earth, only distantly connected to the stars.

To love.

I don't know what I did to deserve this kind of pleasure—the all-encompassing, soul-deep kind—let alone a life with this man. Maybe it's recompense for generations of trauma, or maybe it's just coincidence.

Whatever it is, I'll be forever grateful that my demon followed his instincts to stalk me.

THE END

Want more Chaotic Paranormals?
Read about Raya and Asher in Book 1: Love (Literally) Bites,
or check out the bonus content on the website. I've got both
spicy and sweet scenes for you to choose from!

Sneak peeks, spicy character art, and extra scenes are sent to
my newsletter subscribers first.
Sign up at www.authorcorinabair.com

ACKNOWLEDGMENTS

Stalking ~~Not~~ Required (the not being crossed out is how I wish I could have copyrighted it, but alas, they didn't like that) is the FOURTH book I've written, which is absolutely wild. It's also the easiest book so far. These characters were dying to leave my brain and the words simpyl flew onto the page. I had a blast writing this story, and I hope you enjoyed reading it!

Thank you for reading my book, and if you have shared or told anyone about it, created content or recommended it on social media, left a rating or review, thank you so very much. It means more than I can express with words on a page at the end of a book. I hope you enjoyed riding along with Lor and Ro on their chaotic adventure.

There are a few people I'd like to specifically thank.

Alex, as always. Thank you for always being ready to chat, read, re-read, re-re-re-read, toss ideas around, solve problems and fill plot holes, complain, vent, and generally keep me sane. I appreciate you so very much.

To my beta readers and authenticity/sensitivity readers: Gabs, Alisha, Cat, Hannah, Jamie, and Michelle. Thanks to all of you for your thoughtful critiques and helpful feedback in making this story what it is!

I'd like to acknowlege the local Friday morning author group. Meeting up at the library to write together each week has been delightful, inspiring, and encouraging. We really need to come up with a fun name to call ourselves.

Andrew, for being my rock. Thank you for being there

every step of the way, no matter how early or late, and for always listening to my wild ideas. Your support is unparalleled. I love you!

Lastly... one more thanks for the romance readers!

ABOUT THE AUTHOR

Corina writes feel-good love stories with tension-building spice, funny and relatable characters, and Happily Ever After's that feel like a hug in book form. All of her novels take place in queer-normative worlds.

When she's not reading or writing, you can find Corina forcing snuggles on her dog, rollerblading with her husband, or soaking up the sun like a plant.

Check out Corina's website and newsletter for info on upcoming romance novels:
www.authorcorinabair.com

Connect with her on socials:
@CorinaBairBooks on IG
Corina Bair, Author on FB